Barry Unsworth won the Booker Prize in 1992 for *Sacred Hunger*; his next novel, *Morality Play*, was a Booker nominee and a best seller in both the United States and Great Britain. His other novels include *After Hannibal*, *The Hide*, and *Pascali's Island*, which was also short-listed for the Booker Prize and was made into a feature film. He lives in Umbria with his wife.

BY BARRY UNSWORTH

THE PARTNERSHIP

BARRY UNSWORTH

W. W. Norton & Company
New York • London

Copyright © 1966 by Barry Unsworth
First published as a Norton paperback 2001

Library of Congress Cataloging-in-Publication Data

Unsworth, Barry, 1930–
    The partnership / Barry Unsworth.— 1st American ed.
        p. cm.
    ISBN 0-393-32147-9 (pbk.)
    1. Cornwall (England : County)—Fiction. 2. Garden ornaments and
furniture—Fiction. 3. Partnership—Fiction. 4. Businessmen—Fiction.
I. Title.

PR6071.N8 P36 2001
823'.914—dc21   2001030471

W. W. Norton & Company, Inc.
500 Fifth Avenue, New York, N.Y. 10110
www.wwnorton.com

W. W. Norton & Company Ltd.
Castle House, 75/76 Wells Street, London W1T 3QT

1 2 3 4 5 6 7 8 9 0

For Valerie

1

Foley directed the thin jet of sealing fluid over the pixies at point-blank range, aiming the spray carefully and with growing viciousness at their grinning identical faces, as though instead of merely closing up their pores he intended to disfigure them for life. He experienced this futile hatred for each new batch, as he neared the end; a rage at their numbers, their sameness, the mechanical accuracy of their reproduction. Tray after tray of them came up to him from his tireless partner Moss below until he sometimes felt an urge, not however so far obeyed, to befoul their plaster composure in some way, by spitting on them usually, though grosser defilements had occurred to him. He had not confided these impulses to Moss and did not intend to, not because of shame, in fact he was rather proud of this dark, elemental side to his nature; he was reticent in the matter because he had come to believe that the less Moss knew about him the better, generally speaking.

It was the last tray he was on, anyhow; this dozen completed the two gross and made up the order. Two hundred and eighty-eight lucky pixies, each sitting grinning on the rim of a mottoed ashtray. All they needed now was the paint; three colours would do the lot as long as they were bright enough. The faces were most difficult: you had to have people to paint them who would follow the intention of the moulding and not attempt to mitigate the hideousness of the features. Usually only an experienced painter of pixies had the necessary self-control. It was, though, essential that the face should retain that leer that holiday-makers demanded, the authentic lucky pixie-look of slightly lecherous domestic complicity that was considered to augur well for the year to come.

The spray kept up a faint but steady hiss. The liquid itself was too finely dispersed to be visible – the pixies' faces were not discernibly moistened by it – but its force, playing over the bench on which the pixies were set, caused flakes of plaster and small particles of gold-leaf to sidle about the room, briefly and with apparent circumspection. It was still April and quite cold outside, though the room itself was close because Foley had put on his electric fire when he started work that morning. Warm currents, weighted by the acrid exhalations of the spray, rose slowly, misting over the closed window.

Foley's eyes were stinging a little from the fumes and as soon as he had finished the spraying he went over to the window and opened it, remaining there for some moments to look out across sloping sheep-fields to shrub-green cliffs and the pewter-coloured sea beyond. He had felt of late some spleen against the sea, against the whole view in fact, for its refusal to be more dramatic. When, three years before, they had moved into this house and set about converting it for the pixie business he had been excited by the sea view, coming as he did from a basement flat in Battersea. He had secured this room for his own to work in, relegating Moss and his ovens to the dark room on the ground floor. Moss had, of course, been more amenable then, more open to suggestion in every way. Foley had congratulated himself at the time on his shrewdness and tact. Now he was not so sure. At any rate he had failed to live up to the landscape, beginning quite early to miss the minutiae, the changing scenes of life, to which years of living in London had accustomed him. It was true that nothing sordid or petty here distracted the eye; the trees scattered between the house and cliffs were undeniably impressive, especially in the drained or pallid light of certain days when, outlined against the sky, they had an arresting hallucinatory grace, due to the stunting effect of the sea winds which in the course of many winter offensives had combed their branches back against the natural bent, tortured them really, but invariably into the semblance of order, into beauty, like the delicate, impossible trees on Japanese ceramics.

For all this Foley envied Moss his lowlier view of the farmyard and a segment of lane. Indeed he tended now to hold the whole thing against his partner, as though that former tractability had been the result of cunning foresight on Moss's part. Moss could see hens from his window and hikers or campers occasionally; he could see Royle the farmer, their landlord, going to and fro about his business; he could watch Phyllis the farm girl feeding the hens and observe, if he felt so inclined, the progress of the strong black hairs on her legs. It was not much, perhaps, but compared with what he had himself, a feast of life and colour. He never saw signs of human life from his window at all, unless you could count the intimations of ships on the horizon. Thirty miles to the south, miles of tangled headlands webbed by rocky inaccessible bays, was the capital town; and in the other direction, only two miles away but completely hidden by the curve of the coast, was Lanruan, whose shops supplied them with groceries and took a good part of their pixie out-put.

Relieved at having come to the end of this particular lot, Foley allowed his distaste for the pixies to soften into the feeling of superior discrimination which he had cultivated in order not to feel circumscribed by the work he did. Turning from the window he regarded the pixies steadily for some moments. Moss and he were assisting in an outrage against the whole human race, he thought, with some pleasure at being able to include Moss. These creatures were, after all, made in the human image, though fashions, he conceded, changed in pixies as in all else. They had begun with an idealised, pre-Raphaelite type, wistful of feature and attenuated of frame, but this had slowly coarsened into the present more truly native product, less elegant, lewder, with cunning hints of deformity, and some elements of the comic postcard superimposed, particularly in the bottled vacuousness of the expression.

He was tempted to descend on Moss and ask him straight out whether in his opinion three years of making plaster souvenirs for summer visitors was not bound to affect the health of the psyche, stopping up, for example, certain essential sympathetic responses; or, putting it another way, whether he and Moss could go on immersing themselves in the acid of seasons without being corroded in the end. He had a habit while working of devising such questions, sometimes in elaborately metaphorical form, for Moss, phrasing and re-phrasing them with great care so that they might be perfectly clear and comprehensive and allow no scope for evasion on Moss's part. But by the time they had reached this chiselled perfection there no longer seemed any point in putting them, they had lost the quality of interrogation. In any case he was quite aware that Moss's casuistry was a fiction of his own devising, his partner in fact being an unsubtle pedestrian person who would regard such issues with solemn indulgence and no play of mind whatever.

This time the temptation passed almost before the question had been framed, certainly before it had been polished. It sufficed to summon Moss to mind as he would doubtless be at this moment, in his room below, prising out further pixies from the moulds, constantly patting things with his big dusty hands, patting the warm pixies, patting the tops of the ovens to gauge the heat, breathing heavily. Before such an image all query quietly died. Besides, Moss was always wounded by slighting references to the pixies, and it would be a bad mistake, he felt, to bring up just now any subject that might lead to disagreement. There was still some strain between them, a certain wariness, since their quarrel of three days ago, when Moss had upbraided him for staying out late, a mistake this, because although Foley was a malleable person he would always fly into anger when forced into a corner and his dignity threatened. The quarrel had been momentous in that it was the first to mar their three years' association, the first time, at least, that recriminations had been explicit. Though it was he himself, Foley reflected rather uneasily, who had done most of the recriminating; Moss had simply gone quiet and hurt. And it was he who had subsequently retreated, becoming even more secretive than before. Moss had simply remained himself, if possible more intensely so. Moss had been difficult lately. It was as though the spring had contained some ingredient indigestible to him, an irritant, an intestinal grit that darkened his outlook, souring his former solicitude into a sort of domineering fussiness.

Neither of them had since made any healing reference to the quarrel, either humorous or apologetic, which might have made it public and manageable, part of the folklore, so to speak, of their association. The whole incident, Foley felt, would have to be left

4

alone now. But it was certainly not a time for needless irritations; it was a time, quite clearly, for tact.

Dismissing Moss's sensibilities from his mind for the time being, Foley began to pack the pixies into a number of large cardboard boxes. This he did with great care, covering the bottoms of the boxes and each layer of pixies with a thick pad of packing straw, making sure that no two pixies were touching, since breakages were expensive. He enjoyed packing. It was an activity exactly suited to his cautious, treasuring, pattern-forming nature. He liked packing anything: even the loathed pixies took on a preciousness with their fragility as he bedded them in the straw. This morning, however, he was not able to enjoy the process for itself alone, since it brought him up against a problem which until then he had been deliberately avoiding. It concerned the choice of a painter for the pixies.

Later on, when they were really busy, they would use all available painters, but at this time of the year they had a sort of rota system, which seemed fairer. It was the turn of Albert Smart, who lived by digging graves and doing odd jobs. There was nothing against Albert, a lanky respectful man, good with his hands. Moreover he was more or less constantly in need, since deaths were not so very frequent in such a sparsely populated district and he had a number of small children to support. Look at it how he would, Foley could not deny that all considerations of justice and humanity were on Albert's side. But if he ignored these claims and took the pixies into Lanruan instead, and gave them to someone there to paint, he could call on Gwendoline, not only today but on Friday too, when he went in to collect them, and Moss would be hoodwinked because it was a blameless business trip.

Albert's sad claims faded as Foley nestled one after the other of the pixies down into the yielding but springy straw. Something in this, something intimate and exploratory and at the same time systematic, gave added force to his desire to see Gwendoline. He might sit on the floor, on her red carpet, watching her move about, that big-boned yet graceful and curiously docile body of hers. It was this doe-like softness he sensed in her, together with her narrow-eyed, sleepy expression, which had attracted him first. He was quite sure she was still a virgin, despite her aspect of fecundity.

5

Planning seductions was an occupation extremely agreeable to him. He engaged in it frequently, even when through a dearth of suitable acquaintance he was obliged to imagine his heroines. Like packing, it made a strong appeal to the scheming orderliness of his character and it also gave him a long-drawn-out illusion of mastery. He had, however, never succeeded in seducing anyone, if seduction is an unremitting manipulation of another personality. He had some of the qualities: he was good-looking, ready of speech, sensual enough and not given to pity — more capable indeed than many of ignoring inconvenient appeals to chivalry. In spite of these natural advantages something always went wrong, something in himself. He invariably succumbed to the response he aroused, lost his impetus. He could not help posing himself and waiting in a flame of self-love for the over-stimulated moth to immolate herself on his candle. Sometimes this happened, sometimes it did not, but it was never clear in the end who was seducing whom, and Foley found this, however enjoyable at the time, retrospectively lacked the true qualities of a *campaign*.

With Gwendoline at least he felt he had made a good start. On his previous visit, in parting, he had rested his hand for a moment in the small of her back, in that hollow formed by the spine and the first convexities of the buttocks. He had felt the grain of her silk blouse slide under his palm against the softer, more resilient, flesh beneath. Today he would wait for some accidental proximity, and kiss her. If she rebuffed him he could put it, with an air sufficiently respectful, down to passion. This would do him no harm. No woman could fail to enjoy being the provoker of ungovernable impulses, provided they turned out to be governable. If, on the other hand, which he felt on the whole more likely, she acquiesced, the kiss could become habitual, and a prelude to better things.

Foley finished the packing in a voluptuous heat. Carrying the boxes down to the rear door, ready for loading into the car, the harsher aspects of life again obtruded. Moss now would have to be encountered. Not being kept informed of what was going on was one of the things his partner had lately shown himself to resent. Pausing only to assemble his features into an expression of duty shouldered, he went into the casting-room.

As he had visualised, Moss was bending over the big work-bench in the middle of the room, extracting baked pixies from their lemon-coloured rubber moulds. He had his back to the door and did not hear Foley come in. Footsteps were inaudible in this room because of the thick deposit of plaster dust and shavings which covered the floor. From some source not immediately traceable Moss's wireless was emitting gusty orchestral music.

'I have to go down to the wretched village again,' said Foley. Moss turned the moment he began speaking, and straightened himself. He was a big man, a full head taller than Foley. The front of him, his jersey and denim trousers, were white with fine grains of plaster, and a floury dust adhered to his cheeks and eyebrows and the ridge of his nose, giving him a farcical doomed appearance. Beneath this mask Foley saw two distinct expressions pass over his face one after the other: a sort of automatic solicitude, evoked by the tone of the words, and then, almost immediately, as their meaning came home to him, a wary blankness.

'What a bore for you, Ronald,' he said in his customary deep and rather resonant voice, luxuriant with the vowels of his native Essex.

Foley stood silent for a moment, seeking uneasily for inflections of irony in the remark. 'Yes, isn't it?' he said. 'But we must keep things going, you know, Michael, we must keep our end up.' A sort of subdued heartiness based on cliché was his habitual conversational stance with Moss whenever, as now, he was conscious of practising a deception. 'Spread the good word,' he added, scanning Moss's face. It was amazing, he thought, how that face suggested gullibility, a willingness to be favourably impressed. It was largely a matter of those round, blue, believing eyes and the unusually high arch of the brows above them, but the mouth too added to this impression by its fullness, its appearance of innocent greed. Only if one disregarded the credulous mouth and eyes and dwelt on the largeness and bluntness of the head, the heavy, prominent bones of temple and jaw, might it have been surmised that Moss was an extremely obstinate and inflexible person. Particularly so in the matter of human appraisals. His acquaintance was not extensive, but they all had a sense of being

7

netted in his opinion of them and they usually suffered in his presence, fluttering into insincerities as they tried to express themselves without coming into conflict with his almost invariably inadequate conception of their characters. Foley, on the other hand, being preoccupied with himself, found it easier to approach people tentatively. Indeed he kept an open mind for so long that in the end he often lacked the interest or energy to close it.

'You seem to go down there often these days,' said Moss, again without any apparent intention of irony. 'Is it really necessary for you to go today?'

'Well, yes it is, as a matter of fact. It's the ashtray pixies, you know, the lot we've just finished. The people want them for this Friday. Why I don't know, there's nobody about yet, but there you are. It's important we should be on time with them because this is the first order.' He was conscious of having been too explanatory.

'Of course I know all that,' Moss said. 'It's that woman who wears wooden beads that knock against one another, and the man is bald.' He had resumed work on the pixies. Foley watched for some time in silence, impressed as always by the tenderness with which he handled them. His thick blunt fingers released them from the clasp of the rubber with an amazing gentleness, a continuously renewed care, as though he were delivering them from the cramping womb. They were all mutants on emerging: these moulds were old now, their edges worn and blunted, and this caused accidental and sometimes monstrous accretions, little ridges and humps, swellings, goitres, phalluses. Sometimes the pixies came out like drowned things, seaweeded or encrusted with dredge. All this had to be put right by Moss, who had a small file for the purpose.

'Whose turn is it for the painting, someone in the village?' he asked without looking up.

'I thought I'd take them to Graham,' Foley said.

'Is it Graham's turn again already?'

'Well, yes it is, as a matter of fact.' A furtive anger was beginning to rise in Foley at the other's graceless persistence in these questions, which had driven him now to a direct falsehood. 'I thought I might call in on Barbara Gould at the same time,' he said. 'She is back again now, for the summer.'

'Barbara Gould,' said Moss. He crumbled away with his fingers a thin ridge from the pixie's shoulders. 'I don't think we should have much to do with her,' he said.

'Why not?'

Moss assumed his special worldly manner, forbearing and censorious, which he kept for those times when he felt Foley needed some coaching in the facts of life. 'The life she leads, Ronald. It's common knowledge in the village.'

'What has that to do with us?' Foley demanded warmly. His guilt and annoyance, diverted into the defence of Barbara, had become, he felt, a generous emotion, one which ought to be sustained. 'There's no common knowledge in that village except how to fleece the summer visitors,' he said, 'and no uncommon knowledge at all.'

'I have heard that she is insatiable,' Moss said, as though it were something like leprosy.

'Who on earth says that? Anyway, it would be a misfortune, surely, if it were really true. Her morals don't concern us in any case. What does it matter to me how many men she sleeps with? I like talking to her, she gives me the London news.'

Before this burst of frankness, Moss's air of wisdom had wilted a little. 'Everybody knows about her in the village,' he said. 'It's up to you, of course.'

'It's not catching, you know,' Foley said. 'Do you think I'll be corrupted, or what? Michael, you simply can't consider people in this way. People aren't just so many moral vitamins.' Foley's precarious sense of advantage led him into something like a sneer. 'Tom's all right, he's a nutritious character, but keep away from Dick, he'll constipate you, he's deficient in citizenship, he has an uncontrollable impulse to expose himself on public commons and heaths.'

He paused for a moment to struggle with his idea. Moss was silent, as though staggered by this figurativeness.

'Anyone can be poisonous, actually,' Foley said. 'People don't give other people what is wholesome for them necessarily, even wholesome people, I mean. It's a sort of surplus, whatever it is the person has a lot of. It depends on the system of the receiver whether it's poisonous or not.'

His vehemence seemed finally to amuse Moss, who actually began to chuckle a little. 'You must keep one foot on the ground, you know, Ronald,' he said. 'Idealism is all very well, but it doesn't get the work of the world done.'

'Idealism?' Foley was sometimes bewildered by Moss's apparent shifts of ground, suspecting some design in them; but he was always forced to acknowledge that so far from cunning was this inconsequence that Moss wasn't even aware of it. Now, for example, he had simply fallen back, perhaps out of self-defence, on his role of hard-headed practical man.

'I wasn't being idealistic at all,' Foley said, making an effort to break out of his own allotted role of fanciful fellow, in which indeed, because of Moss's conviction, there was something hypnotic, compelling assent. 'I was only trying – '

'Never mind, never mind,' said Moss, still smiling. He seemed in great good humour now, and Foley knew that this was because he himself was behaving in character, in Moss's view at least. Moss had assigned to him from the beginning an Artistic Temperament – it was typical of him to think in broad categories – and this apparently implied a sort of picturesque ineptitude for the bread-and-butter aspects of life, rather than the possession of any definite talents. But in Foley's case there was talent too, as Moss would have been quick to point out to anyone who seemed unaware of it. Was it not Foley who designed the pixies, made the models and the moulds? And he himself who did the heavy work, the crude preparatory processes, and kept the accounts?

Foley had found his elevation comfortable enough on the whole, and had acquiesced in it. But it was frustrating to be trapped, as he was now, unable to descend and explain his ideas without their being discounted in advance, dissolved in Moss's indulgence. And it had had a subtly demoralising effect on Foley over the course of time, causing him to adopt poses gratifying to Moss – rather like a dog with a good trick. He moved vaguely towards the door, uttering in a declamatory tone, 'There are more things in heaven and earth, Horatio, than are dreamed of in your philosophy.' Suddenly afraid that Moss might think he was being mocked by being called Horatio, he added quickly, 'That's a quotation.'

'I thought I recognised it,' Moss said. 'Wasn't that the person who held the bridge?'

Foley was aware that having wrought on Moss he should leave immediately, but at the door he found himself insufficiently resolute for this, and plunged into further explanations.

'I thought, you see, that if I took them down now the painter would have the rest of today and a clear day tomorrow and I could deliver them on Friday morning.'

'Yes,' said Moss, 'and if we're prompt in getting them in, and they are satisfied with them, they might be interested in this new design of yours, the one sitting on the Cornish pasty.' He was constantly urging Foley to break new ground, conceiving it his duty to provide the drive, the dynamism, of the business. At one time he had even gone out with samples, but something too strenuous in his advocacy of the pixies had tended to put people off. Foley now did the prospecting for new business; his aloof approach usually succeeded very well. If this had wounded Moss he showed no signs of it.

Foley agreed with him about the Cornish-pasty line. It had definite possibilities, since it could so easily be adapted to demand. The pixie would remain the same, of course, no point in changing that, but the pasty itself could be changed into a little tray for putting things in, or a money-box. Also, he felt that the distinctively Cornish nature of the thing would be a selling point. People liked to have this regional reminder of their holiday. It was a peg for the year, a piece of evidence. Beside their far-flung hearths, on winter evenings, they would catch the eye of this Cornish-pasty pixie, and remember the wind and sunshine of their holiday, the boarding-house bed that creaked, the scandalising cockroach in the bathroom. Things ugly in themselves can none the less suggest beauty and perhaps for many this pixie leer would evoke the flight of gulls, the envied life of fishermen, a golden hitchless passage of adultery or a dazing win at Bingo.

'You'll be taking the car, I suppose,' Moss said. 'I hope you'll drive carefully, Ronald.'

'Yes, yes,' said Foley, wincing inwardly. He hated discussing the car with Moss. It was a topic which made him feel particularly vulnerable. His partner's last words had been a reference to the two minor accidents he had already had this year, caused by his habit of alternating when driving between exaggerated caution and euphoric abandonment, either of which moods was liable to descend on him at any time without warning, other than a tendency to whistle through his teeth during the latter. Moss himself was an unspectacular but steady driver who had never had an accident in his life.

'Go slowly along those lanes,' Moss said. 'It's better to be safe than sorry.'

Of course, thought Foley, it was too much to expect that Moss would see it was a distasteful subject, one that caused pain. Perceptions of that kind were foreign to him.

'Well, I'll be off then,' he said, as stoically as possible.

'That's right, Ronald,' Moss said. He turned back to his work-table, but almost immediately looked round again as though to add something. Foley, however, had gone.

Moss stood still, listening to the sounds from outside. The shed doors were unbolted, there was a brief pause and then the car coughed and stopped, coughed again in a prolonged manner and picked up. The engine ran while Foley put in the boxes, then the doors slammed shut, the gear jarring harshly a moment or two later, as he engaged bottom too vigorously.

Had he wished, Moss could have watched the car emerge from behind the house and turn up the lane that led to the road. His window gave him a view of all this. He did not raise his head, though, until the noise of the engine had completely died away. For some time longer he stood upright beside the bench, while into the silence left by the car's departure a number of familiar sounds came seeping back: the cries of sheep from the surrounding fields, the faint bickering of gulls, the respirations of the hot ovens. Somewhere on the farm one of Royle's dogs yelped as though in pain.

He resumed work in a deliberate manner. One after another he took the pixies out of their moulds, holding them gently, almost caressingly. The full daylight was flooding into the room now, sea-light, austere yet benign, without subtlety, blanching the filed pixies that stood in neat ranks on the bench before him.

While he was working he went over the conversation he had just had with Foley. On the whole he was inclined to be pleased with his part in it. He felt that he had shown tact, and tact was of paramount importance with Ronald, who had been so touchy lately, not like himself at all. Someone was getting at him, of course, but you couldn't ask him right out. Ronald couldn't be reasoned with. He had shown that clearly enough the other night, flying up in the air like that and shouting so that all the dogs barked. Royle had probably heard every word. A wave of unhappiness swept over Moss as he thought of that quarrel, its pointlessness, Ronald's pale indignant face. Ronald had looked at him as if he were an enemy. There had been no way of showing that what he wanted, wanted more than anything, was to help Ronald, advise him for his own good. He had had to stand there helpless, watching the antagonism in Ronald's face, the terrible misunderstanding that was developing between them.

He thought of Ronald on his way to the village, nearly there by now. Four times in the last ten days he had made completely unnecessary trips to Lanruan. Moss counted them over again in his mind: one, two, three, four. He liked enumerating, marshalling the facts. There was no doubt about it. Ronald was seeing somebody down there, some girl. Nothing mattered, waste of petrol, loss of time. And the lies he told! Did he really think that he, Moss, whose finger was on the pulse of the business, would be ignorant as to whose turn it was for painting? It was Albert Smart's turn. Even if he hadn't known he had only to check up on the rota-sheet. A chill of fear struck Moss as it came home to him how careless and flimsy Ronald's excuses had been. That could only mean he wanted desperately to see this person. Moss tried to concentrate his mind, to discover by a sort of intuition what she could be like, fighting as he did so the sick incoherence that was descending on his thoughts. He tried his hardest to be objective, to bear in mind her humanity, complex and irreducible; but in spite of his efforts he was unable to separate from this unknown girl the idea of flaccidity, the familiar female complement of Ronald's slimness; soft, plasmic, absorbent. Striving to contain his disgust, Moss felt a prickle of sweat break on his upper lip.

He set the pixie he was holding, smooth now and indistinguishable from the others, carefully down on the bench. He felt the silence of the house all around him, like an invitation. The disagreeable thoughts of the girl receded, and a feeling of excitement began to stir him. After standing a few moments as though undecided, he went slowly out of the room and upstairs. He walked down the passage, past Foley's workroom and his own bedroom, and stopped at the far end, at Foley's bedroom door. After a long pause of complete immobility he opened the door and went in. He stood just inside the room looking round. This is seven times I have done this, he told himself, and out of habit checked the times over, beginning with the cold January day when the idea had first assailed him: one, two, three, four, five, six, seven. It was incontrovertible and gave him, he felt, a certain prerogative.

Foley kept his things always very neat, the bed made up, the floor swept, the room well aired. Near the window was a white-wood table surmounted by an oval mirror in a gilt frame. Foley used this table for his toilet accessories. On it were laid, meticulously arranged, his twin blue-glass eye-baths, his big blue tin of Nivea, his bottle of after-shave lotion and a pink plastic cup with a tube of toothpaste and a yellow tooth-brush in it. There was also, set a little apart from these, a large bottle of Cologne. Moss lifted this and read the manufacturer's label. Then he removed the glass stopper and sniffed at the neck of the bottle. The sweetness expanded in the cool room.

After seven visits Moss had become very familiar with all these objects and he would have noticed immediately if anything had been missing or not in its accustomed place. They were like an extension of Ronald's personality, attributes only observable in this way, in the silence of their owner's absence. All Moss's movements in this room had a complete, an almost ritual, certainty. After soothing himself at the dressing-table, he went over to the mantelpiece to look at Foley's photograph, the only picture in the room, taken four or five years previously, in Foley's fabulous past, before they had met, when he was a photographer's model in London. It had been taken for circulation to the agencies and was a studio portrait, full face, with Foley smiling slightly. The photographer, an expensive West End one whose name was embossed in gilt letters on the frame, had cleverly caught a characteristic tension in Foley's face between conscious charm and faint anxiety. It was a very attractive face, perfectly regular without being at all insipid. Something aloof and almost severe about the dark level brows and narrow eyes was mitigated by the sweetness of the small, well-shaped mouth. The fine, straight hair was parted carefully and swept back over the ears in smooth waves.

Moss studied the picture intently. Then he turned and went over to the wardrobe, which had little bone handles on the doors. When he opened it a smell of lavender came out. He knew why this was: Ronald always put lavender cubes in the breast pockets of his jackets when he was not using them. He stood for quite a long while, allowing these emanations to reach his nostrils. Then, very delicately, with his arm fully outstretched and his finger and thumb quite rigid, he pinched one of the empty sleeves.

2

Meanwhile Foley drove fairly contentedly towards the village. The road, which descended gradually to sea-level, was narrow and winding. The high banks and thick hedges admitted no view of the surrounding countryside. It was quite impossible to see what was coming and necessary therefore to proceed slowly, hooting loudly almost the whole time. Motoring under these conditions resembled a sort of vociferous tunnelling.

The car was old and capacious, with a long square bonnet like a snout and that appearance of brutal decorum which streamlining has taken from more modern cars. Now, with its speed controlled by the low gear and no need for acceleration, the engine was so quiet that in the intervals between hoots Foley could hear through the open window the occasional notes of the sea-bell. He could sense, as though it were an activity faintly clamorous, the general sappiness and effluviums of spring all around.

This effortless progress and the protection afforded by the high banks gradually induced in Foley feelings of security and confidence. He was able for the moment to still all his misgivings, or rather it was as though he had been secreting as a by-product of these misgivings and the anxious summarising of his life and prospects in which he was more or less continually engaged, some gummy substance which under these conditions was released and stopped up all the little conduits of worry, making him feel for the time being impregnable. This feeling of impregnability was the nearest he ever came to happiness.

Life had never seemed particularly easy to Foley. He had seen the way some people forged ahead without taking even elementary precautions, and yet nevertheless seemed to prosper. He had envied these charmed careers but would not have dreamed of trying to emulate them. For him life was something one more or less painfully, using whatever materials were to hand, wrought; a laborious, unending process of construction, harassed by a diversity of saboteurs. It had always seemed so to him, even as a child, when novelty had appalled him with the chaos just beyond it and successive developments had had to be endured with secret misery until sockets could be found for them to rest in; only when fixed in relation to the familiar could he regard anything as achieved. At the age of ten he had been given an elaborate Meccano set and he had prized this before all his other possessions. He remembered it lovingly still, for the absence of mystery in its components, the builder's complete control at every stage. At school among his fellows he had cultivated bravado as a means of self-protection, a subtle bravado based on understatement, which had impressed without provoking challenges and even gained him a reputation and a modest following. But this technique had had to be abandoned in the more sophisticated societies of later life in which the threat came almost entirely, as it seemed to him, from the carelessness or malignancy of other people. He had found the answer in an assumed complaisance. Protecting the structure depended on not revealing it, and this in turn made necessary, not a poker face –that merely invited closer scrutiny – but a highly developed capacity for dissembling, a refusal to force issues. He had slipped into this role easily and sustained it without discomfort, even with self-approval, except on the rare occasions, when, cornered by unmannerly insistence or direct rudeness, he flew out at his persecutor with a bitterness that surprised even himself. It was as though his previous evasions had, after all, been accompanied by rancour.

Foley suffered a good deal, since he was only able to enjoy his adroitness when he did not feel threatened, and this was infrequent. But these moments, when they came, had a purity, a quality almost of contemplation. The present was one such. His life seemed inviolable, all his schemes bound to fructify. He thought of Gwendoline, unseduced it was true, unattained as yet, but only as imminent holidays are unattained in childhood, no more in doubt than these.

Most splendid of all, however, far beyond any merely carnal

17

satisfactions, was his vision of his studio back at the cottage, that large quiet room under the roof, filled with the golden cherub lamps which would enable him before long to escape from his servitude to the pixies and the wheel of seasons, into prosperity and enhanced status. Three winters he had worked on them until he now had what could only be called a showroom up there, a wide selection of lamp stands and bases and bracket supports; all plaster casts of cherubs, with a pagan admixture of cherubic Cupids, Loves, and *putti*; their variety lay in their differences of posture, and was considerable. He did not know exactly when the idea had first come to him; it was as though he had always had it, like a heroic virtue waiting for the stress of circumstance to call it forth. He had plotted himself into fevers to obtain the models and spent money that should really have been ploughed back into the pixies – as Moss had sometimes pointed out – nosing out what he wanted in a score of junk shops amid the scourings of a debased baroque; convoluted salvers, wreathed and curly fruit-bowls, the borders of looking-glasses. Perhaps his purest pang of gratitude was to that dealer who, standing to gain nothing, had allowed him to take a cast from a genuine eighteenth-century Spanish bedpost. Now he had enough. He was in a position to turn out large numbers of them at a low cost. This winter he could invite representatives to visit his showroom, or he could go out himself with samples to the big stores in Plymouth and Torquay and even London. He felt sure that people would be interested. It was, after all, an original idea; and there was a demand for the ornate these days. People were getting bored with the austerities of Scandinavia.

Foley's feeling of security began to fade as he approached the village. It never lasted long in any case and always disappeared when encounters threatened. This morning it vanished quite away when he noticed how many of the houses along the road into Lanruan had already put up 'Vacant Accommodation' signs in the windows, although it was not yet May. He always watched for signs of the approaching season with apprehension. It was like an extremely searching annual personality test; every year he was afraid he might fail, impossible demands might be made on him. Besides, it was difficult during these months to conceal from oneself that one was battening on a taste one despised. Though you could hardly call it battening, he reflected, in view of the firm's resources.

He began to arrange the calls in his mind. Graham first, of course, with the pixies; his house was on the way in any case. A few minutes there, a look at the painting, then on to Gwendoline. She would probably give him coffee, he would find an opportunity for the over-mastering passion gambit. Finally Barbara Gould: half an hour there to bring her up to date with the latest Mosseries, and home for a late lunch.

In order to call on Graham it was necessary to turn off just before reaching the main part of the village and start climbing again up a loosely gravelled lane which led to Graham's gate. The car had to be left here but the journey was by no means over: to reach the house itself you had to pick your way some hundreds of yards along a very narrow overgrown footpath, intersected at one point by a wide and deep stream. The only way to get over this stream was to walk along a plank, green, slippery and rotten with age, which Graham in periods of world-weariness or heavy debt pulled up like a drawbridge, making his house virtually unassailable.

Foley left the pixies just inside the gate, having no intention of struggling down the path with them: the going was difficult enough even when one was unencumbered.

The single-storey wooden shack in which Graham lived was invisible from the road above and the village below because of the screen of trees around it, planted for purposes of concealment by the former owner, who either through shyness or distaste had cut down his human contacts to the minimum necessary for survival, and had kept bees and planted a lot of aromatic herbs, flowering shrubs and fruit-trees in the few acres of sharply sloping ground, which surrounded the house. Graham had kept up the misanthropy but totally neglected the garden. Most of the flowers planted so carefully had seeded themselves into a decline long ago and the fruit never sweetened now. But no neglect could affect the fertility of the place, the constant presence of water, the sunny, sheltered slope. In full summer the place swooned with germination and the tangle closed one in completely, despite the steepness of the slope, but now there were several places along the path from which one could get a view of the village. Immediately after crossing the stream, during which he slipped and almost fell, Foley stopped for a few minutes to look down and recover his nerve.

Lanruan lay below him, divided into its three separate zones. There was the old village, narrow houses with red-tiled roofs and well-spaced windows, clustered round the harbour, the quays and the fish market. Stretching back from the harbour on both sides of the road were new brick houses with neat gardens and strips of flagged path and bay windows, which looked at this distance like the bulging eye-cases of inert red beetles. These houses were nearly all used as private hotels or guest-houses during the summer. Thirdly, scattered over the cliffs above the harbour were villas, built in a variety of styles, whose terraces and rock gardens climbed yearly higher, driving back the gorse and fern. Plate glass twinkled at Foley from among forsythia, mock-orange trees and puny palms. Beyond all this was the sea itself, within the wall of the harbour pretty and manageable, gay with the reflections of small pleasure boats, glinting fish-nets and flexing spirals of light on the stone quays; outside this wall pale and featureless, another element altogether.

Foley continued his way along the path to Graham's door, noticing as he did so how the ash-trees seemed to lean in towards the house. Their branches almost touched the windows, the sharp black buds split already by the fleshy leaf inside. Something ravenous in the appearance of these buds impressed Foley disagreeably. He did not knock but shouted, 'Graham, hallo Graham,' and immediately Flossie, Graham's marmalade spaniel bitch, began to bark loudly. Foley heard the sound of a bolt being withdrawn, then Graham peered out warily from below the peak of his cap. Recognising his visitor he drew back without speaking and Foley followed him into the long narrow room in which Graham ate and slept and worked at his picture. It was untidy in a sordid way, littered with odd garments and scraps of food. Almost the whole of one wall was covered by two bed sheets which had been tacked together.

'How are you, Graham?' said Foley. 'I've brought you some

more pixies, two gross. They have to be ready for Friday morning.'

'Right you are, boy,' Graham said in his hoarse, knowing voice which always made Foley think of a groom, or some sort of coach – a person, at any rate, intimately acquainted with form, mettle, temper; an insider's voice, despite Graham's solitary life, yet at the same time untrustworthy.

'I left them at the gate as usual,' he went on, watching Graham closely, trying to engage the warm brown eyes under the shadow of the cap. It was like trying to catch the eye of some intensely alive but completely unco-operative mammal; a resemblance intensified by Graham's diminutive stature and the furry brown corduroy jacket he always wore. 'You can do it for Friday, I suppose?' he said. 'Usual colours for the pixies, black for the ashtrays, with "Here's Luck M'dear" in white paint round the rim.'

Graham did not answer directly but said after a moment, 'I'm a bit down on the paint.'

'You'll have enough for this lot, surely,' Foley said. He had been aware for some time that Graham was using part of the paint supplied to him for purposes of his own, but unwilling as always to disrupt established practice he preferred to condone this, so long as Graham was moderate in his pilfering.

'I'm a bit down generally this week,' said Graham, putting the discussion on a broader base. 'Any chance of an advance on this lot? Half down now, say, and the rest when you collect?'

Foley said, 'You know that's not the way we do things, Graham.' It distressed him just a little to have to refuse but there had not really been much hope in Graham's voice. After a decent pause, but before Graham had time to get round to asking for a personal loan, Foley put the question which of all others was calculated to take Graham's mind off scrounging. 'How's the painting going?' he said. 'I see you keep it covered up now.'

Graham became alert immediately. 'I shall have to make a few changes,' he said. He walked over to the wall and pulled at one corner of the sheet, which fell away, partially exposing a gigantic canvas crammed with painted forms. 'I keep it covered all the time now,' he remarked as he crossed to the other side. 'Except when

'I'm actually working on it. Otherwise I find it gets me down.' The whole sheet now fell to the floor and at once the room seemed to shrink. Foley had the feeling of not being able to get far enough back from the vast painting.

It was a painting of the whole village with its harbour, its new residential district and the creeping villas on the cliffs. The lines were refracted as though seen through a blur of heat and this gave to the whole a sort of sliding disintegration, not, however, uniformly advanced since some of the houses still appeared to be intact while others were listing or buckling already, their walls veined with delicate fissures. The inhabitants, nearly all of whom, despite the brutishness with which Graham had endowed their features, were clearly recognisable as local people, had been arrested at a particular moment and were in various stages of disarray. Many had gathered in the streets outside their houses, others stared vaguely at the sky from upper windows. Some faces showed merely a dull surprise, others were blubbered with tears; while here and there were black, open and perfectly rounded mouths of terror. Splintered 'Vacancy' signs spun wildly in the air, together with pieces of masonry and household articles. It could be seen that some tremendous centrifugal force was being exerted on the village. In spite of this, on a slope of the cliffs in a shaft of sunlight, a pair of lovers lay embracing, their faces happy and calm; and elsewhere a group of children played unconcernedly together. The gay, banal holiday colours of the village had been preserved, emphasised. Sky and sea were clear and luminous, and sheep grazed on the hills around. But among the villas were pockets of yellow flame and some small figures could be seen waving wildly. Graham had called the painting 'Crack of Doom at Lanruan' and he had been working on it now for more than two years. It was remarkable for its scale and the energy of execution. Above all, perhaps, for the sustained malignancy of the numerous portraits it contained.

'Here is where I mean,' said Graham, pointing out a group of women at the far right of the picture who were clinging together in attitudes of helpless fear, all wearing night-dresses as though they had been roused from some kind of communal day-bed.

'I don't quite see what you mean at the moment,' Foley said, looking hard at the distraught faces, prominent among which were the alcoholic barmaid at The Fisherman's Arms and the highly respected wife of the vicar.

'The figures aren't defined clearly enough, boy, they merge too much together. They look like wraiths already in those bloody nighties, do you get me? Not what I wanted at all. Hell is waiting for them all right, every one of them, the bitches, but this is just the first hint of it. Everything has got to look more or less normal. The normal caught short. Do you get me?' Graham paused for a moment, smiling. He smiled rarely, which was fortunate, because his upper teeth were wide spaced and unusually tapering and this gave to his smile an unpleasant gloating quality and narrowed down his general mammalian appearance to the rodent branch. 'That would be another painting,' he went on. ' "The Inhabitants of Lanruan in Hell." I could do it after this one. But there's a lot to do to this one yet. It's nowhere near finished. I might put in some shiftings in the cemetery.' His hand indicated an area of the canvas.

'That sounds a good idea,' said Foley. In spite of this talk of other pictures he felt sure that the painting would never be finished. Every time it looked about to be, Graham found changes that had to be made. The truth was that Graham wanted it to go on for ever; he needed it as a means of concentration, in the way that the Orthodox devout use ikons, as a focus for simultaneous discharge and replenishment; the only difference being that Graham kept himself charged with loathing. Every alteration he made was in intention punitive; he was not so much painting a picture as indulging in a process of retribution against the population of Lanruan. What the ground of his grievance was Foley had never discovered. He probably disliked the people to begin with, since he disliked everybody; but dwelling on them had engendered hatred. It was as though some revelation of human nastiness had been made to him in the silence of his shack. The element of caricature in the painting had grown steadily more savage and would soon, Foley felt, become pathological. Though caricature perhaps was not the way to describe it. These faces could not be dismissed as exaggerated. By subtle shifts of emphasis Graham had realised them, brought out the animality that lurked behind the decorous masks.

23

Conversation about the painting was satisfying for both of them. For Graham because it was the most important thing in his life, for which he scraped and dodged and sacrificed all comfort, and he had few people to discuss it with; and for Foley because the painting could be regarded as a constant factor in his life. At different times, sometimes when far away, it gave him a curious pleasure to think of Graham working on the painting. It would have dismayed him now to find it completed.

'Think of it,' said Graham. 'A day like this perhaps, an ordinary day with everything just as usual, sea and sky behaving properly.' He paused, but Foley said nothing, warned by the malevolent fluency. 'The cafés marking up their prices for the season, the cosy widows in the guest-houses getting ready, with clean white pinnies and knees clapt close, the young couples with Vision sticking up the "Available" signs in the Seaview windows. Grasping their bloody teapots.' Graham smiled again. 'Teapot graspers,' he said, 'do you get it? To *grasp* something and – '

'Yes, I get it,' Foley said.

'There you are, then, everything in order. Polish up the "To Let" board and back into bed again for a tumble with the wife. They're the finest in the land, these lads, they can ride for hours; every time they're getting near it they just have to think of the money they're going to make in the season.'

'Thinking of wirelesses is not a bad way either,' Foley said. 'If you know anything about wirelesses.'

'The old phoney fishermen down at the harbour practising being local characters so the fools in the pubs will stand them drinks, practising their Cornish burr. Burr!' said Graham with a shiver of disgust. 'You know as well as I do they don't go fishing. They hire their boats out by the hour.'

Why shouldn't they? thought Foley, but he said nothing. He did not want to excite Graham, who was proving milder today than usual, perhaps because he was pleased with the pun he had made. Sometimes his rhetoric got out of control and then he would only stop when clogged by his own obscenities. What disturbed and rather fascinated Foley was the way Graham seemed able to contain his venom, keep it in the lonely vessel of himself, without allowing it either to leak internally and vitiate him with melancholy, or spill over into incidental and ill-timed rantings in public places which might have caused him to be arrested or certified. He simply poured it steadily into the mould of his painting and into the ears of people like Foley whom he had assumed to be sympathetic because of their acquiescence.

'And then the first tremors, you see,' continued Graham. 'They are interrupted in their domestic duties, working out how to save on the breakfasts, extracting the meat from the pasties, watering down the cider. Suddenly the houses shift on their foundations, the sea darkens. This itchy-palmed, feuding, calumnious . . . They don't know what's happening at first, it's never happened before. And the beauty of it is, it's too late to do anything about it, too late for repentance. The bastards have nowhere to run to . . .'

'My goodness yes,' said Foley. 'It would be quite a sight. But we wouldn't see it of course. I mean, it would be happening to us too, wouldn't it?' He waited for a few moments, but there was no answer and looking at Graham's face he found it closed in a sort of rapt complacency. It was impossible to tell whether he had heard the words.

'Or are we exempt?' said Foley, more loudly. He felt a need to assert himself, as though Graham by this insulting finality had somehow broken the rules of their intercourse, which required at least a token deference. But Graham's expression did not change, nor did he look towards Foley. After a moment he turned back to the picture. 'I'd better cover it up,' he muttered. 'It gets me down if I don't.' All at once Foley knew that Graham despised him, regarded him simply as a receptacle, a sort of stooge; and with this perception there came a cold irresistible urge to wound Graham. He thought of the people of the village as he knew them individually. Reviewing them thus he could not immediately fix on anyone whom he would much mind seeing involved in cataclysm. There was Gwendoline, of course, but she could hardly be classed as an inhabitant, she was merely a visitor, and besides he had taken her out of all other conceivable contexts, given her a previous engagement which made it impossible for her to be present even at Doomsday. Suddenly he thought of the girl who had just started work at the post office in Lanruan. She was very young, about fifteen he supposed. This would be her first job

25

after leaving school. She was slow and made mistakes and people quite often became impatient and spoke to her sharply or sarcastically. At such times she blushed darkly and her eyes regarded the customers through her little wire grill with a tearful lustre. It would be a pity, Foley decided, for her to be engulfed.

'I suppose there are exceptions,' he said at last, keeping this vulnerable face in his mind, feeling the excitement of being about to deal a blow at Graham, the unsteadying excitement he always felt when going against the bias of another person's will, risking enmity. Graham was beginning to hang up the sheet again. He had to stand on a chair to hook the top corners.

'What are you getting at?' Graham said, without looking round.

'I should have thought it would be obvious. They can't all be lost souls down there. Some people, apart from you I mean, must be worth saving. If they've all had it, where do you stand? I mean, in that case you'd be either less or more than human.'

Graham had turned now to look at him, but still made no move to get down. His face looked different from below, dignified, mournful and undernourished. The peak of his cap stuck straight out from his forehead like a knightly accoutrement.

'Which are you, Graham, sub or super?' asked Foley, straight up at this strange face.

Graham got down from his chair slowly and came up close to Foley with a very serious expression. 'Are you defending the bloody Cornish?' he asked. There was an intensity in his tone which Foley did not care for.

'I was only saying – ' he began.

'I never thought I'd hear you defending the bloody Cornish,' Graham said, this time with a sort of horrified reproach, as though Foley had been guilty of some racial infamy. His eyes looked quite quenched.

They were beautiful eyes, Foley realised, now that he was seeing them so close, completely without kindness, with little flecks of gold in the irises. He saw that Graham had no intention of attacking him. His feelings had been hurt, that was all, and he didn't for the moment quite know what to do. His own satisfaction at having paid Graham back was fading rapidly as the suspicion grew that he had been unwise. He had not expected to make such a palpable hit. The damage to their relations might well be irreparable.

'I didn't mean it quite like that,' he said in an attempt at appeasement, but Graham had retreated into a corner of the room and would not answer or look at him. After two further attempts he gave it up and took his leave.

Even before reaching the car his sense of having spoken up for humanity had lost its power to please. What was the girl in the post office to him? Besides, he had not disagreed with Graham for her sake, but because he had felt himself slighted. With a little more restraint he could have had it both ways, kept his sympathy for the human race, and Graham's confidence. He felt his latter loss as extremely serious. It had the element of unresolved discord which he hated; it considerably increased the chances of Graham cheating him; and he now ran the risk of being put into Graham's picture. It was particularly disagreeable to think of his own face, whose every lineament he knew so intimately, undergoing the distortions suggested by Graham's malice.

It was not in this way, however, that he was putting the matter to Gwendoline a few minutes later, esconced in one of her armchairs while she sat across the room facing him in another.

'I couldn't let him get away with it, you see,' he was saying, with an assumption of manly forthrightness. From the first he had simplified himself for Gwendoline, presenting the sort of obtuseness which he thought most likely to succeed with her, by giving her scope for the female wisdom she seemed rather keen on. It was a flattery more telling in the long run, he felt, than mere compliments about her looks. To keep it going had meant doing some violence both to his innate secretiveness and to his habit of seeing all sides of a question; and he was not absolutely sure yet that it was the right course. But at least he had discovered that Gwendoline liked the issues as broad as possible so she could get to work breaking them down. This was an activity she enjoyed very much, even when it concerned people such as Graham whom she had never met.

'I felt I had to tell him, you know,' he said.

Gwendoline looked seriously back at him for some moments

without replying, as though she already saw more in this matter than he did. It was an attitude which might normally have irked him but he was still too taken up with Gwendoline's appearance to bother about it much. He thought she was looking particularly attractive this morning. Her hair, which was brown with glints of unapplied auburn, was pinned up on her head in the rather careless way he thought of vaguely as being French. It was a style very becoming to her because it showed to advantage the strong, graceful curve of her neck. Everywhere you looked at Gwendoline there was this satisfying fullness. She was a *meaty* girl. She would have been a gift to the sort of painter that likes painting women getting in and out of the bath. This morning she was wearing a fawn dress of some linen material which shone softly at the points where her body pressed against it, at the shoulders and the high full breasts and along her monumental thighs when she shifted helplessly in her chair. It was the suggestion of helplessness, a sort of unease, as though her body needed soothing, that Foley found most stirring; there was something in it still of the anguish of girlhood where the poise is precarious and seems to depend on the charity of the beholder. He had never found this hapless appeal in thin girls, who find it easier to be all of a piece and have to be content with mere fragility.

Her self-distrust, however, was entirely of the body. It never seemed to affect her belief in the accuracy of her judgements; a fact which she demonstrated now by saying very positively, 'He won't forgive you.'

Foley showed his teeth in a smile and held it for some time. 'That doesn't worry me,' he said. Privately he found her remark presumptuous, especially as it expressed his own misgivings. It was a great pity, he sometimes felt, that girls like Gwendoline, otherwise admirable in every way, so often set up as specialists in people's feelings: it prevented them from giving support to a man when he needed it. 'I should worry about *that*,' he said. 'Ha, ha.'

'No, but listen,' said Gwendoline. 'I mean you have *told* me about this, haven't you, and what I feel about it is this, that you ought not to have waited so long before saying that to Graham. You should have made your position clear from the start. You let him feel that you agreed with him all that time, don't you see that, Ronald?'

'Yes,' said Foley. 'Yes, I do.' In his relations with women he nearly always got bogged down in this sort of insincerity sooner or later, because of his fatal habit of trying to be what people seemed to expect. He had felt sure that what Gwendoline would most like in a man was a sort of virile predictability, plenty of fodder so to speak for her intuition. Instead of rupturing himself in the effort to achieve this he should, of course, simply have behaved naturally. He tried briefly to picture himself behaving naturally, but could not manage it.

'Graham is a very good painter, you know,' he said, with some idea of restoring his own credit by praising Graham up a little. 'He did one painting I like very much, of his dog Flossie. He adores her, it's the one love of his life. He wants to have something to remember her by when she dies. The whole painting is just Flossie's face looking at you full on. I never realised before I saw it what tragic faces dogs have. He'll never sell it, of course.'

'Artists,' said Gwendoline, 'are different from other people, they feel things more.'

Foley experienced a temptation to point out to Gwendoline that Graham would detest her too if he knew of her existence. He saw now that he had made a bad mistake in rushing to her in this dishevelled manner, claiming a false triumph. He should have known that there are some things a woman should never be directly invited to comment on, especially such a judging girl as Gwendoline. It would be time for him to go soon and he was no further forward. He felt it as vitally important that he should kiss Gwendoline this morning. It was on the meticulous observance of such details that the ultimate success of the whole plan depended.

He eyed her stealthily. She was looking dreamily at the carpet beside her feet. Her mouth was full, slightly pouting, a delectable mouth, but he felt no desire to kiss it: all desire had been lost in the terrible necessity for action. She was only a few yards away, but it might as well have been miles. How to find some way of navigating the pitiless expanse of carpet, getting within range? The whole operation seemed incredibly difficult. All very well, the sudden impulse, when bodies were close: closeness after all would condition her to some extent. The thought would surely be in her mind too. But he had not realised that morning, mapping the whole thing out, how very rarely, in the normal course of things, bodies come to rest in this proximity for long enough to bring off such a *coup*.

He got up from his chair and walked over to the bookcase in the far corner of the room. 'Are these all your books,' he said, 'or do they go with the house?'

She made no move to join him. 'Some of them are mine,' she said. 'The ones that were here before are all pretty ghastly. I had to bring some of my own.'

Foley read out one of the titles at random: '*The Snow Goose* by Paul Gallico. That must be one of the landlord's, isn't it?'

'It's one of mine, as a matter of fact,' said Gwendoline coldly.

He felt himself blushing. Bending further down, he began scanning the books on the bottom shelf. 'There's one here I can't see the title of properly,' he said.

'Which one is that?' said Gwendoline. 'Do you mean the red one with the torn cover? That will be one of the landlord's.'

After hovering over the books a few moments longer, Foley gave up and went towards one of the prints that adorned the walls. 'Do you like Modigliani? he said. 'Why do his people always have such long necks? Is it signed? Perhaps they don't put the signature on reproductions.' Instead of coming to show him she got up and went over to the bookcase. She took out the tattered book and looked inside. '*The Compleat Angler*,' she said. 'Did you ever?'

Foley abandoned his scrutiny of the print and moved quickly towards the bookcase. Before he could reach her Gwendoline had replaced the book and gone round the back of the chair into the middle of the room. 'The signature is in the right-hand corner,' she said. 'I can see it from here.' She sat down in her chair again and gloomily Foley resumed his. The thing to do was to rise unhurriedly and saunter over, sit on the arm of her chair. As effortless as a bee settling on a flower. He was beginning, in fact, with a rather terrible sense of weight, to raise his buttocks from the chair again, when Gwendoline suddenly spoke:

'It seems to me from everything you say,' she said judiciously, 'that Graham has integrity at least.' Integrity was a word she used a fair amount. She glanced as she said it round the square

30

sitting-room, at the Modigliani prints on the white walls, the green glass lobster float in its cradle of brown cord which she had found on the beach one day; as though these things quietly demonstrated her own. 'He is all of a piece,' she added, thinking perhaps that the term needed elucidating for Foley.

'Yes, he is, he certainly is,' Foley replied, with a heavy imprecation on Graham's head. The moment had passed; he did not feel capable of nerving himself for it again. Quite suddenly he was given over to a deep depression. It was not anything complicated in the business which daunted him; he liked complications, they justified his habit of scheming. In this case the sheer simplicity of the thing was defeating him, the absence of cover. 'It's time I was going, I'm afraid,' he said, beginning to rise from his chair.

'There's something you must see before you go.' Gwendoline said.

'What is it?'

'It's something you don't see in a girl's room every day.' She spoke in the tone of one who wishes to provoke curiosity. Foley with some difficulty kept up the expression of interest he had immediately assumed. Was the girl actually going to ask him to guess?

Gwendoline held his gaze for a short while, smiling. The enigmatic was the effect she generally aimed at and it worked well enough when her face was in repose or only just smiling, helped by the slow-moving, heavy-lidded eyes and the full mouth. But when she allowed the smile to broaden, as she did now with pleasure at her secret, the whole effect collapsed into a sort of primitive rejoicing, a prolonged and soundless chortle, which was entirely captivating.

'It's a *toad*,' she said. 'I've got a toad in the house. In this room.'

'Good Lord!' exclaimed Foley, startled. 'What are you doing with a toad?' He glanced quickly down. 'Did you say it was in this room?'

'Yes, it's in a kind of tank behind the sofa. Come and look at it. You don't mind toads, do you?'

'No,' Foley said. 'I don't mind them. But why have you got one? Do you like them very much?'

'I have to draw it for a book. I haven't started yet though. I'm still studying it.' She went across to the sofa and kneeling on it looked down over the back. 'Come and look,' she said.

The tank was a metal water cistern, speckled with rust. The sides were a good two feet high and slippery, so the toad probably could not have escaped; in any case it had clearly, for the moment, stopped trying. It sat in one corner looking at them unwaveringly, in a posture which, though inert at present, promised a rather gruesome sprightliness. Not by any apparent increase of tension did it acknowledge their regard.

Gwendoline said: 'Don't you think he's rather sweet? I have to keep him indoors because toads must be kept warm. Warm and moist.'

'Warm and moist,' Foley repeated. 'I didn't know you were illustrating a book.'

'It's a book for children, all about toads, or rather one toad; by a woman called Dove-Gibson who is a friend of an uncle of mine. That's how I got the job, through my uncle. He thinks I can draw anything because I was at art school for a year. Toads are difficult, though.'

As they leaned together over the back of the sofa their shoulders touched. Gwendoline did not move away. Immediately, the normal symmetry of Foley's sensory equipment was wrecked, all sensation flowed swiftly to that little patch of eager skin where beneath his own three layers of clothing and Gwendoline's probable two this warm pressure – surely slightly firmer now? – persisted.

'I'm getting quite fond of him, believe it or not,' Gwendoline said. 'He's absolutely no trouble at all, no dirty habits.'

The toad continued to regard them with beautiful dark eyes under avuncular bulges. Bronze-green pimples like minute bubbles of lava covered its back and sides; and a softer, livid pouch below its throat sagged and distended regularly, marking the pulse of its life. Keeping his eye on the toad, Foley shifted his position cautiously until the whole of his upper arm was pressed closely against Gwendoline's in a manner which could no longer be regarded as accidental: and still she did not move. Now, he told himself.

Gwendoline said: 'He would make a good pet if he was house trained. Toads are intelligent.' Her voice was perfectly composed. Foley uttered a sound that could have expressed incredulity or assent or derision. 'It's true, they *are* intelligent,' she insisted, turning her head with what seemed sudden vehemence towards him.

Foley, with a sense of imminent suffocation, bent his head and kissed her on the corner of the mouth, then worked round gradually until he was kissing her full on. Her lips parted during the latter phase and she leaned suddenly and heavily against him so that he would have fallen if it had not been for the back of the sofa. The kiss was a long one. When it was over they did not look at each other. They remained for some moments with the sides of their faces pressed together. Neither of them said anything. Foley tried to make his breathing less noisy by distributing the breath equally between mouth and nostrils: it didn't seem to make much difference. Then Gwendoline declined her head and he began to move his mouth softly backwards and forwards across her nape. He kept his eyes open throughout, which helped to give him a feeling of detachment. The drooping angle of her head enabled him to see a little way down the back of her dress, a silky tracery of blonde spine hairs, the blunt sprouts of her shoulder-blades. Raising his eyes he had a last impression of the toad pulsating away in its corner, its webbed feet still as stone, before he yielded to the irresistible logic of the situation which demanded, despite his limited aim being well accomplished, more decisive action on his part – action which he now set under way by a gentle but firm pressure on Gwendoline's left shoulder and a gradual reclining of his own body, two manœuvres designed by their cunning coincidence to bring her down, drugged and docile, beside him on the sofa. But this trend to the horizontal was evidently not a logical consequence for Gwendoline, who stiffened and drew away.

'No, don't,' she said, in an incisive, not at all pleading tone. 'We mustn't.'

Foley brought himself up abruptly to a sitting position. He was for a few moments filled with a sharp accusatory resentment. But as he cooled down he began to find her reluctance reassuring. It had all been provided for in the plan. It had in fact the encouraging quality of a partially fulfilled prophecy. With a flash of complacent insight Foley now understood her seeming composure of a short while before. It had ruffled him vaguely at the time that she had not been more tremulous, but now he saw why: she simply did not know what it was all about.

'Why mustn't we?' he asked. She had begun tidying her hair, a sure sign that all, for the time being, was over.

'Because it would be Wrong,' she said. With a hairpin held in her teeth it came over indistinctly but with unimpaired moral force.

He did not press her further, thinking he knew the answers she would make. It was a fairly standard line, after all. Besides, he was unwilling to offend by the gross suggestion that there could have been any real prospects for him, on this the occasion of their very first kiss. He was somewhat surprised indeed that the matter had been raised at such an early stage. But perhaps she had been told by her parents or guardians that kissing led inevitably to *that*.

He conducted the farewells somewhat clumsily, falling, in his anxiety to avoid all marks of vulgar jauntiness, into an excessively social manner. 'We must meet again soon,' he said, as though merely anxious not to lose touch. An unfortunate and ill-judged attitude, as he realised at once. She came out of these exchanges at the door considerably better than he did, with her narrow-eyed, enigmatic expression fully reassembled. He collected himself at the last moment, and remembering that girls like to know where they are with dates asked if he could call again on Friday, for which visit, of course, he had already established an alibi with Moss. She said with unflawed composure that that would be lovely. Friday morning then.

3

Despite the uncompromising beginning to the visit and this slight raggedness at the end, Foley was distinctly pleased with the way things had gone. So much so that as he walked back to the car he was able to dwell on his own part in it without any of the usual misgivings. He was compelled to recognise a certain debt to the toad, but how adroitly he had seized the occasion. He wondered with momentary uneasiness whether Gwendoline's view of the matter quite coincided with his own, but decided that it couldn't possibly not. Of course, she would not have a wide range of comparison.

The harbour was for the moment deserted. Foley stopped to watch a crowd of herring gulls disputing some fish offal in the shallows near the quay. They appeared to dispute, that is, but in fact they were taking turns at it and shrieking just for form's sake. There was only room for one at a time to alight, so each had to shred off quickly what gobbets it could, before being dislodged, and there was a constant flux of cursing gulls in the air above the offal. Foley watched them for some time with a sort of growing protest. The unseemliness of their haste affected him disagreeably; he was struck by the contrast between their grace in the air and their nastiness on alighting. Up there they were beautiful and assured, fractionally avoiding collisions, wheeling with marvellous precision as though on palpable slipways of air. But when they settled, balancing clumsily on the putrid prize, in those few stationary seconds each in turn was revealed for an unclean scavenger, betrayed by the vulturous shuffle of the wings, the carrion glaze on the beak, the rheumy, stupid eyes.

Foley clapped his hands together loudly, stinging the palms, producing thus a sound different from all those the gulls had accustomed themselves to in the life of the harbour; in the silence of panic they all rose and with superb lunges of the wings climbed rapidly and almost vertically into the softly nacreous sky. And as though that clap had been a summons also, an enormously fat man appeared at the opposite side of the harbour and approached him rapidly with a smooth, rolling motion. When he was still about twenty yards away Foley noticed that he had begun speaking, but at that distance the words were indistinct.

'What did you say?' he called.

'Are you Mr Foley, Ronald Foley?' enquired the fat man, drawing nearer. He spoke in the flat, self-protective accents of the Tees-sider, with a certain nasal plangency superimposed, which Foley could not immediately identify. He owned to his name and the man's face seemed visibly to increase in extent, to spread with relief and a kind of triumph. He gave a breathy sigh and spoke on the ebb of it: 'My name is Bailey,' holding out at the same time a large white hand. In allowing his own to be engulfed in it, Foley was aware of a disagreeable moistness, an adhesiveness in the contact. 'Glad to know you, sir,' Bailey said.

Foley murmured, 'How do you do,' by degrees withdrawing his hand, which the other seemed disposed to retain. As well as being very stout, Bailey was a tall man, taller than Moss even: Foley had not only to raise his eyes but to tilt his whole head back in order to look into the other's face. He observed, with the unnerving distinctness sometimes experienced in dreams, that despite the great expanse of the face, the actual features, though properly formed, were freakishly minute; the round, almost lashless eyes and button nose formed the points of an inverted equilateral triangle; far, far below the apex of this, at a point where the face was already overdue for ending, moved a tiny excitable mouth; still further south the chins, a separate study altogether. Over that face Foley felt his eye might travel for ever and find no significant lodgement, no repose.

'You see,' Bailey went on in an explanatory manner. 'You see, what I need are skulls, as a matter of fact,' and while Foley still regarded him dumbly, he added: 'About a dozen or perhaps fifteen.'

There was a short silence during which Bailey's eagerness was audible. Then Foley said 'Skulls?' and smiled painfully. 'I'll see what I can do.' he said.

'That's just not good enough, I'm afraid,' said Bailey, with a sudden briskness that nearly had Foley recoiling. 'I want to know whether you can do it. Come on now, can you or can't you? Life-size they'll have to be and I want them painted with that phosphorescent stuff.' A cagey expression wandered over Bailey's face. 'I'm prepared to pay a fair price,' he said. 'I suppose it goes by weight?' He regarded Foley steadily, and now that money had been mentioned, rather reproachfully, as though he had finally established himself as being in the right.

'You mean you want me to *make* some skulls? Plaster skulls?'

'That's it. They told me . . . You were pointed out to me as the man for the job. I won't say by whom . . .'

'Well, it doesn't matter, does it?'

'I won't say by whom, because I am not at liberty to do so. You must respect confidences, in business.'

'Quite so,' said Foley. 'And, besides, I am not curious.'

'I believe,' Bailey said, 'in dealing direct, going straight to the source, as you might say. You're the man for the job, right-oh. It's a principle of mine, that is. No middlemen, gentlemen's agreement, see what I mean? Our word is our bond, they say that in the Stock Exchange, nothing else needed. Bloody marvellous, isn't it?' Bailey suddenly beamed with pleasure. 'I know a bit about it, you see, I know a bit about commerce,' he said. 'I could say I've *studied* it.'

'All the same,' said Foley, 'I should need an order properly made out.'

'No red tape,' said Bailey. 'Too darn much red tape these days.'

This last epithet, with its homely but alien force, finally cleared up for Foley the mystery of the other's accent: that occasional, disturbing vibrancy was transatlantic; Bailey must have visited the States at some time or other.

'But I should require a properly made-out order,' he repeated.

'Here,' said Bailey, becoming confidential. 'I've bought that place over there.' He pointed across the harbour at a low, broad-fronted building with a narrow terrace approached by a short flight of concrete steps.

'You mean The Harbour Café?'

'No,' said Bailey. 'I don't mean The Harbour Café. I mean The Smugglers' Den. Oh, I know all about it, believe me, I could say I've *studied* the history of the place. That's a principle of mine, get hold of the facts. It was a fisherman's cottage to begin with, then it was The Wishing Well, then Lanruan Crafts, six months that lasted, after that it was The Kit Marlowe Tea Shoppe and then The Harbour Café.' Bailey paused. He seemed to have a good sense of timing, or perhaps he had said all this often before. 'Well,' he continued, 'it's The Smugglers' Den now. A white elephant, you might say, but you'd be wrong. I was told there was a jinx on the place. Balls. No such thing as a jinx, not in business. People don't realise that what a place like that needs is Atmosphere, something out of the ordinary. I saw it myself, right away. I know what this place needs, I said to myself, it needs a bit of Atmosphere, but I didn't let on, of course, mum's the word till you've got it in black and white, that's a principle of mine.'

Bailey threw back his great head suddenly and narrowed his eyes with rapturous shrewdness. 'Drape some fish-nets about, barrels for tables, ships' lanterns for lights, and there you are. And the skulls, of course. The skull and crossbones, you know, the jolly old Roger. I bet they did some rogering, too, up and down these coasts.' Bailey winked vulgarly.

'That was pirates,' said Foley. 'Not smugglers.'

'Comes to the same thing. People on holiday, they like something a bit different. The place was noted for smugglers, wasn't it, in the old days?'

Foley uttered sounds of polite assent. He rarely questioned views so emphatically expressed. Besides, he could see that this was reasoning the other had lived closely with for some time. All the same, Bailey did not inspire confidence. He was too voluble for one thing. There was a fatal air of eccentricity about him. Of course it happened from time to time that somebody came to Lanruan, started something up and made a lot of money quite quickly. Lanruan was that sort of place. But these successful persons never expounded their intentions beforehand. Nor, in Foley's experience, did they refer at all frequently to principles. Bailey's, in any case, had largely cancelled one another out.

'I'm prepared to offer,' Bailey said, 'for twelve skulls in good condition painted phosphorescent white – '

'In view,' Foley said firmly, 'of the fact that a new mould would be needed, which would have to be scrapped immediately afterwards, since you will appreciate that it's not every day we are asked for skulls, not to mention – '

'Ten pounds the lot,' said Bailey. He began a sort of smooth withdrawing motion intended to indicate finality.

'Quite frankly,' said Foley, raising his voice slightly as Bailey was now some yards away, 'it would not be worth our while for less than a guinea a skull.'

Bailey came to a halt. 'You don't mean to tell me,' he said, 'that there's anything very tricky about a skull. Christ!' he added, reproachfully.

Foley said: 'I don't think you quite realise the amount of work that goes into . . . A skull is a complicated structure, anatomically speaking. And I take it you want yours to be realistic.'

'How much then?' Bailey asked, closing his eyes for a second in assumed weariness.

'Well, it would be twelve guineas, wouldn't it?'

'For fifteen?'

'No, for twelve.'

'Knock off the odd twelve bob,' Bailey said moodily.

'All right. Twelve pounds then. We can't begin till next month, I'm afraid, because of previous orders. We could have them ready by about the middle of May if that's all right.'

Bailey recommenced his withdrawal, still facing Foley. 'That doesn't matter so much,' he said. 'There's a lot to do to the place yet. I don't expect to open till the beginning of July.' He was quite a long way off now and beginning a slow and ponderous turn.

'Isn't that rather late in the season?' Foley called.

'Just in time for the peak period,' said Bailey over his shoulder. 'Well, goodbye for now.' The turn completed, he put himself in rapid motion, but not the way he had come.

Foley walked slowly back towards the car. With the advent of Bailey he felt that the season had definitely begun. Every year they appeared, with the swallows, people on the make, people on the run, pedlars of every sort. From the middle of May to the middle of September, Lanruan throbbed with financial aspiration. Some, like Bailey, came with an Idea, others for pickings generally. Yet others – quite a numerous class this – were refugees from metropolitan involvements, brought to a halt on these shores by the impassable character of the Channel. They lingered for a summer, sustained by some hope or ambition, and vanished without trace.

Foley hated to think of this seasonal wreckage, the anguish of these persons drifting without a hold on the future, without a plan. By some process impossible to prevent, this became his own anguish too. Perhaps it was simply that he had himself quite recently emerged from a similar existence – his life in London with its expedients and uncertainties. Only the pixies lay between him and resubmergence in that element. Only the pixies kept his life plugged – and his cherub-lamps, of course. Thoughts of these were always comforting. He thought of them now, softly refulgent in the quiet attic, the suspended ones trembling very, very slightly, the light shifting on their antique rotundities. A different class of thing from the pixies altogether.

He drove along the far side of the harbour. Barbara Gould's house was the last one, and faced out over the open sea. The road ended here, dwindling to a footpath which led over the cliffs to Tollynt, the next village, about five miles further down the coast. Foley left the car outside the house and proceeded down the path to the front door. He rang the bell and listened. No sounds could be heard from the interior. After a moment Foley opened the door himself and stepped into the passage. Here he coughed several times and tapped his feet. Barbara's voice called from the sitting-room, asking who it was. Foley infused his own voice with a reassuring resonance. 'It's me,' he called through the wall. 'Ronald Foley. Long time no see.' He regretted this last expression terribly, the moment he had said it. There was no reply, which meant at least that Barbara was alone: if she had been entertaining some man or other she would have told him immediately to go away. This had happened several times before. Foley opened the sitting-room door and walked in.

When he had not seen a person for some time Foley was always apprehensive of finding some radical change in character or appearance; and he had not seen Barbara since the previous October. Thus for the first few seconds after entering the room he looked at her with anxiety. She seemed to be the same.

'How was London?' he said, knowing she would not let herself be thus interrogated. She was sitting near the window with a black towel round her head like a turban and a sort of pale blue wrap on, which Foley immediately decided was a kimono.

'A few minutes earlier and you'd have found me in the bath, or just getting out,' she said. 'What would you have done?' She had a voice that went with her plumage, harsh and carrying. Foley smiled, pretending to consider. 'So far it's always been tradesmen who have caught me in the bath, particularly grocers,' Barbara went on. 'Most disappointing. I always hope for the best, of course. But I see their faces change, through the steam. They say things like Oops! or Oompah! and bolt for the door. Grocers in particular I have found to be a most timorous class of men. They must use up all their nerve manipulating those bacon-slicers.'

Foley kept on with his amused, considering smile. He knew of old Barbara's habit of getting people where she wanted with this sexual talk, always more pronounced with strangers, or people she had not seen for some time. It was her way of keeping the initiative. The present subject was one he had no wish at all to pursue. Besides, he needed time, as always, to adjust himself to the extreme bareness and starkness of this room in which everything, except Barbara herself and the black divan against the wall, was white, flat white, without even a gloss: the ceiling, the walls, the sparse furniture, all dead white and shadowless. There was nothing, in fact, for the eye to rest on, except Barbara and the divan, a conjunction which Foley had ceased to regard as accidental. Reflected light from the sea directly below accentuated the blanched effect, but even without this there was scarcely anything that could have mustered a shadow. The thing one noticed almost at once was the complete absence of objects: there were no little boxes or bottles or receptacles for things, concessions made to the passing of time. Time indeed was not acknowledged in this room, even as inimical. There were no mementoes, no photographs showing Barbara's younger faces, no clock. It was a room sealed off and curiously clinical, like the

41

white rooms in hospitals where time is only a graph at the foot of the bed. Through the open window the notes of the bell-buoy sounded with absolute regularity, like the pulse of the sea. It would not have been possible to guess that this was a woman's room, there was no female scent or spoor in it, no hairpins, no elastic, no smells of drying nylon. The room held out no intimacies save the ultimate one suggested by the divan against the wall, which was of a useful breadth and velvety black and which Foley had never so much as sat upon: reclining on it was inconceivable, unless for the recounting of old traumas or for some sort of operation.

He sat at the table, still holding on to the smile, though he felt it was becoming rather frayed. 'It might be a subject for research,' he said. Barbara regarded him in silence. The towel concealed her hair completely, emphasising the beaky opulence of her features, the large, almond-shaped eyes. The folds of the kimono, or whatever it was, covered her slight form and only her bare feet showed, still rosy from the bath; they were beautiful feet, narrow and proudly arched at the instep; the nails were painted scarlet. Foley thought of saying how much he liked the kimono, but said nothing in case it turned out not to be one. The sight of Barbara's red toenails immediately revived an old speculation as to whether she painted her nipples. He only wondered this about Barbara, not about any other women he knew. It would be with some gentle, non-abrasive lacquer, if she did. Milky-rose would be the shade, or gold, or that lovely silver-grey he remembered using years ago as an under-coat for model aeroplanes. The dark nipples would glow through . . .

'You'd probably be just as bad,' Barbara said.

'As bad as what?'

'As bad as all those grocers. Judging by the voice you put on for me when you came in, I'm afraid you'd be even worse. *And* without the bacon-slicer excuse.'

'What voice do you mean?' enquired Foley, to gain time.

'You know perfectly well what voice I mean. That breezy, respecter-of-womanhood voice. It makes me feel elderly. Do you suppose I start worrying about being raped every time I hear muffled noises in the passage?'

Foley tried to counter this with a sustained humorous gaze, intended to make rebuttal unnecessary, a mistake on his part, since Barbara proceeded to outstare him.

'I do it to reassure myself, not you,' he said at last, giving up the struggle to beat down those rigid lashes and lowering his own gaze instead. He was conscious of having somewhere else that morning encountered a similarly luminous and inhuman regard, but could not immediately decide where. 'I *know* I'm doing it,' he added, and the familiar confessional feeling began to come over him, derived from all the previous occasions when he had sat in this uncomfortable room and fluttered his ego in Barbara's cold sunshine with the bracing sense that everything he said was sealed off from the world by her contemptuous discretion. Not that he trusted Barbara – he trusted no one at all – but he needed a hearer from time to time for the incessant dialogue he carried on with himself. It helped to clarify the issues, especially at times of stress. And in Barbara he felt he had found the almost perfect confidante. He was sure she never spoke of him to anyone else, no one that mattered anyway, partly because her local contacts were so slight. She divided her year between this cottage and her flat in London, and even her men visitors were not of the vicinity but came from far places wearing corduroy caps and silk cravats, details which distinguished them from the local bucks as effectively as if they had been from another planet; all this had incensed public opinion against Barbara but increased her security value from Foley's point of view – he didn't in the least mind people talking about him in Fulham or Pimlico, for example – wherever Barbara's admirers came from; anything likely to affect the local trade concerned him. However, the main reason for his belief in Barbara's discretion was her unfeeling way of bottling up people in anecdotes and then putting them away. She was only interested in the quintessential, and that only in order to dismiss. She lacked the compulsion of the real gossip whose interest in the subject is coextensive with life itself, who desires above all to impress others with special knowledge, special sources of information. Barbara would have seen little point in that. So Foley kept his relation undramatic – that part at least which referred to himself and Moss and the business – and felt safe, and pleased with himself too.

43

Time, moreover, had proved him right: in the course of three summers nothing had come back to him. It was, he felt, quite long enough.

'I *hear* myself doing it, you see,' he went on. 'I suppose everybody has a sort of private armoury of tones from which they choose to suit the occasion. I know I have, at any rate. And they're all genuine, it seems to me. I've behaved quite differently with all the people I've seen so far this morning. Why, only just now, just a few minutes ago as I was on my way here, a man stopped me and asked me for some skulls . . .' He told her about Bailey. He was not a very good mimic, being far too wrapped up in himself, but he managed to bring out Bailey's unwieldly, conspiratorial delivery and the horridness of that request.

Barbara laughed harshly. 'Did you say he had a very small nose? I have a theory about men with small noses, a theory of correspondences. It's still only in the experimental stage, of course, but some day I shall publish my findings.'

Foley smiled again, on a smaller scale, waiting for the ripples of these remarks to die away. It was part of his policy with Barbara never to take up such allusions, partly because they led away from himself to some other subject of discourse, and partly because he sensed they might damage the essential chastity of his relations with her. After some moments he said:

'Nobody knows much about other people's tones. One always tends to think that the tone employed towards oneself is the true one, that is, the one most expressive of the other person's nature. But the person I know with the smallest range of tones is Moss. He only seems to have one.'

'Ah, yes, Moss. Still going strong, is he?'

'He certainly is,' said Foley, with feeling. He paused again. It was Moss he had been wanting to talk about, but he felt unable for the moment to go on. Discussing Moss was not something to be entered on lightly. It was difficult, for one thing, to know where to begin. There was no one but Barbara with whom it would have been feasible to discuss Moss at all.

'You're the only person I can talk to about it,' he said. 'As you probably know,' he added, looking gratefully across at her. This acknowledgement should gratify her, surely. He wondered suddenly whether Barbara really did know how much these visits meant to him. He knew very little, really, of what she felt, but he didn't wish to know more. She suited him so well precisely because he did not care unduly about the impression he made on her. By not attracting him, she freed him from shams. There was, in fact, something in the composure of her figure, the bony deftness of her hands and feet, the hard, almost warrior-like, sexuality she exuded, which repelled and at times even horrified him a little. He liked soft, exploitable women within whose indulgence he could machinate. Barbara was too avid, too discerning, too experienced. But the absence of tenderness between them was favourable to the austerities of his self-analysis. Sometimes, it was true, because he could not help looking for pitfalls, Foley grew uneasy, wondering what she got out of it all.

'I feel at ease with you,' he said. 'I suppose it's because you expect nothing from me.'

'But I do, dear boy,' Barbara said. 'I expect great things from you. Not that it matters now. Tell me about Moss.'

Foley thought for a moment, or rather, while he paused, into his mind came a vision of Moss as he had been that morning, his features constructed round the habit of jovial surprise. He said: 'Moss has been behaving very oddly lately. This morning he actually seemed to resent my coming to see you.' He told her briefly about his argument with Moss, sharpening up the epigrammatic quality of his own observations, reducing the offensiveness of Moss's.

'And you defend me against him? That is very touching. He was quite right though, in the main.'

'Well, I can visit whoever I like, surely.' Foley brooded for a moment. 'I have the feeling that he's watching me all the time these days, as though he suspected me of something. It's making me terribly secretive. I never tell him a thing now if I can help it. What can it be, do you think?'

'I don't know. Perhaps he's worried about you, seeing your weaknesses.'

'That's exactly what he doesn't do. He thinks I've got quite different weaknesses from the ones I have. Actually he doesn't see *me* at all. He made up his mind about me a long time ago. You know, when Moss gets an idea of you, it's just like being lassooed. Well, he decided that I am a completely irresponsible person. Glamorous, in a way.' Foley spoke deprecatingly to disarm Barbara's irony. 'My own worst enemy, that sort of thing. He's always trying to protect me. The trouble is, he hasn't a clue himself really.'

'Well, he's certainly wrong if he thinks that about you,' Barbara remarked. 'You're a schemer, if ever there was one.'

'Perhaps I am,' said Foley, rather pleased. 'The trouble is, though, that I played up to Moss at the beginning. It seemed easier, then, to get together a few working suppositions about each other, not necessarily true, but viable – comfortable, so we could get on with things.'

'And now you're beginning to find his idea of you oppressive?'

'It's not that so much,' said Foley. 'Of course, in a way I always disliked him a bit for thinking he understood me so well. But I was very anxious that nothing should go wrong. It meant a lot to me that we should make a success of the business. It meant a lot to him, too. So I was prepared to put up with things, you see. And then Moss believed in his idea of me so much that I began to myself, a little. It was quite pleasant, really. I mean I knew what I was like and I knew what Moss thought I was like, so it gave me something – an extra dimension. And I never had to do anything disagreeable to back it up. No, it's not that. But now Moss is turning sour on me. He says nasty things to me. Only the other day he asked me if I didn't sometimes worry about what would happen to me when my looks were gone. He suggested I should start building up what he called "inner resources". "I've got plenty of inner resources already, thank you very much," I told him.'

Foley stared at Barbara solemnly, to mark his sense of outrage.

'You two are so dissimilar,' Barbara said. 'It always amazes me that you should have gone into partnership at all.'

'It *was* largely an accident. We didn't know each other before. We met here in Lanruan. I had this idea, you know, for a pixie business, and I needed someone dependable to go in with me. I happened to meet Moss just at the right moment.'

'You must have summed up his character very quickly.'

'I suppose it *was* taking a chance,' Foley said. 'But we have to sometimes, don't we?' He smiled at her, his Old Campaigner smile, which involved stretching the lips without opening them, and screwing up his eyes attractively. He did not find it necessary to add that in any case the chance had not been taken by him, but by Moss, since Moss had put up all the money.

'He's getting so possessive too,' Foley said. 'We had a real row last week. It was that I wanted to tell you about. We went to the "Jubilee" for a drink. We sometimes go there mid-week, you know, it's really the only place we ever do go together, during the season. Lesley Garland was there. I don't know if you know him. He used to be in a cabaret act, "The Top Hatters" they called themselves, very crummy. Then he married one of the Richmond girls. Gentleman farmer he calls himself now, but he does nothing much except hang about the pub and natter about the doggy old days. Not a bad chap. Anyway, he asked five or six of us at closing time if we'd like to come back home with him for a few drinks, and I said straight away, "Yes, thanks very much we'd love to, wouldn't we, Moss?" Moss had hardly opened his mouth all evening. Now, after I'd already accepted, mind you, he said he thought we'd better be getting back home, we had work to do next day, and so on. You don't know how sort of *heavily* Moss can say things like that, as though everyone else is idle and frivolous. The others all looked at me in a most peculiar way. I felt *embarrassed*. In the end I said I'd come anyway and Moss could go home if he wanted. He did go home too, which I hadn't expected. He was waiting for me when I got back. I didn't want to argue but he started on at me the moment I got through the door. He said didn't I know there was such a thing as loyalty and I said he had no right to try to dictate to me. We had a regular set-to. I don't think he had expected me to answer back, because I don't usually, you know, but this time I got very cross. Moss went as white as death and kept swallowing. It was terrible.'

An enterprising but misguided bluebottle had got in through the window; after one brisk tour of the aseptic walls its buzzing contained a trapped note. Behind Barbara's head Foley saw the sea, green and glistening and faintly corrugated, salted in patches with motionless gulls.

'It was terrible,' he repeated. 'We haven't really recovered from it yet. In point of fact,' he added with an excess of candour, 'I would have gone back with him if only he'd given me a loophole. As things were, I couldn't, it would have been too undignified. But that's Moss all over, it would never occur to him to make things easier for one. He's got no tact.'

'Was it a good party?'

'What? Oh, no, not very. There was another row at the party, only I wasn't in it. We met Max Nugent outside the pub, or rather we didn't meet him. We found him there. He was drunk.'

'He is always drunk, isn't he? At least he never seems to show himself unless he is. He is a sweet man, I think, don't you? I think it's very wrong of that actor of his to keep him cooped up all alone here in the country. It's like buying someone's life.'

'Simon Lang you mean, yes, but he pays Max's rent and keeps him, you know. I don't know what would happen to Max if Simon stopped sending the money. It must be twenty years since there was anything *physical* between them.'

'I don't think you quite see what I mean, Ronald. Never mind, tell me what happened.'

'Well, as I said, we found Max outside. He was on his hands and knees in the shrubbery that runs alongside the car park. He said he was looking for a pair of yellow woollen gloves. It wasn't cold enough for gloves, you know. We all started looking and someone asked him where he had dropped them, and he said he hadn't dropped any, he was just looking for some. In he end we took him with us. It wasn't so bad at Garland's at first, we all had some whisky, but he would insist on playing these old records of "The Top Hatters" – terribly dated, and feeble anyway. It became rather a bore, because Garland kept laughing out loud at these ghastly songs and expecting everyone else to laugh too. Then Max suddenly started saying that Simon Lang was a great artist and Garland was annoyed at having his songs interrupted and said Danny Kaye was a greater artist and Max got absolutely furious and started shouting and one of Garland's children woke up and cried and Garland told Max to clear out. Max slammed all the doors and that woke Garland's other children up – he has four altogether. Garland jumped up and went after Max but Max had disappeared, and in the confusion one of "The Top Hatter" records was broken. No, it wasn't a good party, really. Perhaps that's why I flung out at Moss as I did.'

Barbara asked suddenly, 'Has Moss had many girl friends?'

'I've never actually met any in the flesh,' Foley said. 'We both go up to London fairly frequently in the winter. I don't know what he gets up to there. There's a photograph of a girl in his room but I've never asked him about it. He told me once she was in South Africa. We never discuss that kind of thing. I somehow can't picture Moss actually *doing* anything. It seems to daunt the imagination, it's like blasphemy, difficult to explain really. I've always thought of him as a confirmed bachelor.'

'It doesn't do to go by appearances,' interrupted Barbara. 'He might be quite a thruster. My first husband looked good enough to be used for stud purposes, a high-coloured man he was, with the most *sensual* mouth. He really looked capable of *feats*. He was in a body-building club, too. Twice a week they used to go and lift weights and talk to one another about their laterals and things like that. I was only eighteen then and I had led a sheltered life. I was crazy about him. I'd have done anything he wanted. I *told* him quite frequently during our engagement that I'd do anything he wanted, but he said he respected me too much. He was waiting for our wedding-night. I thought at the time he seemed a little too resigned. I expected him to *chafe* more, because it was quite a long engagement, but I didn't know very much about these things.'

Barbara paused, fixing Foley with a regard of ironical steadiness. 'You'll hardly believe it,' she said, 'but I was still a virgin after the honeymoon. He only managed it half a dozen times all the eighteen months we were married and even then I hardly knew it had happened.'

'Probably something psychosomatic,' said Foley.

'Call it what you like,' Barbara said, 'but there was all that gorgeous hulk, quite useless. I'd have been better off with a randy dwarf. He used to kneel down beside the bed and pray every night before he got into bed with me. I always wondered what he was praying for. It was wearing me down, seeing him there night after night, kneeling in his night-shirt. He always wore a night-shirt. God, how I hated those big strong shoulders of his and his hairy

49

legs. What I wanted more than anything to do, was creep up behind him while he was praying, lift up his night-shirt and jab him as hard as I could in the bottom with my finger. I was a very high-spirited girl.'

'Good Lord,' Foley said, 'what an extraordinary impulse!' He glanced at Barbara's nails, blood-red and of inordinate length.

'I don't know why I wanted to do it so much,' Barbara said. 'It was something that mounted up night after night, seeing that great big back turned on me.'

'Did you do it in the end?'

'Oh yes, I did it. I had to do it.'

'What did he say when you did it?'

'Well, what with wanting so much to do it, and wondering all the time if I was going to do it that night or the next night, and putting it off, when I finally did it I was overcome. I jabbed him as hard as I could and then I just burst into tears. He turned round and looked at me. I was crying so hard I could hardly see. "I am saying my prayers, Barbara," he said in a sort of *reproving* voice. He didn't say anything else. I hated him after that. I hate him now, terribly, although he's dead.'

Barbara looked down for a moment at her fingers. 'I suppose I could have got a divorce for denial of rights or incompatibility or something, but the war came. Victor had been a keen Territorial and he was commissioned immediately in the Somerset Light Infantry. He looked marvellous in his officer's uniform. He grew a little blond moustache. It must have suited him down to the ground while it lasted. All those comrades and no sex to bother about. Doing press-ups and having showers. I should think he was in his element. He was killed in the second year of the war. In France. They gave him a medal with a ribbon. Well, they gave it to me actually. I mislaid it years ago. D.C., I think it was, but I always get it confused with the electric currents. Victor had behaved with what they called conspicuous gallantry. It seems he gave his life to retrieve a wounded lance-corporal who shortly afterwards expired.'

Barbara smiled and looked unblinkingly at Foley. 'Poor Victor,' she said. 'He was always a bungler. I didn't really know what I was missing in those days . . .'

Foley cleared his throat. There were times when Barbara's sheer lack of piety filled him with something like awe. Such vindictiveness made her seem for the moment more than mortal. Ever since the day he had died she must have been punishing Victor. Over and over, whenever people tolerant enough were gathered, she must have told her little story of the impotence and the night-shirt and the praying and the pointless death. Hatred for Victor had disturbed her judgement and she did not see that dying for somebody is not ridiculous even when it is pointless. Foley thought of Victor, big and fair and red-faced, some of his stuffing mislaid no doubt, but not that which determines courage. Perhaps he had insisted on dying, just as earlier he had insisted on praying. 'Well, it's time I was going, I'm afraid,' he said. 'I'm coming down again on Friday morning so I'll drop in again then, if I may.'

'Yes, do,' said Barbara. 'By the way, those skulls you were talking about – do you think you could make an extra one and sell it to me? I sometimes think this room needs a bit of brightening up. It would do as a *memento mori* too, wouldn't it? Whenever I felt tempted to join a book club or keep a budgerigar, I could look at it and remember that I'm going to die some day.'

4

Before setting out on his Sunday afternoon walk, Moss always spent half an hour or so in his workroom, engaged in what he described to himself as reviewing the incidents of the past week. Sundays had an objective quality which made them best for this. Lately, however, he had not been very successful at marshalling the facts and getting them into perspective: efforts to do so seemed to stir up an emotional residue, a kind of silt, which clouded everything and took a long time to settle again. Today he felt it was particularly important, indeed vital, that he should keep his calm – not an acquiescent calm, but the poise of a wrestler – because today for the first time Ronald was bringing the girl home. He had been hinting at the possibility of this for almost a month, and now that it was happening at last Moss felt the need for complete self-possession. Not that he expected to be favourably impressed by the girl. Her very name, when he had finally learnt it, had seemed to confirm his worst fears about her. He said it softly to himself again now, Gwendoline: the bogus lisping homeliness of the opening syllable, the mindless pause in the middle, the factitious sweetness of the close – in which there seemed to lie also a threatening, abrasive quality. It was no good saying anything to Ronald. He had already departed to collect her, far too flimsily dressed for the time of year. May wasn't out yet after all, but it was no good saying anything. The two of them were to go for a walk first and come back about tea-time, the actual provision of tea being, of course, his concern.

Count your blessings, Moss told himself. He was fond of adages and all pegs for thought. At least the business was doing well. They had enough work already to keep them going through the summer, more than enough. People from further and further away were asking for their work; they were getting a name. It had to be admitted that Ronald was good when it came to business, very good. He never minded working hard and he was keen too, full of ideas. Take the money-box line for example, that had been a first-rate idea of Ronald's – as an idea. He had wanted to embark on a difficult, complicated group of pixies clustered in different attitudes on top of a large hollow toadstool, each pixie to have a little slot for sixpences in its belly, so that all the coins slipped down into the toadstool. But he had listened, that was the point, he had taken notice when Moss had suggested instead a single, large pixie with a crafty sack over its shoulder, the slot for the coins at the neck of the sack; so much easier, and cheaper too. 'You are right, Michael,' he had said, just like that. He recognised the value of a cooler judgement. That was the way things should always be between them, give and take. That was what a partnership was for.

If only Ronald would take his advice about other things too. Reluctantly Moss's mind reverted to the impending visit. It marked a dangerous advance in intimacy, either a lowering of resistance or a hardening of intention on Ronald's part. Moss could not think of this without intense alarm. She was just the girl, he felt sure, with a name like that, to assume a domestic demureness for the occasion, insinuate the need for a woman's touch. Well, he swore to himself, she should find no bachelor squalor here. She would find that men could look after themselves perfectly well, *and* without a lot of female clutter. Silly, dirty clutter that women left everywhere like droppings . . . His mind flinched away. Women's clothes should all be white and loose-fitting and made of cotton, not slippery silk, and they should be boiled for a long time. He grasped this vision of shining hygiene, and was about to get up when, without any preliminary warning this time, he had one of his flushes. He had time for nothing but a glance at his watch.

As usual, the immediate sensation was one of complete inability to move; as though he was out of his depth in some thick, warm fluid which buoyed him up vertical and motionless, enfolding him in an outer layer of heat and climbing at the same time with a terrible agility the internal rungs of his helplessly suspended body.

The early stages were not unpleasant and there was one point at which he experienced, briefly, a sort of subjugating sweetness; but as the heat rose, threatening to engulf him, his breathing became constricted and his vision blurred. Always at this stage he felt that he could not survive, that he was in process of drowning, of dissolution; but this was the culminating moment. After this the flush ebbed and the little gasps that Moss uttered were sounds of relief mainly, as he felt himself once more above the surface. He looked at his watch again.

Still gasping, but at longer intervals, he went upstairs for his scarf and beret. He wore a scarf and beret until the beginning of June, no matter what the weather.

Outside the cottage the sun halted him immediately. He stood still at the door with a vivid sense of his body recuperating. He felt planted and growing there, and with this confluence of energies came a rare sense of wonder at the miraculous interplay within him, between the eddies of his blood and his compact flesh. He pressed his hands flat against the frontal convexities of his thighs, pleased by their hardness. He raised his right arm and clenched his fingers slowly into a fist. The knuckles whitened under his gaze. Moss knew himself to be extremely strong. He regarded his strength as an identifying attribute, like the colour of his eyes. It had grown without any special effort or training on his part and had not resulted in any particular skills. It was simply there, almost in the abstract: a capacity to lift and heave, impose his will on inert things.

He was still half turned towards the cottage, and when he raised his eyes from his fist, he saw for the first time in his years of living there that the stone of the wall supported a film of minute mosses, a seeping pale green tide pricking roots thinner than hairs into the seams of the plaster and even, where there was an irregularity in the surface, battening on the tiny pockets of dust left there by the wind or the decay of tissues. Such tenacity amazed him. There must have been a network of roots spiring through the masonry of the house like the burnished tendrils of a tumour. Strange, too, that he had never before noticed this intense life. He was about to take a closer look when Royle, their landlord, appeared, driving before him a black and white bullock with heavy blows of a stick.

He was cursing in a soft, accomplished monotone. Moss guessed that the bullock had disobeyed some order, and was being taken to the punishment paddock for a beating. The punishment paddock was behind the farmhouse on the seaward side. The offence must have been serious, Moss thought, to have so incensed Royle that he could not wait until they reached the appointed place. When he drew level with Moss he looked up briefly. 'We s'll have more rain, I do believe,' he said, in a soft voice, his face purple with rage. Moss nodded, not believing this. Royle proceeded on his way and was soon lost to sight, but the sound of the blows continued.

Moss took a step nearer to the wall and scrutinised the plants. It seemed to be some kind of fungus mostly, but here and there, skeining the wall, was a different sort of plant, a creeper with glossy, denticulated leaves, gummy hoop-shaped tendrils and tiny dark blue flowers like microscopic violets. Moss advanced his face close to the wall, possessed by a kind of ardour. The little blue flowers were beautiful, bell-shaped, and each one had a speck of yellow, only just visible, in the centre of its throat . . . Suddenly Moss saw that they were actually rooted in previous clumps, putrescent now, and in fact extracting from these a sparse ooze; all over the wall, as it seemed, a swampy efflorescence was taking place, the new plants hooked into the nourishing corpses of the old. Simultaneously with this perception, and quite unmistakably, there came to his nostrils a stench of decay. The surface of the wall, from this close, smelled like a clogged drain. Disgusted, he stepped back quickly. No doubt caused by the high degree of humidity in the atmosphere, he thought, seeking for a formula to neutralise the indecency.

Slowly he walked down the farmyard in the direction of the sea. The feeling of disgust persisted. He thought of the fertilising and corrupting moisture, invisible droplets of it in the air all around him, breeding plants that stank, fleshing the gum-pink undersides of mushrooms on the cliffs, fattening the fungoid umbrellas in the crotches of trees, that rotted as they grew and ended as malodorous puddles. Hang a piece of meat out in this air and the maggots would be at it before you could snatch your hand away.

Beyond the farm outhouses he passed through a wooden gate

and followed a faint track across two fields, then down through a narrow gully made by a dry stream bed. Entering this gully was always a strange sensation for Moss, a descent deliberate but curiously clandestine, away from the open fields, the arid certainties of the sea. The high banks enclosed him, the chestnut trees with which the banks were planted met overhead. Their great candles of flower were full out now and their scent filled the air. From time to time Moss was obliged to duck his head to pass beneath the branches. A blackbird, possibly with a nest in the vicinity, followed him, repeating a single fluting note at exact intervals. At its lower end the gully widened and led into a regular, bowl-shaped declivity about two acres in extent, in which there was an orchard of ancient, maimed apple-trees, bounded on the far side by a screen of hawthorn bushes. This was the farthest limit of Royle's cultivable property; beyond it the gorse and broom began and the land took a steep tilt towards the sea. It was the place on the whole farm that Moss liked most. Except for him no one seemed to come here. Certainly, no one bothered about the trees. The small, sweet apples were allowed to fall year after year and the wasps got boozed on them. The trunks of the trees were scabbed with pale green lichen, and lichen draped the lower branches in petrified swathes giving the whole orchard the appearance of a marine grotto: one would not have been surprised to see fish at eye-level swimming about among the branches. Above this, however, through the crust of algae, the trees had thrust their blossom with improbable abundance, as though conscious of dying.

Moss stood among the trees looking up through the gushes of blossom at the pale blue sky. The noises of the farm and the sea reached him here with an effect of reassurance, sustaining but not involving him. The hills around spluttered with the invalid cries of sheep. Out at sea and invisible the bell-buoy recorded the swell. Quite close, hidden among the leaves, a bird that he could not identify began to sing; the sweet, intensely inhuman phrases trickled through the foliage like something shed or spilt which could never be gathered again.

He sat down at the foot of a tree and rested his back and the back of his head against the trunk. Bees were rifling the flowers above him; he could hear how their drone was deadened when they entered the cups. The ravished stamens gave off heady waves of scent. By degrees, amidst this sweetness, Moss became aware of a darker strand of odour, sweet too, but muskier, different from yet not altogether alien to the smells of propagation all around. He was still trying to identify this smell when quite suddenly thoughts of Lumley came into his mind and the familiar narrative began again, with its attendant apprehension and regret, began, it seemed, without his volition, as though in these surroundings there was some irresistible stimulus or reminder. He could not think of Lumley now except as part of this narrative, beginning with the straggling double file of schoolboys walking through the cobbled streets towards the swimming baths. Habitual recollection had fixed an emotion to every point of the story and he could sense again after all these years his clumsiness among the others, the cap too large and worn absurdly straight on his head, the grey flannels hitched too high, flapping round his ankles. Preedy leading them, striped prefect's cap at a knowing angle, blazer tight round substantial buttocks. Lumley somewhere in the file, unknown then except as the others of the form were known, a slight, unassertive boy with a pale, oval-shaped face and very red lips, who had once made the whole form laugh by imitating the mannerisms of the organist, pulling out the stops with terrible grimaces; only this little spurt of mimicry in all that year redeeming him from complete obscurity.

Once more at this customary point Moss paused to wonder at that obscurity and to feel gratitude for the boon of intimacy which had been granted him; because during that walk to the baths and during the changing in the cubicles, all that time Lumley had been afraid and no one else had known it; the vibrations of his fear reached no one at the time. Only afterwards was Moss given the privilege of sensing it, and it almost certainly would never have entered his range of perceptions at all without the feeling he had come to have for Lumley.

The sequence of his memories, orderly up to the entrance to the baths, was broken and confused among the clanging doors of the cubicles, with their scratched, corroded sides, the pencilled slogans and drawings of copulations in defiance of anatomy which covered the inside walls; the steamy echoing pool, the hissing green water that slopped in the gutter all the way round and caused the cracks in the cream-tiled floor of the pool to squirm like eels as you stood looking down from the matted springboards.

Lumley had been an inveterate shallow-ender; he would always have preferred to dabble about in the water, waist high, no more, jumping up and down to try to keep warm, head held rigidly back from the slopping surface; engaging from time to time in little shrieking battles with his peers.

On this day for reasons of his own he had wandered along the edge of the pool to where the water was deep and the surface bobbed with sleek heads, threshed with flailing back strokes, dangerous. Why he did this on this particular day Moss had never discovered. Only since that time, during the years when it was no longer possible to ask, had it occurred to him to wonder. And on this day Preedy was in charge, who no doubt believed he was doing his duty, getting the shirkers into the water, but who was known most to enjoy duty when it meant pain for the timid or the inept.

Preedy must have noticed Lumley at that moment, as he lingered at the edge watching the lordly ones in the water. Preedy would have observed immediately the dry swimming trunks, the dry hair, the clear whites of the eyes. Here was a boy who hadn't even been in yet. And Lumley had not of course obeyed the order to get into the water at once – the water was six feet deep there. He must have attempted to edge back to the safety of the far end, but found his retreat cut off. Then Preedy had started flicking at him with the wet towel to drive him over the side – idly at first and then, roused by Lumley's mincing passiveness, more deliberately. A wet towel, used as Preedy knew how to use it, was as good as a whip. From where he was standing halfway down the pool, Moss had seen the pain and shame on Lumley's face, the absorption on Preedy's.

Moss raised his face and looked up through the foaming branches. Inside some of the flowers he could see the dark furry shapes of bees. The musky smell that was not from the flowers nagged him with something familiar in it which he could not yet determine, something which began at last to arouse a definite repugnance in him, a sort of protest. He was held back, unwillingly, from the memory of how he had saved Lumley. Instead, from Lumley's tormented face in the swimming baths, his mind swung over to Lumley's dying face as he had seen it the following summer, white and pinched in the pillow, only that vividness of the lips proclaiming blood in the body. And that, precisely, had been the reason: Lumley was losing all his red blood.

The word *leukemia* meant nothing to Moss at this time, when he heard it applied to Lumley. Not till later did this particular conjunction of sounds assume such a soft, avid, insinuating quality. It was then only a word, a definition in a dictionary; it might have done for a girl's name. What in his boy's mind – already intensely obstinate and pragmatical – he decided was happening, was that Lumley's blood was being turned white and that when this process was completed even Lumley's lips would be white and then he would die. Vague agents of blight were doing this inside Lumley's body, so that his life all that summer was draining away without wound or pain. He had been dying then, while Moss looked down at him holding the useless squashy grapes he had brought. Lumley's face had worn no particular expression and yet it had been quite changed. Even when he smiled with those bright lips, his eyes had not seemed to be looking at Moss. Below the grief and awe he had felt, below the sobbing of Lumley's mother heard in a room below, a feeling of horrified distaste had stirred in Moss, a disgust he was helpless to repress, to think that Lumley's blood was whitening all the time in his body under the fluffy, white blankets. On a little round table beside the bed was a bowl of bronze-coloured roses. Their cool, decided perfume hung in the air. Underlying it there had been another, coarser odour, coming from the folds of the bed, from the reclinations of Lumley's body. To Moss it had seemed that this must be the smell of Lumley himself, who had been so many weeks dying . . .

He got up and after hesitating a moment began to walk slowly through the trees. Beyond them there was a gap in the hawthorn hedge. He passed through this and after pausing again briefly to sniff the air, turned right and followed the hedge for a few dozen yards in the direction of the sea. The smell grew stronger as he proceeded, less ambiguous; it was no longer possible now to confuse it with the burgeonings of spring. It was a smell of animal decomposition. The line of bushes thinned as he went on until they could not really be regarded as a hedge at all, but grew unkempt and straggling at intervals of several yards. Beyond the protection of the hollow nothing much grew save these wind-swept thorn-trees and the tough broom. Moss's feet struck against rock. Suddenly he became aware of the pale, unruffled expanse of sea again and with surprise he saw at practically the same time where the smell was coming from.

On the very last of the thorn-trees three dead foxes were hanging, roped together by their necks. The light wind moved their dangling feet continually through a brief arc. Clearly they had died by violence. The throat ligaments of the middle one had stiffened, wrenching its head up, so that the tortured muzzle pointed vertically to the sky. The others looked out to sea, submissive forelegs raised to the soiled white bibs on their breasts, as though begging; a docility not congruous with the rictus on their faces. Moss thought that perhaps they had spent some time alive in gin traps before being found and shot by Royle. He could see no wounds on them, but their brushes had been removed, only limp membranes, scaly with dried blood, remaining. The sun reddened their pelts; and the stink of them seemed like the fumes of this slow combustion. They grinned and swayed there under his gaze . . .

Preedy's face had changed, that day at the baths, from absorption to anger, when Moss got between them. He had acted without a plan. Then Preedy's anger braced him. Preedy advanced his face, narrowed his eyes, in an attempt to intimidate, but, of course, by this time Moss had known he was bluffing. Their eyes had been on a level in spite of three years' difference. His eyes had seen the uncertainty in Preedy's. Just below the mouth, below the right corner, almost on the line of the jaw: that was where he would have struck with his balled fist which knew it could smash Preedy and Preedy knew this too, knew he must act quickly, retire with dignity before a crowd gathered, making a fight obligatory.

'I'll settle with you later,' Preedy had said at last, and turned his back on them both. But no settlement ever came. Preedy avoided him thereafter. Preedy in fact, at this point, his connection with Lumley severed, his introductory function performed, ceased altogether to exist – Moss had no further recollections of him.

He could not remember any form of words that had passed between Lumley and himself after Preedy had gone. Something they *had* said to each other, but nothing so appropriate to the occasion as thanks or disclaimers. He had turned to Lumley still with the light of battle in his eyes and had possibly in these first moments seen the other boy as the prize for which he and Preedy had been contending. As indeed in some measure Lumley had been, was: to hurt or console, a victim in any case. But it was he himself who was conscious of being placed under an obligation at the time. He had felt so indebted to Lumley for allowing himself thus to be protected. So although it was tempting now, in a way, to imagine a firm handclasp at the edge of the pool, in fact all he remembered was this gratitude and Lumley smiling at him, luminously, through tears of pain. His face had worn the same smile when a little later, the swimming period over, he came carrying his clothes over his arm along the row of cubicles to Moss's, to share it with him, a thing which particular friends did sometimes . . .

The foxes seemed to have preserved some alertness. The bodies of all three were quivering slightly at the end of the rope, and their sharp muzzles appeared responsive to the scents of propagation all around. There was no blood anywhere on them except the pink strips of tail, but there was this inexplicable suffering on their faces . . .

Lumley's naked body in the cubicle, mottled red by the cruel strokes of the towel. Thin red welts followed the curve of the ribs and there were angry red patches in the hollow of the flanks above the sharp hip-bones. Memory, grown now exact and intent, as though filling in a familiar mosaic, experienced again minutely the falling to the ground of his own water-heavy swimming trunks as he trod heavily on the wet brown duckboard; the water running green into the runnel below the duckboard; both their bodies patterned by the light through the slatted cubicle doors; the stillness between and around them which thickened into something almost tangible so that reaching towards Lumley was attended by a strange sense of effort and aspiration. Silence thickened round his own limbs as he ran the tips of his fingers gently along the weals that Preedy's towel had left. That silence – heavy, sacrificial – throbbed now in his memory. There could be no words or sounds between them, because the walls of the cubicles did not reach the ceiling. Everything could be heard, and this lack of privacy gave an urgency and a sort of skill to everything they did as though these gestures in precisely this order had been many times rehearsed, even up to that moment when Moss, braced back against the cold side of the cubicle as though fighting for life, felt that the silence must finally be violated by the sobs bursting inside him, racking his body and contorting his face under the scrutiny of Lumley's calmly smiling one. It was the first orgasm of his life: anything before, that he had inflicted on himself or endured in dreams, could not be counted. And it was Lumley who had shown him the power for pleasure that dwelt in his body. Lumley, who had culled from this stealthy occasion such dexterity and grace; Lumley, in whose own body the blood was already bleaching, whose smell would before long be sickening the odour of roses . . .

Moss stared straight before him at the foxes. Once again he tried to understand this paradox, but was stopped as always by the pain of it. The budding sprays of hawthorn were shaken by a light gust from the sea. The foxes swayed on the rope, their paws appeared briefly to scrabble for the ground. The movement intensified the smell of decay that came from them. Numbers of very small black flies were reposing on their bared teeth and gums. Suddenly Moss understood the agony of their faces, the supplication of the forelegs, the absence of wounds. The foxes had been strung up living, strangled in fact. This last hawthorn was a deliberately selected gibbet. Somehow the foxes had become part of Royle's elaborate ritual of revenge on the brute creation. Moss could not prevent himself from wondering at what stage they had been stripped of their tails. Certainly Royle must have been set on lynching, to have extracted them alive from the traps, and run the risk of bites. They would hang there and stink till they oozed out of the ropes that held them.

He turned and walked fairly briskly back along the hedge towards the apple-trees. He did not pass through the gap again but continued on the outside of the hedge until he came upon a faint track which led up diagonally across the fields above the farm. This path would take him by a roundabout route back to the cottage in time to get the tea ready. As he climbed, with his back to the sea, he began to think about Ronald again. He had never spoken to Ronald about Lumley, never pointed out how similar the two were in manner and appearance, though Ronald of course was a grown man and Lumley had died at fourteen. Ronald was more handsome but they both had the same diffidence, the same gravity of expression, the same fineness of feature and something else which Moss found less easy to define; a kind of aura, really, a sort of luminous quality. That evening in the pub, three years before, Moss had noticed the resemblance immediately, before Ronald had even spoken to him. So that when Ronald did look across and smile and say good evening, it had been in a way as though – without himself knowing it – he had confirmed this connection; and Moss too had been less constrained than he might otherwise have been, thinking of the precedent for friendship established between them all those years before. He would for ever remember how elegant Ronald had looked, out of place in the public bar, in his chocolate brown suit and pink tie, his narrow fastidious face raised aloof. His own clothes never had this distinction, least of all on that evening, right at the end of the holiday. How lumpish he had felt and how unlikely it had seemed that such a person as Ronald, even though resembling Lumley so closely, would have anything more than this bare greeting to say to him. But Ronald had actually moved down the bar, started up a conversation, seemed interested in him, really interested, not just polite. Moss had talked more freely than he usually did to strangers or indeed to anyone, and all about himself too, about his holiday at first and then about his clerk's job in London, the others at work, and above all how much he hated being in an office all day, how he had always liked working with his hands. In the course of that evening, as they stood each other half-pints of beer, he had confided to Ronald his terrible attacks of restlessness which resembled hysteria. He did not know what to do with himself at such times. He had even hinted that one day he would 'break out' and thus perhaps revealed to Ronald how closely unhappiness was allied to violent impulses in his nature. To all this Foley had listened with grave courtesy, and made suitable rejoinders. Later, when the conversation turned to business matters, he grew more animated, dwelling on his need for two hundred pounds. With the repetition of this sum his eyes shone. He made his own lack of it seem somehow noble to Moss, who of course, although he did not immediately avow it, had this amount and something over; he had always been the saving sort. So out of casual talk of souvenirs, and holiday spending habits, the amazing proposition emerged, made by Ronald actually, though Moss had helped out by a series of inspired guesses. Once again Moss marvelled at this impulsiveness of Ronald's in making such a suggestion to a complete stranger. He had seen then how unwary Ronald was. Another person might have taken advantage of him. Walking back alone to his boarding house, Moss had felt, beneath his excitement at the prospect of change, a return of that gratitude as he thought that here perhaps was someone needing protection.

Reaching the crest of the rise Moss paused for a moment to look down, before beginning the slow descent to the cottage. Somewhere among the cliffs or down at the shore Ronald would be walking with Gwendoline. Perhaps he would be speaking to her in that smiling, aloof way of his, or they might be walking along quietly, holding hands. They might be lying down together somewhere . . . Moss averted his mind from this possibility. He realised suddenly that the whole business of Gwendoline, and the estrangement between Ronald and himself, were simply the results of a failure of sympathy on his own part. He had been too reserved. He should have confided more in Ronald, shared his thoughts and experiences. These foxes, for example. He would tell Ronald about them, describe their appearance. He often saw interesting things but till now he had kept quiet about them, because he was not naturally a talkative person. Talking about himself, particularly, always made him feel uneasy and ashamed. But he would make the effort. He would force himself to do it, and surely after a while it would be easier. At all costs he must show

Ronald that he mattered, that he was included. Everything, he now saw, depended on this. He began the journey down, with sober resolution. As he drew nearer the cottage an optimism bred of his new plan grew in him. He began to whistle 'Roamin' in the Gloamin'' very loudly and piercingly.

5

Returning from the village Foley and Gwendoline left the road and took a path which would lead them by degrees to the cliffs. This path at one point passed close enough to the cottage to give them a view over the farmyard, at sufficient distance however to prevent their being recognised by anyone looking up from below. As they were passing they noticed a person, made small by distance, who appeared to be examining intently the wall of the cottage.

'It's Moss,' said Foley. 'I'd recognise that beret anywhere. What can he be looking at, do you think?'

By common consent they stopped to see what Moss could be looking at. Royle passed up the farmyard, steadily beating a bullock. The sound of the blows carried up to them quite distinctly.

'Why do you suppose he is hitting that animal so hard?' asked Gwendoline.

'He is always hitting things. He hits doors for not opening.'

'Country people are so cruel, aren't they?'

'Royle is,' said Foley. 'Royle, I honestly think, is possessed by a devil.'

They saw Moss draw nearer to the wall and then recoil and begin to make his way down the farmyard in the direction of the sea.

'He must be going for his walk,' said Foley. 'I wonder what there is so interesting about that wall. Look, since Moss has obviously gone for his walk and won't be back for at least an hour, let's go down to the house now and I'll show you round while he's away.'

They had a look at the wall before going in, but saw nothing remarkable about it.

'Perhaps it was a lizard or something he saw,' Gwendoline suggested.

'Ah yes,' Foley said, 'that would very probably be it.' His interest in the wall had waned. He was now full of self-approval at his brilliant opportunism in getting Gwendoline into the house without Moss anywhere about. It had been a masterly stroke and one which required to be followed up with all diligence. The thing to hope for initially, of course, was that she should be stirred up by the atmosphere of maleness in the house. Glancing hastily round as they entered, he had to admit to himself that there was very little specifically masculine about the place at all. Moss seemed to have given it a particularly good going-over, and it was really just like any other well-kept room. And immediately Gwendoline herself confirmed this impression.

'You've done it up very nicely,' she said, looking round at the apple-green covers on the armchairs, the giltwood sofa, the little arched recesses painted in dove-grey Walpamur and the water-colours in white frames. 'It isn't like a bachelor place at all,' she said.

This was not promising. It even sounded a little like a reproach. Foley wished suddenly that there were a few rugged, manly things scattered about, like oilskins or studded boots.

'We get along as best we can,' he said.

'You get along very well, it seems to me.'

'Moss did everything,' said Foley, not quite knowing whether he was bestowing praise or blame. 'You've no idea,' he continued earnestly, 'how Moss *worked* on this place. When we first saw it, it was absolutely filthy. It had been neglected for years. No one had lived in it for a long time. Royle had been using it for storage, and the downstairs part as a hen house.'

As he was speaking Foley drew close to Gwendoline and put his arm over her shoulders, a gesture which he felt to be appropriate, since he was sharing his precious past with her. He definitely felt now that he was only giving Moss his due; this was one of the few subjects that allowed him to be unreservedly enthusiastic about Moss. Besides, he himself was always proud and stirred when he spoke of these pioneering days, the way they had taken this derelict cottage and built up a business by sheer hard work.

'I would have given up the idea of taking the house,' he said. 'It looked so unpromising. But Moss saw the possibilities of the place immediately. It has plenty of rooms, which is what we needed — we couldn't afford separate premises for work. Moss worked night and day, literally. He is immensely strong, you know. Personally, I've never seen anything like the way he worked at this place, scrubbing, plastering, painting. Well, it's not too much to say that he transformed the place. He — '

'What were you doing all the time, supervising?'

Gwendoline said this rather sharply. Coming from a girl he was half embracing Foley felt it to be a particularly ungracious remark.

'I did my part, of course,' he said.

Gwendoline laughed. 'Goodness!' she said. 'You do get stately when you're put out, don't you?'

Angry words rose to Foley's lips but he suppressed them at once. No sense in ruining everything just out of pique. Besides, he would be even with her in the end, he assured himself. Getting her to bed would pay off all these scores. It occurred to him that in many ways he rather disliked Gwendoline. With an access of sadism he pictured her floppy and moaning and himself heaving her into the right position. The vision set his teeth on edge slightly. 'I'm not put out at all,' he said. His arm was still around her and by a gentle pressure he brought her face to him. 'I just wanted to explain,' he said softly, 'how much this place means to us.' He kissed her and at the same time nudged forward until Gwendoline had her back against the wall. In this position he could exert a steady and continuous pressure over the maximum surface area and have his hands free at the same time: two things always difficult to achieve in conjunction unless you were lying down or had something to stand the girl against. Besides, such a position gave the girl a cornered, irresponsible feeling, and encouraged her to feel she was not participating until she had ceased caring.

Abandoning the lips for a moment, Foley put in a little work on the right ear-lobe and the side of the neck. Returning by way of the pulse in the throat, he found things steadily improving: her mouth was opening under his kisses now; she was even advancing her tongue a little; he met its soft pressure with his own. It was all, he could not help thinking, exactly like knowing where to press a doll to get the squeaking sound. This fancied, doll-like helplessness of Gwendoline roused him more than anything else. Certain physical changes now occurred in himself which inclined him to crouch slightly. He had taken careful note of her dress earlier that afternoon, when they had first met; opening down the front, a hook and four buttons. No trouble at all. Finding she had nothing under it but a brassière inclined him to crouch further. He did not want to lose any time over the tricky little hooks at the back, so he looped his hand up and tucked his fingers into the top of the silk cup, working them in slowly until his straining fingertips touched an alert nipple. He now experienced the frustration of not being able to feel the breast as a whole, take the weight of it in his hand, and wished he had undone the hooks after all. Too late now, though. He was beginning to knead Gwendoline's nipple between two fingers when she panted suddenly, her stomach heaved against his and the next moment he found himself pushed vigorously back and Gwendoline with a flushed face was doing up her dress again.

'I've told you time and time again,' said Gwendoline.

'But that's exactly what you haven't done,' Foley said.

In fact Gwendoline's refusal to elaborate on this basic position of hers, steadily maintained despite minor concessions during the past two months, was beginning to worry him badly. He had seen himself overcoming all her objections by logic and cajolery, reinforced by a more or less constant tactile persuasion. He was primed for the usual demure, the I'm-keeping-it-for-the-man-I-marry and you-wouldn't-respect-me-afterwards gambits. But such rebuttals cannot be made in a void. And for him to anticipate any of these points would be a fatal mistake, equivalent to admitting their force. It was an impasse. And the strange thing was that Gwendoline was obviously crying out for it.

'It doesn't hurt, you know,' he said. 'It doesn't have to hurt.'

'No,' she said. 'I don't suppose it would hurt.'

'Well, then?' demanded Foley.

'Will you show me round the workrooms now, please,' Gwendoline said, with a sudden queenly condescension that Foley found intensely irritating. He maintained his urbanity with an effort.

'Of course,' he said. There was always the possibility that visiting his bedroom might produce some result, if they could get there before the warmth of the present moment had quite gone.

They looked into the casting-room first, at the ovens against the wall, the gelatine moulds, the muffling of plaster dust everywhere. 'This is where Moss works,' Foley explained. 'Mixing the plaster, keeping up the ovens, that sort of thing. Moss does the actual casting, what you might call the primary process. I do the finishing, upstairs.'

He got her out of there as quickly as possible and up the short steep flight of wooden steps that led to the next floor where the two small rooms were in which Foley himself worked: one for special painting jobs, the other for checking, sizing and packing the finished pixies. Both his and Moss's bedrooms were on this floor too, but Foley changed his mind at the last moment and led her past his room to the far end of the passage and up another flight of stairs. They were now on the floor immediately below the roof. They went down another, very narrow, passage, which ran along the seaward side of the house. Foley stopped at a bright green door. He turned to Gwendoline a face in which caution battled with a sort of solemn pride. For this, he felt, even the bedroom could wait. 'In here,' he said, 'is my showroom.' Adding nothing to this, so that the place could make its full impact, he opened the door and ushered Gwendoline in before him.

She gasped, homage pleasing to his ears, but for the moment said nothing. They stood just inside the large room, in a rich ecclesiastical dimness, lit here and there with shifting gleams of gold. Round the walls in diverse attitudes and sizes she made out cherubim, maturer angels and little unfledged *putti* in dimpled nudity, all dark gold. Brackets had been fixed to the walls and from them, sometimes suspended, sometimes directly attached, they hung in attitudes of blandishment or adoration – it was impossible to say which. Glancing up she saw a golden swarm in the gloom above her, the wires that held them to the roof-beams invisible so that they seemed to be actually in flight. Some, more delicately balanced than the rest, or perhaps in the track of a draught, swung through an unvarying arc and gleamed at regular intervals exactly as if at fixed points in their trajectory light pricked their plump limbs.

'Impressive, don't you think?' said Foley. 'Most of the originals were genuine antiques. These are all copies, of course, but I think you get the effect. Oh yes, quite definitely, I think you get the effect.'

'But how do you get the gold on them, this dark gold,' Gwendoline asked. 'It looks antique. I mean you'd never think they were modern.'

Foley's habitual secretiveness reasserted itself. 'It's a special process,' he said. 'You wouldn't understand it, even if I told you.' After a moment or two, however, he could not resist adding: 'It's gold-leaf, actually. You use a special sort of very thin glue that seals off the plaster and acts as a base for the gilt. Then all you do is flake on the leaf just with a finger-tip, smoothing it over. The glue darkens the gold, you see, and gives it a bit of body, takes the newness off. If you get good quality gold-leaf you can put a sort of patina on, just by rubbing over with your fingers.' No harm in telling her this much, he reflected. There was nothing she could do about it anyway. 'There'd be no point in anyone else trying to do it,' he said. 'You have to have the special formula for the consistency of the plaster, everything depends on the plaster. You see – '

'You don't think, do you,' Gwendoline said, 'that I'm after your trade secrets? I mean, quite honestly, I'm not all that *interested*.'

'No, of course not, of course I didn't think that. Besides, you couldn't do it even if you wanted to, it's not as easy as it looks, believe me, the plaster – '

'For heaven's sake,' Gwendoline said.

'Look at that one over there,' Foley said, struggling free from his jealousy. 'That is one of the best of them.' He pointed to a large and particularly rotund cherub in ascending flight against the wall, with spread wings, blind curly head braced back on plump shoulders.

'He looks,' said Gwendoline after a moment's scrutiny, 'as if his bottom were wreathed in smiles.' She uttered an artificial laugh.

Foley smiled stiffly. 'Expensive, of course,' he said. 'All the moulds had to be made specially. That costs quite a bit, you know. And we haven't had anything back on them yet! We will in time, of course, and not just seasonal sales either. It will get us out of

71

this cheap souvenir business altogether, before much longer. I'm only waiting for the season to be over – '

'Forgive what must seem my stupidity,' said Gwendoline, still tinkling slightly, 'but what are they actually *for*?'

'They are lamps,' he said. 'Most of them aren't actually fitted up yet, but one or two are.' He went over to a switch near the door and with a click selected areas of the room sprang into prominence. 'Wall lamps, table lamps,' he said. 'No use for outside, of course, although they could be used in porches and verandahs. To go with either a traditional or contemporary interior.'

Several of the flying figures were now irradiated and Gwendoline saw their limbs swirled into dark blue lampshades as though by suction.

'We've got our own way of threading the flex and fitting sockets so that it hardly shows at all. There's really no end to the possibilities of these lamps. I'm just waiting till the season's over to take a trip round with a few samples. Plymouth, Torquay, London – there's no reason why someone like Peter Jones shouldn't be interested in them.'

'No reason at all, I'm sure,' Gwendoline said. 'And it doesn't really matter that they're imitations and only made of plaster, does it?'

Foley looked at her with concealed resentment. The heavy-lidded, insolent expression was well in evidence. It was her lack of response to him personally that he minded, not her failure to be impressed by the cherubs. They were beyond the verdicts of such a faulty taste. But he had laid himself out to flatter her by this inclusion, to get her on his side; and he had to admit that he had failed. His enthusiasm seemed merely to make her more sceptical. Her character, he thought, would have suited a more angular frame.

He glanced round the room again, with renewed pride, at the radiant figures flying up into their blue shades. He experienced at times, standing among them thus, something of the loving absorption of the original artists, those obscure carvers whose names he would never know, who had cared nothing for naturalism nor even relevance, lost as they had been in the sheer proliferations of the flesh, the passionate intricacies of knee and navel. There was in these very excesses, he always felt, a spirit of devotion. Why after all should angel-boys be skinny? Really healthy religious feeling should take, surely, forms voluptuous rather than austere.

'You don't seem to care for them much,' he said, and now his anger was swallowed up in pity for her denseness.

'Oh, I don't mind them,' Gwendoline said. 'They seem a bit overdone to me, but I don't *mind* them. It just seems a funny sort of way to get a living, that's all.'

This remark so wounded Foley that his manners for the moment quite deserted him. He switched off the lights without another word and held the door open pointedly. He knew something about funny ways of getting a living. It was precisely from a life devoted to such shabby expedients that he had fled here from London, built up a business, become established. It was to funny ways of getting a living that failure here would doom him to return. After all his efforts, to be criticised in this way, and by a person he was trying to impress. After his scheming and his incredible luck in meeting a person like Moss, gullible and unattached, and with a bit put by, exactly at the right moment. Just when he was beginning to feel some confidence in his status as craftsman and business man. He recognised, however, that it was all his own fault for showing Gwendoline how much he cared about the cherubs, how much they meant to him. True, he had hoped to get something out of it; but that made no difference really, self-betrayal was always a mistake.

So mortified was he that he quite failed to follow up the bedroom aspect of things. He only half opened the door and said, 'This is my bedroom,' without even trying to get her inside. Gwendoline stood in the doorway and took a quick look at the bed with its Royal Stuart tartan cover, the dressing-table with its oval mirror, and the sea-green walls. She was already turning away when she seemed to see something through the bedroom window. 'Who on earth is that old man?' she said, actually advancing into the room of her own accord. 'Who is it, Ronald?' she said. 'A most extraordinary-looking old man, all covered with flour, with no shirt on, only a vest.'

'Plaster, not flour,' said Foley, following her to the window.

'That's Walter. He comes in from the village from time to time to help move the sacks of plaster about. I'm not really clear what he does. Moss takes care of the plaster, you see, getting it in and shifting it about and so on. He gets in this old chap to help him. See that barn-looking place over there, near where he's standing? That's where the plaster is kept. He must have just come out of there, that's why he's standing still like that. It's probably rather dark inside, you see, and he's just getting his bearings.'

'He seems very old to be lifting heavy sacks about,' said Gwendoline. 'And he's all doubled up. Why doesn't he stand upright?'

'He's very strong, you know,' Foley said. 'The money he gets from us supplements his pension. He wouldn't miss coming here for the world.' He had exchanged barely half a dozen words with Walter and did not in the least know how he felt on this or any other issue, but he felt bound to defend himself against the implied charge of exploiting the aged and infirm. 'It gives him an interest in life,' he added.

'But why is he doubled up like that?' Gwendoline persisted. 'Why won't he stand up straight?'

'Well, because he can't of course,' Foley said rather impatiently. 'Surely you can see that?' He felt that he was still being got at by these questions, but when he glanced at Gwendoline he saw that she was completely absorbed. Her face had a startled, almost stricken, look.

They stood together side by side at the window watching Walter who had not, except for a slight weaving motion of the head, so far budged. He seemed bemused this afternoon, as though not sure where to go next. Perhaps the bright sunshine had dazed him. It was impossible to tell from his expression why he was standing there, because his face and indeed his whole person were thickly covered with plaster dust. His eyes and mouth made three dark holes in it like stick-holes in snow. He did not change his position, but the swaying motion of his head intensified slowly in what seemed an endeavour to get a look at the sky. He would never now regain an upright posture, but his aged and dwindled head went on trying to right itself, constantly straining at the rigid harness of the neck, moving from side to side in efforts to circumvent his affliction. The exercise had highly developed his neck tendons and given him a blind, weaving appearance like a charmed tortoise.

'Why doesn't he move? What's the matter with him?' Gwendoline said, in tones of horror. 'Is he going to stand there all afternoon?'

'He'll move when he's ready,' Foley said. But Walter continued to stand there.

'He is the grotesquest thing,' said Gwendoline, slowly and judiciously, 'that I have ever seen in all my life.'

Foley too was struck by the awfulness of Walter's appearance. But he felt impelled to deliver the male rebuke, play the thing down. 'Oh well,' he said. 'No one looks their best when they're covered all over with plaster dust. He is really quite presentable, you know, when you see him dressed up.'

Gwendoline pressed herself suddenly against his side. 'I wish he would move,' she said.

She really was upset, Foley realised. A faint hope was reborn in him. One sort of emotion can easily lead to another. The more general souping-up the better. Perhaps he would yet have cause to feel grateful to Walter. Casually he put an arm round her waist. He said, 'He's probably enjoying the sunshine, you know, after lumping sacks of plaster about inside that barn.'

'Look, he's starting to move!' cried Gwendoline, in excited and fearful tones as though she were assisting at the resuscitation of some sort of unpredictable animal. 'Where's he going now?'

Foley paused for a moment or two before replying. The steady pressure of Gwendoline's hip against his own was beginning to work its own, remorseless, resuscitation.

'He's going to wash himself down at the pump,' he said carefully. 'Over there at the side of the barn.'

Walter crossed slowly over to the pump and having first placed the metal bucket under the tap, began to work away at the wooden handle.

The water came out with a sudden thick gush and flashed in the sunshine as it tumbled down into the bucket. Walter went on pumping steadily until the bucket brimmed and spilled over into the stone basin. Then he began fumbling with himself in the region of the right hip eventually producing a small piece of yellow soap.

'Everywhere he goes he carries soap around with him,' Gwendoline whispered.

'Cleanliness is next to godliness with some of these people,' Foley said, shifting his position slightly. In an effort to distract her he kissed her on the temple but she hardly seemed to notice it, so absorbed was she in the successive phases of Walter's ablutions.

'I think I preferred him covered in dust,' he heard her say after some moments and glancing out of the window again he saw Walter, all clean and veinous, rubbing his head with a piece of grey material which might have been a towel, though where it could have come from was difficult to see. The old man's biceps must once have been considerable: they moved slackly now, with the movements of his arms. His face emerged at last from the towel, ferrety and sharp nosed; he cast a final denunciatory glance over the farmyard and then, towel over shoulder and soap back in pocket, slowly took himself off.

Gwendoline at last allowed herself to be turned and held closely, a position in which the extent of Foley's excitement must have become obvious to her. No recognition of it, however, appeared on her face, which wore an abstracted look.

'I've never seen an old man's body before,' she said. 'It's rather horrible, isn't it? When you think of death, of actually being dead and buried, what do you think about mainly?'

'I don't know, really,' said Foley.

'Well, it's rotting I think about,' said Gwendoline. 'You know, sort of liquefying. That's what makes the thought of it so awful: to me, at any rate. But seeing something very old makes you think it's not like that at all. That old man is so dry and stringy, isn't he? He looks as if he'd go hard, like leather.'

Nothing could have seemed to Foley at this moment less apposite than reflections on death and decay; but he felt slightly ashamed of the irrelevance of his erection to these universal themes. For this reason he felt constrained to respect her desire for an exchange of views.

'I don't honestly see that it matters,' he said, 'once your breath is stopped, whether your flesh runs off you or gets pickled.' He locked his hands in the small of Gwendoline's back. 'It's not our turn yet, is it?' he said.

While he was speaking Gwendoline had begun a slight lateral rubbing motion against him. She raised her head and looked at him without ceasing these movements, and he was surprised to see that her expression seemed to contain no slightest acknowledgement of what was happening: her face in fact appeared to have intensified its abstract and rather theoretical look. He kissed her as tellingly as he was able and found her mouth hot and unmistakably compliant. This rubbing threatened now if kept up any longer to impair his control and he began to steer Gwendoline with a sort of slow tango step back towards the Royal Stuart. The bed caught her behind the knees and she fell rather statuesquely backwards on to it, with Foley on top of her. In falling he caught the eye of his photograph and noticed its mild commiseration. But he soon forgot this and everything else.

There was no question now of persuasion. Indeed he was no longer sure whose the urgency was. With such skilful accommodations of her body did Gwendoline assist him to undress her that Foley experienced a rapturous confusion between subject and object, like a moment of contemplation. He was already sitting his loins with grateful care into the vale of her raised knees when a series of piercing whistles came up to them from below, checking him poised above her. Looking down he discovered an expression of startled conjecture on her face. 'It's only Moss,' he said, with a dim hope of being permitted to continue. But her body had stiffened; it had ceased, by a subtle process, to be available; the warm collaboration between them was lost; after a further moment Gwendoline covered her nakedness hastily with the first thing that came to hand – a corner of the Royal Stuart.

'Moss has come back from his walk,' Foley said, in a wailing undertone. 'Moss,' he repeated in accents of loathing, hissing final s's. Seeing that nothing further was now to be hoped for, he began looking round for his trousers. He felt utterly wretched. The sweet dew of anticipation chilled on his body. His testicles ached with disappointment. The whistling, in which some attempt at an ordered sequence was discernible, continued unabated.

'I'm sorry,' Gwendoline whispered. 'I really am sorry. I'm

disappointed too. But I just couldn't have done it with him whistling all the time like that.'

They dressed in silence. The whistling continued without a break, accompanied now by occasional clattering noises from what seemed to be the kitchen. By the time they were ready to leave the bedroom Foley had decided that it was either 'Loch Lomond' or 'Begone Dull Care'. At the top of the stairs he began speaking in loud and cheerful tones. To anyone below it must have sounded as sudden as a gong striking. 'Well,' he said, 'that's all there is to it, really. Not a great deal perhaps in terms of actual space, but we get through quite a bit of work here, I can tell you. It's a small business of course . . . Oh, hallo, Michael! I *thought* I heard somebody whistling. "Loch Lomond" wasn't it?'

'It was "Roamin' in the Gloamin' ",' Moss said, rather coldly.

'Let me introduce my partner Michael Moss . . . This is Gwendoline Rogers.'

'How do you do?' Moss said heavily. 'What do you think of the place?'

'I think it's absolutely lovely. I'm surprised, really I am.'

Moss's features relaxed slightly. 'Tea is not quite ready yet,' he said. 'It won't be long.'

'Never mind, never mind,' exclaimed Foley. 'Come and sit down, Gwendoline. I've just been showing Gwendoline round the place.'

'Terribly nice,' said Gwendoline, smiling at Moss.

They went into the living-room and sat down. Moss remained at the door for a few moments. 'I didn't know you were here,' he said. 'Until I heard you talking up there.'

'Oh yes, I was just showing – '

'When did you come in?'

'About half an hour ago, I suppose it would be,' Foley said. 'That would be about it, wouldn't you say, Gwendoline?'

'Yes, about half an hour,' Gwendoline said. Foley noticed that Gwendoline's expression was much more alert than usual. Her eyes seemed wider-open and she was sitting upright in her chair with her hands carefully disposed in her lap.

Moss looked from one to the other of them in silence for a moment then he said, 'I'll go and see to the tea then, if you'll excuse me.'

'Of course,' Gwendoline said, smiling graciously. 'He doesn't like me,' she said as soon as Moss had disappeared. 'I can sense it.'

'Oh, you mustn't mind him,' Foley said. 'He's a very shy person, really.'

Gwendoline made no answer to this. After a short interval Moss reappeared, carrying the tea-things, a big plate of sandwiches, and a smaller one of biscuits on a round copper tray.

'This is the stuff to give the troops,' said Foley, adopting an expression of keen anticipation. 'This sea air gives one an appetite.'

'I expect he has a good enough appetite, anyway?' Gwendoline said indulgently to Moss.

'He has indeed,' Moss said, actually smiling.

They got on with the business of having tea; setting up the cups and saucers, discussing tastes.

'Strong, weak or middling?' asked Moss.

'No milk for me, please,' Gwendoline said.

'Ah, no milk,' said Moss. 'Ronald has a little milk and no sugar. I like mine very milky.'

'It's rather unusual for a man not to have sugar. Men usually do have sugar,' Gwendoline said.

'Help yourself to sandwiches, Miss Rogers,' said Moss. 'Cheese and tomato this side, cucumber the other side.'

'Delicious,' said Gwendoline. 'However did you manage to cut the bread so thin?'

'We buy it already sliced. They have one thickness for toasting, another for sandwiches.'

'Oh, that sliced loaf, you mean, wrapped up in paper? A lot of the goodness is lost, they say.'

'We have found,' Moss said, 'that it has answered well enough, in the past.'

'That toad!' exclaimed Foley. 'I never did ask you what became of that toad. Do you know,' he went on, turning to Moss before Gwendoline had time to reply, 'that Gwendoline actually had a toad in her room?'

'Why did you have a toad in your room?' Moss asked.

Gwendoline said: 'I was going to draw it. For a book, you

79

know. But I found I couldn't, and then the toad escaped. Somebody else has got the job now.'

'Did you say for a book?' enquired Moss. He was always impressed by literary references and by people who had anything to do with books.

'Yes, you know the sort of thing.' Gwendoline adopted a shrill, over-refined, declamatory note. 'I am a toad. My *real* name is Bufo, Bufo, Bufo and I live in a chamber-pot at the bottom of the garden . . .'

Moss's slightly puzzled expression did not change. 'You mean it's written from the toad's point of view?' he said.

'You *could* put it that way,' Gwendoline said.

Foley noticed that she had flushed slightly at the failure of her mimicry, and he felt an upsurge of irritation with Moss, for his inability to adapt himself, his obtuseness to other people's tones. 'Have a sandwich,' he said to Gwendoline.

'Thank you, no more sandwiches,' Gwendoline said. 'They're lovely, but I just couldn't.'

'A biscuit then?'

'What sort are they?'

'I'm not quite sure,' Foley said, looking more closely at them.

'You know perfectly well,' Moss said, 'that we always have the same sort of biscuit. I always get shortbread biscuits,' he said to Gwendoline. 'They're Ronald's favourites. Are you an artist then?'

'Not really. I used to think I was. I went to art school but left after only a year. I'm more interested in fabrics, really. Do you always consider Ronald's tastes so carefully?'

'What do you mean?'

'Well, supposing you couldn't bear shortbread biscuits, surely you'd buy some other kind?'

'Michael does all the cooking, you know,' Foley interposed. 'He sees to everything in the kitchen, it's his department. Michael is a wonderful cook. I suppose it comes from being so practical. I'm not practical at all, you see, and I'm sure that must make an enormous difference, in cooking. Timing, that sort of thing. It's organisation, really.'

'I generally find,' said Moss, looking at Gwendoline steadily, 'that we like the same sort of things.'

'That is very fortunate, for both of you. Personally, I'm afraid I should tend to concentrate a bit less exclusively on Ronald's tastes and a bit more on my own. Speaking personally.'

'Ha, ha,' said Foley. 'Would you indeed?' He saw that Gwendoline no longer had the appearance of a young lady being interviewed. She seemed to have settled in rather, and the usual slightly insolent composure had returned to her. He also realised that for better or worse a certain relationship had been established between Gwendoline and Moss during these exchanges, one that would not now easily be changed. He sensed that Gwendoline was secretly outraged by the very thing that Moss took pride in: that their *ménage*, womanless and therefore rudderless, should nevertheless run so well.

'It's organisation, really,' he repeated uneasily.

'Things must be difficult here at times,' Gwendoline said to Moss. 'The shopping and that. You are rather cut off here, aren't you?'

'Yes, one has to plan in advance, you know, everything. If you forget something you can't just pop round the corner for it.'

Moss looked briefly across at Foley, then returned his gaze to Gwendoline. '*He* doesn't realise it, of course,' he said. He gave her a look of solemn indulgence. 'He doesn't *see* these things.'

Foley immediately pouted slightly and turned up his eyes in a look of humorous resignation. 'Oh, Lord,' he said. 'Here we go again.'

'That sounds to me like a rather convenient blindness,' Gwendoline said, without looking at Foley.

'I don't mean he dodges work,' said Moss. 'Did you think I meant that?' He paused judiciously, with eyes lowered. 'The thing about Ronald,' he said at last, 'is that he is at a further remove, if you see what I mean.' He paused again, this time perhaps with an intention of apology for having included Gwendoline in the number of the earthbound; but he did not qualify it and after a moment went on again with her inclusion established. 'He's very difficult to live with,' he said, and now Gwendoline and he were linked, people of good sense, but gross, looking with a sort of humble remonstrance at high-flying Foley. It was not a position that Gwendoline cared for.

'I suppose it's the Artistic Temperament,' went on Moss. 'The girl who married him would have her work cut out. She'd have to know all this beforehand, it wouldn't be fair otherwise.'

'Know all what beforehand?'

Moss looked pained. 'Well,' he said, 'the sort of person he is.'

'We've had our ups and downs, though, since we came here, haven't we, Michael?' Foley said. Why on earth had Moss brought marriage up? he wondered. 'Do you remember that time when – '

'Is he so different?' said Gwendoline. 'She would have to find it all out for herself anyway, surely? No one else could possibly tell her, least of all another man.'

'You don't think, then,' said Moss ponderously, 'that a man can understand another man?'

'But surely,' Gwendoline said, with a little laugh at the obviousness of it all, 'a woman can understand a man in a more complete way than another man, in a positive, I don't mean an analytical, way – that sort of way isn't much use really, is it? Her nature is designed to supply deficiencies in his. Do you see what I mean?'

'I suppose it's this business of intuition you mean, a woman's intuition,' Moss said.

'And what is so remarkable about Ronald? I mean, this hasn't emerged yet, has it?'

Moss regarded her for some time in silence. His face bore an expression of genuine surprise.

'Its high time we stopped talking about me,' said Foley heartily and much too late. 'Michael, why don't you tell Gwendoline about Royle's latest? Royle is our landlord, you know, he's absolutely mad, isn't he, Michael?' Neither of them seemed to hear this. They were looking closely at each other.

'He's absolutely mad,' Foley said. 'He believes that everything has a soul. He does, he really does. He's got this old tractor, ancient it is, from before the Flood. Everything on this farm is . . . antediluvian, as a matter of fact. Well, of course, it never starts on cold mornings. You can hear him in the winter round about seven o'clock in the morning. He talks to it. He calls it his brave girl. That's to get on the right side of it, you know. Then you hear ah–

ah–ah stop.' Foley pressed an imaginary starting button and made a series of staccato noises trying at the same time to imitate Royle's expression of wrathful conciliation. 'Royle mutters a bit, but not too loud, for fear of offending it. Then he tries again, ah–ah–ah–aaah–stop again. Same thing happens five or six times. Then you suddenly hear this great bellow of rage. "You buggering bastard! I'll teach you!" And off he goes raving and cursing and gets this length of chain that he keeps specially for the purpose. Would you believe it, he actually . . .'

Convulsing his features with laughter and leaning forward slightly he looked from Gwendoline to Moss: neither of them appeared to be more than moderately amused by the recital. 'He gives it a good hiding with the chain,' he said, 'every morning, all the winter, doesn't he, Michael? And do you remember that other time when he ate all those snails out of the garden? Someone in Lanruan told him you could eat snails and he went and got a great plateful out of the garden, ordinary garden snails, and ate them all. I've got some photos of him upstairs, doing it, eating raw snails and smiling. I could get them for you now, if you like. I'll go up and get them for you now.'

Foley went up to his bedroom as quickly as possible, not wishing to leave Moss and Gwendoline alone together for too long. He was hoping that the photographs would ease the situation, which was turning out to be even stickier than he had feared. How *did* Moss always manage to get on the wrong side of people? It almost amounted to genius. The album did not seem to be anywhere in his room, although he looked in all the drawers. After some minutes he remembered that he had been looking at it a few days before and had left it in the bookcase in the sitting-room. He descended the stairs rapidly and returned to the sitting-room, to find Moss on his own there and Gwendoline nowhere to be seen. His first assumption was that she had gone to the lavatory, which was on the ground floor at the back of the cottage; but time passed and she did not reappear. Finally, he said casually, 'Where is Gwendoline?'

Moss seemed to be lost in thought and did not answer.

'Michael, where is Gwendoline?' Foley asked again.

'She left,' Moss said in a non-committal tone.

'Left?' Foley was bewildered, and his confusion was increased by a noise from outside in the farmyard of trampling and bellowing mingled with shouted oaths and the excited barking of several dogs. 'Do you mean she just got up and went away?' he demanded, raising his voice to make himself heard above the din, which seemed to be increasing steadily. 'Didn't she give any reason?'

'Not really,' Moss said. 'She said she had to go.'

'Not madly polite, I must say,' muttered Foley. He felt completely stunned by this development.

'I can't hear you,' said Moss. 'What did you say?'

'What the hell is going on out there? You can't see anything for dust.'

'It's Royle, trying to get his bullocks into the big field.'

'But she must have only just gone, this very minute,' Foley said. 'Perhaps I can catch her up. There was something I particularly wanted to say to her.'

'She'll be a long way off by now,' Moss said, with sudden distinctness. But Foley was already through the door.

He had intended to run down the lane and catch Gwendoline before she got to the road; but once outside the cottage he found himself unable to proceed and even in some danger of being knocked down and trampled underfoot, because of a sort of stampede that was taking place there. Pressing himself back against the wall he peered through the swirling dust in an effort to make out what was happening. Royle's bullocks appeared to be completely out of control and Royle himself was shouting in the midst of them. This in itself was not unusual. It was a scene of almost daily occurrence, since very few farm operations, even of a routine sort, were carried out smoothly by Royle.

What seemed to have happened on this occasion was that as the bullocks were on the point of passing through the gate into the field appointed, a small but determined group at the head of them had suddenly become disaffected, turned in their tracks and began battling their way back down the farmyard, apparently to return to the original field, though some of them were already seeking by way of gaps in the fence for new and unauthorised pastures. Losing his temper immediately Royle had begun beating and berating the bullock nearest him which had not been doing anything wrong, merely pressing on towards the new field, but which now, surprised by the blows, was jostling and butting and causing resentment and alarm to spread in the ranks of the still well-disposed members of the herd, some of whom were clearly wavering in their allegiance. The rebel bullocks, led by a robust and evil-looking black with a swishing tail, were at some points meeting the conformists head on, and brisk battles were developing here and there; while the congestion was so great, and the opposing forces now so evenly balanced, that the bullocks in the very middle rotated unceasingly as though trapped in a vortex. Dust rose around the frantically active figure of Royle, now striking out indiscriminately.

'Get they bullocks!' shouted Royle to his three skinny black dogs, but they were already over-excited, then lost their heads completely: two of them fell to fighting savagely, while the third harried the heels of the bullocks at the back, scattering them in all directions.

'Get they buggering bullocks!' screamed Royle. Without pausing in his efforts with the stick, he landed a series of heavy kicks on the two dogs that were fighting, but they merely retreated, still snapping and yelping, under the plunging feet of the bullocks. Surrounded now by the dazed, completely disorientated animals, Royle began to jump up and down, holding the stick in both hands and bringing it down with all his strength each time his feet touched the ground. His swearing reached a rather splendid high-pitched fluency, broken only by occasional choking fits caused by the dust.

Foley edged his way back along the wall and got through the door which he carefully secured behind him. Moss was sitting in the same position, looking just the same.

'Royle will have a stroke one of these days if he goes on like this,' Foley said. 'I couldn't reach Gwendoline because of all those bloody animals.'

'No,' Moss said, 'I didn't think you'd be able to catch her up.' He spoke as if he had known all the time that the bullocks, or something, would get in the way.

6

It was from the day of the tea-party and Gwendoline's strangely abrupt departure that Foley dated Moss's loquacious phase. Up to that time Moss had been pre-eminently a man who could keep his own counsel, not boring other people with the quavers and semi-quavers of his psyche. This reticence, with his predictability and conscientiousness, had been his chief virtue in Foley's eyes. The heavens might sooner fall, he had felt, than that Moss should fail to put in his eight hours a day on the pixies, or forego his Sunday-afternoon walk, or start relating dreams and the remote experiences of childhood.

It began that same evening. Foley had been brooding about Gwendoline. He could not understand why she had left so unceremoniously, and he was also displeased with himself for having betrayed to Moss his perturbation at the time. He was extremely reluctant to allow Moss any insight into the ignominies he was experiencing in his relations with Gwendoline. Because he wished to appear unmoved, he had not gone rushing down to the village to demand an explanation; and also, of course, because he realised that it would not advance his cause with Gwendoline either, if he appeared too keen.

They were sitting in the living-room, each occupied in his different fashion. Foley, wearing the black corduroy jacket which he always thought of as his smoking-jacket, was sitting in an armchair looking through his scrapbook, an activity he usually found soothing, even mildly inspiring, because all the pictures in it were of himself in some guise or other; they had been carefully cut out of magazines during his days as a model. Moss was at a small table near the window doing the monthly housekeeping accounts. It had been understood from the beginning that he would do all the accounts, Foley having early established an exemption by claiming that he had no head for figures. By a series of such uncostly gestures as this Moss's unswerving belief in his ineptitude had been secured. Moss was very bad at adding up too, but he had a doggedness which made up for this. He rarely got things to balance first time and would spend hours going over everything, muttering and becoming very dishevelled; but he never gave up until everything was accounted for; to do so would have meant a lessening of Foley's faith in him.

Because of his anxiety over Gwendoline the scrapbook was not holding Foley's attention as completely as usual, although he still took pleasure in the pictures, especially those in which he appeared alone, coolly smiling in a business suit at the prosperous future now that he was insured properly or presenting an uppercrust profile in sports-wear. He did not usually have the picture all to himself in this way. In the great majority of them he was simply a hovering presence, sometimes no more than an elegant blur, beckoning from a sports car, gazing after some girl who had used the right shampoo, or one of an admiring group of males surrounding a deodorised girl at a party. There was one of him standing shocked beside an undeodorised girl in a Tube train which he did not like so much because the bowler he had had to wear did not suit his narrow head and because he had failed to achieve an expression of disgust, only one of flatulence; but he had included it for the sake of completeness. In some cases he was so far on the periphery of things that only he himself could have known who it was.

Though he sometimes alluded to it nostalgically when he wanted to impress Moss or some stranger with his sophisticated past, Foley had detested this period of his life because one day was never like another and it was quite impossible to see your way, grasp your course as a whole, plan anything. The money was good of course – you might get ten or fifteen guineas for a morning's work – but you could never count on it. You rang up your agent every evening to ask what there was next day. For days, weeks, there might be nothing, and then you had to do washing-up or something and you got tomato ketchup on the hand-woven tie your brief affluence had tempted you into buying. Either this or you found somebody to look after you a bit. Even now Foley could not think of this other than euphemistically; nor could he repress internal quakes and shudderings when he remembered Mrs Burroughs, her homely accent, her propensity for Guinness when she could have afforded anything, the playful way she would fold up a ten-shilling note and tuck it in his top pocket, the gleaming lipstick where there was no lip, the vast freckled breasts. The terrible toil of climbing night after night on to Mrs Burroughs in her bedroom, full of brass objects, in Maida Vale. Mrs Burroughs, together with a remark of his agent's to the effect that people were getting used to his face, had driven him to Cornwall, to Moss and the pixies. He could never, he felt, go back to that life now. But the pictures themselves were satisfying: seeing oneself so variously posed and attired was like a continual enrichment of the personality, and Foley enjoyed the sheer proliferation of his features.

He glanced up again. On the back of Moss's large and powerful hands hair glinted like copper wires. He moved them restlessly in the labour of computing. Foley remembered suddenly an occasion the previous summer when they had been working on the car. A large nut had jammed on the cylinder head. It had not been set squarely on the thread, and he himself had been quite unable to budge it. Moss had taken the spanner and without seeming to exert himself had given it a twist of such staggering power that he had shorn the first inch or so of steel thread completely off the bolt. What Foley chiefly remembered was the expression of surprise on Moss's face and the way the nut slid up and down on the useless bolt.

'Milk,' he heard Moss say very softly, 'milk, milk, milk.' Fat white moths fluttered against the window, beating to be let in. The question of Gwendoline's departure came back into his mind.

'Michael,' he began, but Moss shut his eyes and shook his head. There was silence for several minutes more, then Moss sighed heavily and put down his pen.

'We spent a good bit more than usual on petrol last month,' he said. 'That was because of all those extra trips of yours down to Lanruan.' He regarded Foley with a close and solemn scrutiny. 'Still, it's only once in a while, isn't it?'

'Those were all business trips,' Foley said.

Moss nodded. 'I daresay they were.' He felt he could concede this now. Ronald was looking particularly well this evening. The light was favourable to his appearance, bringing out the serious level-browed look, almost dedicated. The corduroy jacket suited him too, he looked so artistic in it. Moss found it now as ever impossible to dissociate such attractiveness from laudable qualities of character in Ronald: purity, integrity, nobility.

'Do you know who you remind me of,' he said suddenly. 'You remind me of a boy I used to know at school.' Only after the words were out did he really experience excitement, and then he had to control himself, his breathing particularly, at the sheer daring of yoking together in speech these two persons. 'His name was Lumley,' he said, and waited, almost in fear, as though the concentration of his thought on Lumley, his patient, painstaking re-creations of that twelve-year-old experience of battle, love and death, could somehow have been divined by Foley; but no repudiation of the connection appeared on the other's face.

Foley merely said casually and with an air of having something more important on his mind: 'Lumley? That's an odd name. Is that a Christian name or a surname?'

'His name was Lumley Irons.'

'You must be joking,' Foley said. 'Nobody could possibly be called that.'

Moss began speaking rapidly in a flat, unemphatic voice. 'He died when he was fourteen. He had leukemia. All the summer he had it and nobody knew till they got the doctor in. Well, he might have had it for years, for all I know. He used to get very tired, but then he wasn't a very strong boy, he was delicate. They put it down to outgrowing his strength, the tiredness I mean. Nobody knew about it, you see. Perhaps if someone had known, Lumley might not have died, but, of course, that's not true, because it's an incurable disease, leukemia.'

Foley lit a cigarette. 'That was bad luck, to get a thing like that, at fourteen,' he said. He was considerably impressed by this remote and lingering death of the boy Lumley. Moss's manner of relating it, too, had been unusual and rather disturbing: there had been in the hasty yet tireless accents something implacable, rather

89

as though Moss had learned it all by heart, and was determined to get through to the end without mishaps; as though everything had to be said in just that order, or it wouldn't do.

'He was very like you,' Moss said, and paused again. But Foley continued to smoke peacefully. '*Very* like you.' A delightful sense of immunity began to steal over him. 'Same sort of physique,' he said. 'On the slender side. Same colouring, same shape of face. And not only that, not only physical, but you both have the same sort of atmosphere about you. A kind of brightness.'

'How do you mean?'

'The only other person I've seen like that was my cousin Frank and I only saw a photograph of him because he was killed in the First World War. He was a pilot.'

'I'm the only one left, then.' Foley spoke lightly in order to conceal his interest. 'What did you mean by brightness, exactly?'

Moss felt an onrush of this almost choking excitement and was compelled to pause again. Deliberately he deadened his voice. 'It's difficult to explain, difficult to put into words. You are all three of you pale people but you have this spiritual quality, something like light, not a colour I mean . . .'

'A sort of glow?' said Foley, noting the rather curious way that Moss had of referring to the other two as if they were still alive.

'Yes, that's it exactly, a sort of pale glow.' Moss was full of happiness at the sympathetic interest Foley was taking in what he had said and the ease with which they were understanding each other. 'Your eyes are different from Lumley's,' he said. 'Yours are hazel, aren't they?'

'I don't really know,' said Foley, who knew very well. 'They are ordinary brown eyes.'

'You must know better than that,' Moss said. He shifted on his chair and one of his hands came up chest high in a sudden clumsy gesture of expostulation. 'You want to take a look at yourself some time,' he said. 'Just take a look at yourself. Lumley was just the same, quite careless of his own appearance. He often didn't comb his hair even. Once we went for a bicycle ride in the country, just the two of us. It was a very hot day and we got hot cycling. We stopped and bathed in a stream, the water was cold, straight off the hills, you know. We splashed about in it. We took all our clothes off and just waded in. Lumley got his hair all wet but he didn't bother about it.' None of this had actually happened but Moss felt that he possessed the visual essence of it just as firmly as if it had: Lumley's body wet from the stream, the water gleaming on his thin sunburnt arms, the white zones of belly and flanks where the sun had not been, the beads of water caught in the faint hairs on the legs, his head thrown back in laughter, the smell of crushed grass when they lay down together beside the stream. 'Lumley didn't care about things like that,' he said.

Foley looked down into the palm of his hand. He had steadily lost interest since the conversation had veered from his glow. He could not see why Moss kept harping on about this Lumley person. 'By the way,' he said casually, 'have you any idea why Gwendoline pushed off so suddenly this afternoon? Did she seem upset about something?'

There was a rather long pause and when Moss replied his tone had changed completely, returning to its normal, conversational weightiness: 'We were talking about you, as a matter of fact. She suddenly got up and said she had to go. She said she'd be seeing you.'

'I see.' Foley was now further affronted with Gwendoline for having left at such a juncture, when she should have been glued to her seat with the sheer interest of the topic. Finding Moss's eye fixed on him with what seemed mild enquiry, he thought that perhaps he had been allowing something of his pique to show. Instantly he flung his head up and opened his mouth in an *ah*. He held this a moment, keeping his eyes on Moss's face, then slowly narrowed the *ah* down to a recollecting smile. 'Of course!' he said. 'Now I remember. It would be getting on for five when she left, wouldn't it? She'd promised to phone her uncle at five o'clock, I remember her telling me, and, of course, she would know there wasn't a phone at the farm. Imagine my forgetting that.'

Moss's expression had not changed but he now raised his own head and repeated Foley's *ah* on a smaller scale.

'The nearest telephone, of course, is halfway down to the village,' Foley pointed out. He continued to watch Moss but could discern no signs of scepticism on his face. 'That's it then,' he said. 'That explains it.'

Moss leaned forward and seemed to be gathering himself for further speech. Sensing that it was not going to be about Gwendoline, Foley stood up, quickly, tucking the scrapbook under his arm. 'I think I'll go to bed,' he said.

'The only other person that reminds me of you at all is my cousin Frank and I knew him first of all,' Moss said, reverting to his former manner. 'At least, I didn't actually *know* him.'

Foley began moving towards the door. 'Busy day tomorrow,' he said.

'I only saw a photograph of him, at my aunt's house, but he bore a very striking resemblance to you and Lumley.'

'Frank and Lumley and me,' said Foley over his shoulder, and went out. Going up the stairs he sang to himself a little.

'Sleep well, Ronald,' Moss called out after him, as he always did. He was distinctly disappointed at having to break off just when he was starting to tell Ronald about his cousin Frank, but glad on the other hand that he had made such a good start on his new policy of telling things to Ronald. Cousin Frank, though, really belonged in this first instalment and should have been included.

Moss continued for some time to sit at the table, remembering Frank and the pot miner. They had been the twin hearth-spirits of his aunt's house and throughout his childhood Moss had seen them at least once a week: Frank's sad beauty framed in gilt at one end of the mantel shelf and at the other the great ribald grin, protruding eyes and flat cap of the pot miner who was all face, and hollow moreover, and through whose perpetual snarl of clean pot teeth you could put odds and ends, pins, pencil-stubs, buttons, so that he was often crammed to the maw with scraps and threads straggled over his teeth, but his beastly grin never varied. In contrast was cousin Frank's doomed, luminous seriousness, as he looked down in his priestly habiliments of a pilot, the symbolic wings of his order sewn to his breast. The photograph was old and formal, its prevalent tints being brown and mourning sepia, and Frank gazed out of it with sorrowful dark eyes and a pale oval face and straight brown hair. His features had a delicate, sculpted symmetry, rather unearthly, as though someone had known he was going to die and taken his face and chiselled it into a classic shape to serve as the epitaph for a whole generation. He was without apparent antecedents, just as he was without issue; and this for Moss had formed a large part of his fascination; it had been impossible, amidst the jovial blond snubness of the Mosses and the Carters -- the two strains which had gone to compose Frank – to find any remotest trace of him. He duplicated no features of theirs and was impossible to explain, except in terms of a symbol.

His beauty would have been enough. But the aunt breathed a poignant lustre on it by the special voice she used when talking of him. Moss knew every detail of that brief career, knew that Frank had been as a little boy gentle and affectionate and had played much alone; had kept tame rabbits and mourned long when one died. Shot down in flames in 1918 they had recovered him from the North Sea and tried to revive him with brandy but he had vomited it up and died. This was always the highlight of the aunt's relation because it demonstrated Frank's purity and his abstemious nature. 'He couldn't keep it down, you see,' the aunt said. 'He hadn't ever been used to it.' And Moss had known that into cousin Frank's white and wounded body no evil even in the last extremity could be admitted. Frank had died because of his goodness, it came down to that. Moss had never associated him with the life of action, with any lawless freedom of clouds and lightnings, even less had he anything in common with the cynicisms and recklessness of those early pilots read about since. The neat, symbolic wings were on his breast: wings and flames. Frank had taken an Icarus flight, gone too near the sun, but not inadvertently: he had been too good for the world, his purity had consumed him.

And opposite was the pot miner with his vast snarl of mirth. At times it had seemed to Moss that the two faces were simply dual aspects of some divinity, a reconciling of the spirit with the flesh; and although he nearly always found the pot miner repulsive there were occasions when the stress of meeting Frank's high regard drove them into an alliance. For Frank had been an exacting ideal. Because of his purity, the sterilising flames in which he had fluttered to earth, his rejection of the brandy, he was in an unassailable moral position, and backed up, of course, by the whole family. Moss had found him difficult to countenance, with that very faint smile, the irrevocable parting in his hair. So from time to time, driven by a sense of his unworthiness he had veered to the Rabelaisian miner, who was a great accepter of things, whose perpetual grin condoned everything, just as articles of the most diverse nature disappeared through his jaws.

Moss stirred and sighed. There was no sound from above. Ronald must be in bed. He rose and moving in an unhurried manner tidied up a bit, patting cushions, carrying cups through to the kitchen. He put his account books in their accustomed place. Then, making sure that all lights were switched off below, he made his way upstairs. He paused outside Foley's door for a moment to listen. Standing there it seemed to him more than ever a pity that he had not been able to finish what he wanted to say about Frank. Ronald had almost certainly wanted to hear it too but had gone to bed rather than seem importunate. After hesitating a moment longer he crossed to the other wall, moving very softly, and switched off the passage light. Now, standing in complete darkness, he could see that there were no cracks of light round Ronald's door. Fumbling cautiously he found the knob, turned it quietly and let himself in. He closed the door behind him with a slight click and stood just inside the room, listening in the darkness. He could hear no sound of breathing and knew therefore that Ronald was awake.

'Are you awake, Ronald?' he said, in his normal speaking tones. There was no answer. 'I wanted to tell you a bit more about my cousin Frank before I went to bed. I told you you are like him, didn't I? I used to see him nearly every week at my aunt's house. I mean his picture, because he was dead, he died before I knew him. He was shot down in flames and when they tried to get him to drink this brandy, he was sick, he couldn't keep it down. If he'd been able to keep that brandy down . . .'

Moss's voice went on, steady, rapid, without particular inflections. It seemed after a while to abandon all narrative sequence and become circular and spiralling, returning on its tracks again and again like very complicated chamber music. Foley, lying in the dark, his whole body clenched in resistance to the meaning, was unable to ignore the convolutions of sound. And beneath his

sense of outrage, much more potent, a kind of alarm was
uncoiling.

7

'He comes to my room every night now,' Foley said. 'Sometimes he only stops for a few minutes, sometimes for hours, but he never fails to put in an appearance, or rather, no, he doesn't appear, because it's always dark, he materialises, that's the word. It's driving me mad I don't mind telling you. Imagine, just a voice in the dark going on and on.'

'Well, you could always tell him to go away,' Barbara said. 'Couldn't you?'

'Do you think I haven't told him? The other night, for instance, he was just settling down when I asked him would he please, *please* tell me about it all the next day instead, because I wanted to go to sleep. You can't be plainer than that, can you? He didn't take a bit of notice. He just paused a second or two and then went on again as if I hadn't said anything at all. Moss is so obstinate, you see. It doesn't matter what I do, ten minutes after my light goes off, there he is. If I stay up reading or something, he stays up too. Even if he goes to bed first, he lies awake waiting for me to come up. The bedroom door doesn't lock and even if it did a fellow can't lock his door like a nervous virgin, can he?'

Foley looked fixedly at Barbara, trying to convey his sense of outrage. It was not a situation, he felt, with which a civilised man could deal. Moss, merely by blundering through the conventions which protect privacy, had complete command of the situation. 'I'd put the light on, suddenly,' he said, 'if the switch was near the bed, but it isn't. It's just inside the door and that's where Moss always stands and quite frankly I don't fancy barging into him in the dark. Otherwise that's what I'd do, put the light on. I strongly suspect that the light would drive him away.'

'What do you talk about?'

'Good God, we don't have a *conversation*, I don't say a single thing, it's no good, he doesn't listen anyway. He goes on about his childhood, people he used to know, things like that. Sometimes he tells me about things he's seen around the farm. He was on about some foxes, the other night, that he'd seen hanging up somewhere, with their tails cut off, but I never know what he's talking about, really. Sometimes I doze a bit, you know, and when I come to he's gone off on some other subject. And he's very difficult to follow because of the peculiar voice he puts on, different from his normal voice. He seems to know it all by heart, somehow, it's hard to explain. But what worries me is that it's getting worse. Before, at the beginning, he used to continue in the dark conversations we started before going to bed and that was bad enough, but now he saves it all up till the light's off. He prefers to talk in the dark, that's the conclusion I've come to.'

Barbara poured out tea from a pewter pot. 'It is certainly a strange way to behave,' she said, 'Something is upsetting him, obviously. Haven't you any idea at all?' She handed him his cup, looking at him as she did so with a certain curiosity.

'It's driving me mad,' Foley repeated, stirring his cup. He was uncomfortably aware that the weight of Barbara's interest was not distributed as he had expected and would have wished: she seemed to have him under observation quite as much as Moss.

It was a warm day. The windows facing the sea were open. A slight breeze stirred the thin curtains and little strips and blocks of sunlight expanded and dwindled on the glazed white walls. Foley could hear the pealing of the bell-buoy as regular as a clock ticking, although in clear sunny weather like this there was really no need for it, the reef then having its own colour, a band of vivid green over the sharp rocks. On the table between them was the skull that Barbara had asked for, which Foley had just brought for her. It lay grinning straight up at the ceiling, tremendously potent in that uncluttered room, even though too white and porous-looking to be taken for real bone. Foley had another in a cardboard box, that he was taking to show Bailey.

Mrs Gould refilled her cup with neat quick movements characteristic of her, and raised her nose at Foley. 'You mustn't be so . . . passive, Ronald,' she said. 'You must tackle him, tax him,

97

find out what's bothering him. Tell him to go to hell if necessary, rather than lose your sleep. What is obviously needed is something explicit between you. Do you see what I mean, dear boy? You can't go on for ever sagging under this burden of Moss, it isn't altogether manly. Besides, if you lose your sleep your beauty will suffer, won't it?'

Foley remained silent. He disliked flippant reference to his looks. He disliked the whole tone of Barbara's remarks. She was becoming altogether too ready to prescribe, too critical of him. Did she think he came to her for advice? His resentment was increased by the fact – and it was symptomatic of the change that was coming about between them that he did not care to admit this to Barbara – that he was distinctly frightened, physically frightened, by Moss's behaviour, the intensity of which, quite disproportionate to the triviality of his themes, was so painfully conveyed in the unemphatic, droning voice, the lumbering and graceless persistence, and above all in the recent peculiar blindness to his, Foley's, comfort and convenience. This last bothered him most because it confronted him starkly with his own inability to enforce these.

A kind of pride prevented him from explaining any of this to Barbara. Later, when he took his leave, she accompanied him to the door, the first time she had ever done this. It gave a greater formality to the visit and confirmed, in a way he could not yet discern fully, his change of status. Her head came only to his shoulder. Glancing down at her he noticed a thin silver chain round her neck. The skin of the neck was quite smooth and unwrinkled and had a sallow lustre. Whatever hung from the chain had slipped down inside the front of the dark blue linen dress she was wearing and before he could prevent them Foley's thoughts slipped down there after it and he pictured with quite disconcerting vividness the hard, jewelled pendant – keepsake or cross – resting exactly midway between Barbara's breasts, which would be round and glossy and yellowish, something like old ivory, with the dark bruises of the nipples dead centre and a tracery of very fine blue veins . . .

'And if sleeping becomes too difficult at home, my dear,' said Barbara at the door, 'there's always a bed for you here. You might not find it too uncomfortable. And I have a fund of interesting stories. I could tell you about my Swedish friend who is always trying to persuade girls to take a cold bath with him, because the only thing that rouses him is goose-pimples.'

'Why doesn't he just get hold of a goose?' said Foley. He left her smiling and raising her nose in the sunshine and walked back towards the crowded quay.

He had decided to put off his most important visit, to Gwendoline, to the very last, and so he headed directly for The Smugglers' Den. Bailey should be just about ready for business by now, he thought. It was not very far but it took quite some time to reach because the whole area of the harbour was packed with holiday-makers, straggling all over the pavements, diving in and out of shops. He was pleased to notice as he walked along the number of shops displaying their pixies; particularly prominent were the money-box pixies and their latest line, an idea of Moss's, two pixies paddling a leaf-boat. Seeing the pixies actually displayed for sale always reassured him, though they no longer relied entirely or even largely on the shops of Lanruan to take their stuff: all the holiday places up and down the coast were buying from them now.

The 'Closed' sign was still on the door of The Smugglers' Den, but the door was unlocked. The place seemed nearly ready to start business. Bailey, it was clear, had been busy. Holding the box carefully in both hands Foley looked round, at the little ornamental barrels with polished brass hoops that were meant to be used as chairs, and the long boxes stained black and bound with heavy wooden ribs to resemble sea-chests, which presumably were the tables. Brown fish-nets were draped about here and there and strings of painted cork floats looking exactly like giblets hung from the walls. In the window was a huge and apparently genuine ship's lantern with thick green panes. Smaller, less nautical oil lamps hung from the ceiling by slender chains. The only modern note was struck by a vast shiny tea-urn at one end of the narrow counter, and a calendar advertisement for Pepsi-Cola featuring a langorous and deeply cleft girl in a black negligée.

There was no sign of Bailey and at first Foley thought the place was empty. Then, behind him, from the recess just to the right of the door, a hoarse swearing commenced. Turning sharply he saw a small man halfway up a ladder, propped against the wall. The man was wearing a cloth cap and holding a paint-brush. While Foley was looking up the man turned to look over his shoulder and Foley immediately recognised the mournful arrogance of that face below the heraldic visor of the cap.

'Graham!' exclaimed Foley. 'What on earth are you doing here?'

'I'm doing what they call a *mural*, boy,' said Graham. He managed to make the word sound obscene by drawing out the first syllable. He turned his head and continued to climb down the ladder. When he faced Foley, the latter saw that he had a broad smear of paint over the left cheek and the bridge of his nose. His brown eyes regarded Foley with a doggy warmth and remoteness from under the low peak of the cap. 'I only just got started,' he said. 'You haven't been bringing me many pixies lately, boy.' In fact Foley had not seen him since that disagreement over the Cornish; but no consciousness of that quarrel showed in Graham's face.

'We've been going in for some new lines lately,' Foley said evasively. 'How did you get this job?'

'Old fat man came up and asked me himself,' said Graham. 'On foot too, all the way. You should have seen him when he got to me. He was on the point of collapse, boy.' Without otherwise changing his expression Graham opened his mouth wide and panted hoarsely to indicate Bailey's exhaustion. Then he closed it again slowly and drew the corners down to show the deadpan way in which he had played the scene. ' "Can I help you at all?" I asked him. "Haven't you anywhere to bloody well sit down in here?" he said. "Give me a chair, for Chrissake." It was a hot day, that day.' Graham's eyes had begun to shine with pleasure. 'And sweat, I've never seen anything like it. Most people just sweat on the forehead or upper lip, but he had little beads of sweat all over his face. Just like pimples. Every now and then one of them broke and ran down his face into his collar – you could follow it down all the way. I couldn't take my eyes of him. "What the bloody hell do you want to live up here for?" he said. He saw me watching him sweat, you see, and it annoyed him.' Graham smiled gloatingly. ' "Would you like a cloth?" I said. "Or perhaps a towel would be better. You appear to be perspiring rather freely." I didn't look him in the eye at all, just watched his face sweating.'

Despite fairly frequent experiences of it, Graham's unkindness always surprised Foley. 'But since he'd come to offer you a job . . .' he said.

'Oh, I didn't know that at first. As a matter of fact I thought he was from the Council, trying to get some money out of me. He offered me ten pounds for the job and I'm short just now so I took it. I've only just got started. A smuggling or a pirate theme he said, so I started with a ship.'

Foley looked up and saw that Graham had painted a single ship, very small, a galleon in full sail, high on the wall.

'Taken me quite a long time to get that ship right,' Graham said. He advanced his face towards Foley a little. 'I've got ideas for this mural. What were the bloody Cornish so well known for in the old days, hey, boy? Not pirates, I don't see them as pirates, taking their chances with a man o' war, too much bloody opposition. I don't see them as deep-sea operators at all. Smugglers, yes, sneaking up the beaches, bashing the odd coastguard; but the thing they did best was wrecking, luring the big ships on to the rocks with their lanterns and their warm Cornish shouts of welcome. Then they waited a bit and cut up the survivors when they were weak enough. The whole bloody village would be in it. That was your Cornish dodge, specialists at it they were, and it suits their character down to the bloody ground.'

Graham paused, as though inviting comment, but Foley kept prudently silent, warned by the vehement spittle which had collected at the corners of the other's mouth. What chiefly bothered him was a foreboding about the mural as a whole, and a vague commiseration for Bailey, among whose innocent commercial texts there could never have been warnings about people like Graham.

'I believe Bailey is rather depending on this wall-painting,' he said, 'to make the place go with a swing.'

'Oh, he'll get his wall-painting all right,' Graham said. 'Only, I've got a few ideas for it, that's all. He doesn't know what he wants, Bailey doesn't. Pirates, smugglers, wreckers, it's all the same to him. He just wants his walls filling up. That's what he's paying me for, and that's what I'm going to do for him.'

Judging it better now to leave this subject, Foley pointed towards the harbour. 'Lots of visitors this year,' he said in conversational tones.

'You can't blame *them*,' Graham said. 'What can they do, with kids and not much money and only a couple of weeks. They get taken in by the travel posters.'

'Yes, I suppose so. But it's not a bad place, for a family holiday.'

'See that harbour?' Graham said earnestly. 'You just come here at low tide. You ever been here at low tide? Take a walk round the harbour then, and tell me how many people you see snuffing up the ozone. You won't see a bloody soul, and do you know why?'

'Well, as a matter of fact – '

'Because the place stinks, the whole place stinks. All this water goes draining out to sea and there's about an hour when the harbour bed is uncovered. And it's all slime, boy. Nobody goes near it because of the bloody pong. I'm telling you. You won't see any windows open round the harbour at low tide, however hot it is, because the whole place smells of shit, and that's your Lanruan, boy: a nice view and a stink underneath.' Graham sighed, as though in weariness of spirit, but his eyes were bright with heartless energy. 'Of course, it's always high tide on the post-cards,' he said. 'Well, I'd better be getting on.'

At this moment Bailey came through the door at such speed that he very nearly cannoned into Foley and was unable to check his impetus until he had reached the middle of the room. Once here, however, there did not seem to be anything he immediately had to do, so there was no way of telling the reason for his haste. Remembering their first meeting, Foley wondered briefly whether Bailey put on these bursts of speed deliberately from time to time in order to give himself the illusion of high-pressure deals and negotiations.

'Hullo, hullo, hullo,' said Bailey grandiloquently. 'What have we here?' He shot a glance full of dislike and disapproval at Graham. 'Taking a break?' he said. Graham went on climbing up the ladder without answering. Bailey turned to Foley and his manner at once became bland and confident. 'And how are *you*?' he said.

'Very well.' Foley was rendered uncomfortable by this marked difference of address.

'Come through here,' said Bailey. He paused to give Graham's back another long, nasty look, which Foley was obviously intended to notice, before leading the way past the tea-urn, through a door behind the counter, into a long narrow room equipped with a gas cooker and sink unit, a kitchen table with a formica top, and many wooden shelves bracketed to the walls. 'Better in here,' he said, closing the door. 'Never discuss business in front of the men. Besides, I don't trust that man in there. There's something about him that I don't trust. Do you know he lives miles away, in a shack surrounded by undergrowth, halfway up a bloody cliff? I nearly creased myself getting up there and all he did was sit and stare at me. He offered me a towel, as though I needed to rub-down, like a bloody horse. He doesn't know how near I was to thumping him. There's something dodgy, in my experience, about a man who lives in a place like that.'

'You could have written. He'd have been down like a shot if he'd thought there was any money in it for him.'

'Never commit yourself in writing. When you've been in business as long as I have ... The bloody place was filthy too, regular pig-sty ... No, I can't say I like the man, I can't bring myself to like him. Not that that matters, of course. Never let personal feelings get in the way of business, that's a principle of mine. I always go for the best man, in his field, and they told me he was the best.'

Foley wondered vaguely who could have put in a good word for Graham. It was difficult to believe that he had any friends in the village. Whoever it was had probably spoken in malice.

'You have to take people's word sometimes,' Bailey said. 'No time to familiarise yourself with all branches. I was told he was the best, as I say. Personally, I don't see it. At any rate I haven't seen it yet. One bloody boat for a whole morning's work.'

'Artists can't be hurried, you know.'

'He just grunts at me,' Bailey said, with a transition to pathos. 'When I ask him how things are going he just grunts. I told him he could have a tea-break from ten-fifteen to a quarter to eleven, and do you know what he said to me? He asked me if I thought he was a fitter. "A fitter?" I said. "That's a better tea-break than a fitter would get." Now I find him wasting time while my back is turned. No offence to you, of course.' Bailey was silent for a moment, then raised one huge, very pale hand. With the fingers splayed he turned it slowly and let it fall again. The gesture was curiously impressive. 'He better do the job properly, that's all,' he said in a hushed voice.

Foley felt oppressed. Bailey was obviously disturbed though it was difficult at the moment to see why, exactly. Perhaps just having Graham on the premises was unsettling, like knowing there were rats about.

There was a short silence, then Foley said: 'The skulls you ordered are just about ready. I've brought one to show you, in this box.' He handed the box over to Bailey upon whose face an expression of pleased incredulity had slowly been forming.

'My, my, think of that,' said Bailey, looking down at the lid of the box. He shook it a little as though to gauge the contents.

'Aren't you going to look at it?' said Foley. Bailey really was extraordinary; he seemed to be regarding the skull as some sort of gift.

'No, I am not. I am not going to look at it,' Bailey said in immensely emphatic tones. 'And do you know why? Because I trust you. Deliver those skulls whenever you like.'

'The bill, of course, will accompany the goods,' Foley said in deliberately formal tones.

'Think nothing of it,' Bailey said. 'How do you like the place, your real opinion? Do you think it has atmosphere?' He made an expansive, sweeping gesture, with his arm. It was clear that he was once again in the big-time, on the plane of negotiations, released, at any rate temporarily, from such petty concerns as Graham's competence. The increased plangency of his tone indicated this, as well as the amplitude of gesture. It occurred to Foley that Bailey must have a rich and vivid fantasy life.

'Have you engaged any assistants?' he asked.

'Handle it all myself,' said Bailey. 'That's the beauty of it, one-man business, no wages to pay.'

'I suppose you've been in the catering business before?'

'What people don't realise, is that all businesses are the same, basically. What you need is the business brain – and business training, of course. If you've got those, you can run any business.'

'Perhaps,' said Foley, 'you could arrange to pay cash on delivery for the skulls?'

'Opening next week,' said Bailey. 'Just in time for the peak season. I expect a big turnover, cover my costs in a month or less. You can wait that long, can't you?'

'Well, yes . . .'

'Not a matter of life or death, is it?'

'Of course not.'

'Well, then,' Bailey said, very loudly and heartily. 'There you are then.'

On this jovial note they parted, Bailey billowing with farewells, then subsiding suddenly before Foley had got through the door, in order to write rapidly in a little black pocket book he had produced from some fold of his person. Foley said cheerio to Graham as he passed, but received no reply. From what he could gather in a quick upward glance, Graham was busy in the vicinity of the galleon with some dangerously jagged-looking rocks.

He went next to Gwendoline's cottage, as he had planned, but there was no answer and when he tried the door he found it locked, which was extremely mortifying because it was the third time that week it had happened; he had not succeeded in seeing Gwendoline since the day she had come to tea and left so suddenly. Perhaps she was away. But when he looked through the window he saw clothing on the back of the chair, tea-things on the table. The room had the look of a room recently occupied. Quite suddenly Foley was visited by the suspicion, damaging alike to his vanity and his sense of justice, that Gwendoline was not out at all, but lurking somewhere in the house and simply refusing to come to the door. He gave a loud double knock on the door, to show her at least that he was not deceived; but it was impossible, walking away, not to feel routed, ignominious.

His drive home was occupied by bitter thoughts and when he got back he found that Moss too was missing, a most unusual thing. He stood for some minutes in the casting-room, sniffing the austere, baked smell. The pixies Moss had been working on stood stark white in their plaster in a row on the trestle table. The ovens, cooling, creaked intermittently. The room was loud with Moss's absence. It wasn't Sunday. What could Moss be doing, where could he be?

He left the casting-room and made his way slowly up to the attic studio, feeling the silence of the house around him. In here it was quiet, with a whisper of spiders. Foley had washed the windows recently, removing a thick coat of dust and cobwebs, and had been amazed at the improvement in visibility − he had been assuming dusk to be a permanent condition here. Of course you lost the mystery, the selectivity, of artificial light; the sudden golden sprawl of limbs below their shades. But daylight gave a total impact, a massiveness, that in Foley's view more than made up for this.

All the windows were closed. All the morning's warmth lingered in the room. The cherubs and *putti* hung listless on their wires, barely stirring. In this light they were paler, yellower, bloomed with dust. Foley stood still in the middle of the room, breathing devoutly through his mouth. All his doubts and sorrows left him.

It was impressive, no one could deny that. Two years' work in this room. And now, as soon as the season was over, he would be ready. He could get started. He still had contacts in London, from his modelling days. He would issue invitations, on specially designed and printed cards, to visit these showrooms. Agents and travellers for the big department stores would be bound to come, they were always on the look-out for new ideas. He could secure contracts, work all through the winter developing new lines, escape finally from this trumpery trade of pixies, and the tyranny of seasons.

He went over to one corner of the room and took up his long-shanked, specially devised cherub-brush which always rested against the wall there. Much thought had gone into this brush. It had a cane handle several feet long and a tuft of pigeon feathers at the end − not tail feathers, which might have scratched, but the soft, short breast feathers. Wielding the brush firmly yet delicately he skirmished among his creatures, dislodging the dust from their dimples and orifices. His face grew absorbed and his tongue protruded slightly. The touch of the feather set many of the cherubs in motion and Foley, pausing among them with the long brush held aloft, his face raised reverently, resembled a figure in some disordered Assumption.

8

Moss, meanwhile, was walking on the cliffs. He had left his work on an impulse of restlessness increasingly frequent with him in recent days. At times, alone in the casting-room, impatience rose in him, like a criminal impulse. He would grow aware at certain moments of the terrible discrepancy between his outer, observable self, the patient ministrations of his hands, the periodic trips his body made to and from the ovens, and the other part of him which no one could see. This tension could often be relieved, he had found, by whispering words to himself, almost any words would do. 'Testing, testing, testing,' he would whisper, 'are you receiving me?' Or the words of songs passed repeatedly through his mind, impelling him in the end to utter them in the same whispering voice. Quite frequently, too, he was troubled by a sort of arbitrary dredging of his memory, which brought up old, incongruous things connected with his former life, before he had known Foley. Things he did not know he had remembered now attacked him with their irrevocability, the big round clock on a certain office wall, a garden gate with a number on it in white letters, things which had never been important. Yet the memory of them was now attended with anguish; and his heart laboured as though he were engaged in a physical struggle to shift them.

In the midst of this he would experience from time to time a sudden luminous focussing of his thought on Ronald, like a visitation; and then certainty descended on him, a sense of peace in the lineaments of Ronald's face, the face of the photograph in the bedroom usually, so noble and still. He thought of the face always as efficacious, healing; the fine luminous brow, the serious eyes. There seemed to be, while he could cling to this image and keep it pure and untrammelled, a refuge against the violence that rose within him more and more frequently these days, the desire to smash and disfigure things, the tearing urge to be delivered from his own clumsiness and patience. He could never possess this safety for long because however hard he tried to isolate the face, seal it off from its own sneers or the effect of some remembered unkindness, it could not be managed for more than a very short time. Before long some chance remark of Ronald's or simply some remembered movement or stance – Ronald turning from a window, Ronald standing still in a white shirt – would come to destroy his certitude, and he would be possessed by an anxiety which could only increase as similar images came flooding in on him, Ronald in a hundred trivial attitudes and occupations. The result was a kind of unlocalised pain which caused him to frown and whisper at the pixies. At these times everything – even Ronald's enthusiasm and ambition – seemed like dangers to their partnership; and then, at the threat of loss or change, the violence would flush in him again, the revolt at his own acquiescence; and only with difficulty could he restrain his impulse to take the nearest pixie, set it down in some convenient position, and use his fist like a hammer on it.

Such an impulse now had driven him out. He walked slowly, with dogged thrusting movements of his thighs, through the summer vegetation of the cliffs. He had frequently to climb over low walls of unmortared stone which, following the curve of the hills, were edged on either side by a strip of lush green like fat round a bone, contrasting with the paler, quick-wasted grasses on the open cliff side. Gorse blazed in the sunshine, filled the air with its sweet, excessive odour; but the sea-pinks were finished now, spent with May, almost colourless under this leeching sun. Huge, virulent foxgloves had replaced them, their flaring magenta linked the cliffs like beacons, in the midst of glossy nettles and the pale new leaf of brambles. Below, the sea was ridged with small indentations, dappled with shadows that scuttled continuously across its surface as quick clouds moved across the sun. There was a single fishing boat out to sea and in the sky overhead a kestrel loitered on sharp wings. Moss's feet in the bleached grass disturbed hordes of thin brown grasshoppers.

He descended through a narrow rocky cleft lined with ferns and broom. An occasional stunted elder writhed its moribund branches across the path and Moss was obliged to stop and insinuate his body through the branches since there was not room enough to walk round. Several times he did this without thinking. The branches were damp and slippery and a thick green mould rubbed off them on to his hands, and the breast and sleeves of his jacket. Then, as he was half climbing, half crawling through one of the elders, he was halted by the very strangeness of what he was doing, this probably unprecedented and almost certainly never to be repeated series of actions: a man creeping through a tree. And at this moment a cluster of shiny green elder fruit, a few inches from his nose, began to remind him of something. He paused, still involved in the branches, in an effort to remember. For a moment no thought came into his mind. He stilled his breathing. It was as though his whole life was in abeyance, waiting for the momentousness this unusual position had conferred on his body. He waited calmly and after a while he began to remember.

The fruit was like frog-spawn, frog-spawn in brackish pools below allotment gardens near where he had lived as a boy. Fishing in the frog-spawn pools with home-made nets, fishing for the newts that you never saw unless you caught them, because they lived in the dark ooze of the pool bed. You scooped up netfuls of liquid mud, hoping that when the mud had drained away through the meshes of the net you would find the wriggling iridescent reptile there. He had gone fishing there one day with another boy of his own age, a fair curly-haired boy whose name he had long ago forgotten. Two girls had appeared and sat by the side of the pool watching them; bold, talkative girls with sun-tanned legs; nameless, gypsyish girls from nowhere, existing only in that one scene by the pool, before and after too remote even for speculation. They had watched ironically at first and then with open mockery and teasing, sitting at the side of the pool with their skirts up over their knees, loose summer skirts that they twitched and drew forward and flicked back again and which were constantly falling away from their slender, active legs. Moss remembered with shame and a kind of impotent rage his own extra grimness of absorption and how his companion had exchanged gibe for gibe with the girls, leaving the fishing finally to sit near them, talking and laughing. He himself, before a scrutiny now three-fold, had gone on doggedly scooping up the mud, sullen and ridiculous. How old were they all then, eleven, twelve? He had seen one of the girls raise a hand carelessly and scuffle the other boy's hair. 'What lovely curls, you should of been a girl,' she had said, and his friend had laughed. 'I'm not though, am I? I could prove it if you liked. Would you like me to prove it?' So witty and so bold had been this retort, that Moss had not been able fully to believe that he and the curly-haired boy occupied the same planet; and for years afterwards it had seemed to him a supreme verbal felicity. The other girl, though, had perhaps been interested in him, attracted in some way by his aloofness. She had tried repeatedly to goad him out of his silence; but he had remained dumb. And then at last he had caught a newt in his net, seen the creature wriggle free from its accretion of mud and assume its lithe and wary form, its bright, resigned gaze. Turning to the three of them in his pride and loneliness, holding up the net, he had demanded, 'What do you think this is then?' and been amazed, overwhelmed, by their unanimous laughter. Now, after nearly twenty years, he could understand that laughter, see how discordant to their mood his demand had been, how comical. But he felt now there was a more important question behind. Lying against the damp branch, he considered gravely. Those two girls had appeared so promptly by the pool, stayed for that time only. It was difficult now not to think they had been provided specially; but if so he had missed a chance, failed to take an offer that had not been repeated. They had been girls apt for hot experiments, leggy and careless; he remembered their dexterity with the skirts. Perhaps one of those girls, the one that had gone on talking at him (but who had also laughed), if he could have gone with her somewhere quiet and screened from view, might have revealed some joy to him while there was time. Then, in childishness and guilt some essential sweetness might have been shown him, an appetite fostered, a direction set. Then, there had been time.

Slowly Moss disengaged himself and continued along the path. He resolved conscientiously, as he went along, to tell Ronald of this incident in his boyhood at the earliest opportunity. He would try to convey his sense of the irrevocability of that distant retreat.

He looked forward to these sessions with Ronald, the triumphant facility of speech he discovered in the dark, the sense of immunity.

After a few minutes the path broadened and flattened into a kind of marshy plateau, screened on three sides by steeply rising ground and on the fourth by a sycamore of venerable girth and low, sweeping branches, which presumably owed its existence, in that otherwise treeless place, to the sheltered position and the presence of water underground. As Moss emerged from the tangled path, practically the first thing he saw in the clearing was a black-faced ram crouching under the sycamore looking straight at him. What was a ram doing here? And it didn't move even fractionally when it saw him, which in itself was strange. Then he heard a concentrated, stealthy buzzing and saw the glints of flies round the ram's head. Still he was puzzled by its uprightness and thought it must be sick until looking closely he saw it was not crouching but trapped there and held upright by black mud; the spring below had seeped through here and made a bog several yards in extent, which though caked grey elsewhere was gashed black round the ram's body. The creature's legs were stuck fast and invisible, and the mud had risen to its breast and held it firmly braced. Its eyes were open mildly, and so natural and reposeful was its position that the fact of its death was difficult to accept, strangely disconcerting. He could detect no signs of violence or infirmity: its tightly curled, sand-coloured fleece appeared in good condition and the mild, libidinous face was quite unmarked.

He was perplexed by the question of how the animal could have reached that point, since behind it and all around the deep mud was crusted over. It must have come down from the cliffs, perhaps using the same track as he had, to drink at the watery verges of the bog, and waded in too far. One thing seemed clear, the ram had starved to death, not suffocated.

The flies round its head were vivid blue and green and their combined buzzing made a sound like distant adorations; their wings and bodies, traversing the zones of sunlight shafting down through the sycamore leaves, flashed with a brief and gauzy radiance; and this was all the sound, all the movement there was in the clearing.

Turning away from the creature's mild gaze, Moss climbed up

the slope beside the tree, using the lower branches to help him, and abruptly the closed world of the bog was left behind as he once more confronted the great sweep of the cliffs, the immense sea. But all the way home thoughts of the dead ram occupied him, and chiefly the fact that at the moment of death, the moment of release, the ram could not possibly have moved; not even the least bit, since by then it would have been too weak and, moreover, settled in its final position in the mud, posed irretrievably. It had not so much as declined its head or closed its eyes. There had been absolutely nothing to distinguish that moment from any other during the hours and days the ram must have stuck there dying. This seemed wrong to Moss. His mind continued to protest vaguely against it, even when he was back in the casting-room again, working on the pixies. He was affronted by such a meek manner of dying; though he did not formulate it in words he demanded that death should be more marked, more definite. Otherwise, death invaded life. He felt himself, as he chipped away at the pixies, intensely alive. He felt the power in his body and knew how it would struggle and convulse itself before submitting to die.

Certain small sounds overhead convinced him that Ronald was up there with his cherubs, but he did not pause in his work. From time to time his mouth shaped words without uttering them.

9

That evening Moss made pancakes for tea. He made them exactly as Foley liked them, not too puffy, lightly coated with a sweet lemon paste of his own invention. Foley ate largely of them, and said admiring things during the meal about Moss's skill in cooking and efficiency in domestic matters, compliments intensely gratifying to Moss, in spite of his modest disavowals, so much so indeed that in the end he became quite flushed with pancakes and pleasure. It was like old times. All the time he was washing up he whistled piercingly indistinguishable airs, but even this could do nothing to ruffle Foley who had settled himself in the living-room all set for a studious evening reading a Life of Benvenuto Cellini, a craftsman with whom he felt he had a lot in common.

Tonight when the washing-up was over, Moss felt so happy that he wanted to involve Foley in his thoughts without waiting for bed-time. He sat for some time in silence, his hands between his knees, regarding with the accustomed mixture of pleasure and pain the naturally graceful reclinations of Foley's body as he moved in his armchair. 'Oh . . . Ronald . . .' he said.

Looking up from his book, Foley saw Moss's solemnly confiding face aimed at him from the sofa. He knew that look. Moss's mouth moved for a moment without speech as though slightly convulsed by the pressure of its imminent disclosures. Foley sought desperately for some way of eluding the confidences that were to come; but nothing presented itself.

'I had rather a strange experience today,' said Moss. 'While I was out walking. I was going down this path, this very narrow path, and I had to keep stopping all the time because of the trees. They were growing across the path. Elderberry-trees. I had actually to crawl through the trees because there was no room to get round. The path was very narrow, as I say, and these trees were growing right across it. There might have been a way round actually but I found it easier to work my way through the branches. What I mean is, I didn't stop to look for a way round . . .'

A suffocating impatience rose in Foley. He felt an impulse to halt Moss by making some unexpected demonstration – uttering a series of shrieks for example. It was not only the intrinsic boringness of what Moss was saying at that moment, but the accumulation of all their previous sessions. Foley had reached a point at which the mere assumption by Moss of his Ancient Mariner voice, flat, rapid and monotonous, was enough to set him helplessly grinding his teeth and digging his finger nails into his palms. Yet he had so far concealed these frantic symptoms from Moss – out of innate politeness, as he liked to think; but he was aware of a deeper reluctance.

'The path was very narrow,' Moss said. 'So every minute or two I had to stop and sort of crawl through these trees. It's a funny feeling, crawling through the branches of a tree. It's not exactly climbing.'

He paused for so long at this point that Foley was able to bring off a *coup*. Rapidly he narrowed his eyes, dropped his jaw and nodded his head up and down several times. 'That must have been a remarkable experience, Michael,' he said. 'I can see what a remarkable experience that must have been.'

'No, but just a minute – ' Moss began.

'Having to stop like that,' said Foley, 'every few minutes and go through those *peculiar* motions.' He went on quickly, before Moss had time to gather himself. 'I don't feel much like reading tonight, do you? Shall we go down to the "Jubilee?" It was, he thought, distinctly the lesser evil; Moss was quite clearly set for the whole evening. At least in the pub there would be distractions, a less enclosed feeling, the prospect of intruding acquaintances.

Moss was not easily diverted from his purpose, but after a brief pause he agreed. 'I didn't quite finish what I was going to say,' he said. 'But I can always tell you about it later, can't I?' And Foley knew he would, without fail.

It did not take Moss long to get ready for the outing. He put on his invariable sports jacket, an extremely hairy cinnamon-coloured one with large leather buttons – his habit for all festive occasions. He gave his face a wash too; and it shone innocently while he waited for Foley, who always spent much longer preparing himself. Alone in his bedroom Foley was completely immobilised for quite some time by the habitual anxiety as to what should be worn for the occasion. In his mind there was an absolute standard of sartorial fitness, divorced from any actual social context, like a theory of ideal beauty for which there is no correlative in life. He chose finally his fawn, turtle-necked sweater, dark green jacket, tight-fitting trousers with a Prince of Wales check and suède boots. A last glance at his pallor in the looking glass and he joined Moss in the living-room.

Moss drove. He said little on the way, but his sense of responsibility for the handling of the car came off him in waves to mingle with the faint odours of leather and petrol in the dark, draughty and capacious interior. From time to time Foley glanced surreptitiously at his face. Seen thus, in profile, intent on the road ahead, it had an appearance of brooding sadness. There was no trace of that demanding joviality which the exigencies of speech seemed to bring out in him. Foley was visited with feelings of affection and regret. With Moss so firmly concentrating on the business of driving he became more manageable, more negotiable as it were. It had always been at such moments, when the weight of Moss's attention had been diverted from him personally, when he had watched Moss engaged in some neutral activity, that he had liked him best. He experienced, in realising this, a pang of regret for the old pioneering days of their partnership, the days of Moss's reticence. It was not the facts themselves, the actual details of the relations, that troubled him so much, nor indeed their timing – strange though this often seemed – but the way in which Moss delivered them with his whole weight, this curious, disturbing intensity. It seemed that he was not so much being informed of certain of Moss's perceptions and experiences, but invited – obliged, rather – to take on the extra burden of what it meant to be Moss. And this, he honestly felt, was beyond his capacity. He had enough with the constant running repairs his own life seemed to require. Besides, he liked people to keep their lids on; he had never had the slightest desire to pry into things, prise them open. He felt the same as when his seaside companions during school holidays had gone tramping miles along the rocks armed with long sticks with which they levered up the flat stones to see what was under them; he himself had no wish to see what ungainly creatures scuttled forth. School holidays pass quickly; and with that careful self-regard and nice sense of priorities that had always distinguished him, Foley had considered it more important to relax in the sun, fret his toes in the waves, acquire a tan deep enough to gild his acre all winter.

From a long way off they could see on the horizon a diffused pink glow, cast by the 'Jubilee's' huge, neon sky-sign. It gave them a homing feeling, coming out of the wastes to this focus of warmth and companionship. Their engine seemed to get throatier at the sight, like an animal sure of its prey.

The sky-tinting capitals were repeated over the door in sloping blue script and the flagged threshold was bathed in pale blue, which made the face of each appear to the other momentarily ghastly as they paused to consider whether to go into the bar or the lounge. They chose, they had always chosen, the lounge; but that deliberation was part of their freedom and neither would have liked to forego it.

The lounge was already full of people. Its familiar opulence closed round them as they entered, derived not from anything of intrinsic value there, but from the rosy twilight shed by the lamps and the impressionistic use by the decorators of red velveteen and dark oak stain, the whole combining in a sort of dust-free plushiness.

They got pints of bitter and moved away with their drinks into the middle of the room where there was more space.

'Isn't it crowded?' Moss said pleasurably. It took him no time at all to settle down in any gathering. It never seemed to occur to him that he might be out of place, or subject to the speculations of other people, or required to converse with them. His role as he conceived it was always external and, in a curious way, predatory. He appeared to regard the whole thing as a raid on the manners of everyone in sight, during which you stored up as many impressions as possible, till the next time you could get out. Very soon he began to make comments, too loudly, about the inhabitants of the lounge, and to repeat some of the things he heard them saying.

Thus, for the first few minutes, Moss acted as a link between Foley and the outside world. Foley always needed to feel himself into his surroundings, by a process of minute observations and compliances, a sort of settling of the feathers. He had a great horror of being conspicuous in any way.

'Those men over there are something to do with the police,' said Moss. 'I heard one of them say he had been to see Fabian of the Yard.'

'He probably meant at the cinema.'

'No, I heard him say that he had been to see Fabian, to have a word with Fabian he said. That one there, in plus-fours.'

'It's just a name to impress people with,' said Foley. 'That man is too small for a policeman. Keep your voice down, people can hear you.' He was coming to himself now and able to look around with more composure.

Moss went for two more pints. The room was very crowded now and the noise was considerable. The man whom Moss had indicated was talking in a didactic manner and those with him listened gravely. He had an enraged face, like a cockatoo's, and he pecked at the air for emphasis. Most of these people were holiday-makers. In the rosy light they looked assured and prosperous. The men seemed all to have thick necks and confident, slightly snarling voices. The women had touched up their holiday tan with lotion and nacreous ornament; many of them wore light summer dresses and their throats and arms shone softly. All seemed comfortably aware that at home in their suburb the house was secure, the garden well watered. Foley was swept suddenly by feelings of envy and deprivation. These people looked so settled, their comfort and security established beyond question. Why was it that only his own life seemed to require these ceaseless ploys?

Moss returned with the pints. 'There's a funny man at the bar,' he said. 'That woman over there in the green dress, sitting at the bar, she had her handbag lying on the bar beside her and that little man in the yellow pullover came up and asked for a gin, I think he's had a few already, and she just picked her handbag up to make room for him and he said "I wasn't going to pinch it, duckie." '

Foley said: 'She's rather an attractive woman, isn't she? There doesn't seem to be anybody with her.' The woman's dress was cut in a deep vee at the back and Foley noticed a pale strip of skin about an inch wide going across her back at about the third notch of the spine. That must have been made by a bikini strap. As an anodyne for his envy, Foley began to imagine the patterns formed by the sun on the front of her body, the breasts flushed to just above the nipple-line, the crescents below still white, and dazzling by contrast; a dusky tide over flank and belly and thigh – broken only by the faint diagonals at the pelvis where the strings had crossed; gold and white struggling in the roots of the first tender hairs of the hillock itself, and then the milky, inviolate triangle . . .

He noticed that the people at the bar were edging outwards away from the man in the yellow pullover, leaving him finally quite isolated, holding what looked like a gin. A second later he recognised the man.

'It's Max,' he said to Moss, and it seemed to him that a rather apprehensive expression appeared on the other's face. Moss lowered his voice so that Foley could barely hear him.

'You mean the Max who is the friend of that actor?'

'Yes. You haven't met him, have you?'

'The one who has been kept by an actor?'

'Yes,' said Foley, somewhat impatiently. 'Simon Lang. I've told you all about him, haven't I?'

Moss mouthed an 'oh' with exaggerated discretion and looked intently across to the bar where Max was still standing. 'It's funny,' he said. 'I always thought of him as being taller.'

Max's feet were still but his whole body was swaying rhythmically from side to side as though he were keeping time to some distant, reedy instrument played slowly.

'He looks drunk to me,' said Moss, after several more seconds of inspection.

'He nearly always is drunk. I don't think I've ever seen him not drunk. But he doesn't usually come here. He sticks to the pub at the place where he lives – the Tolreath pub. They know him there and they look after him.'

'I suppose it's because he's so unhappy that he drinks so much,' Moss said. There was no doubt in his tone, despite the tentative form of the words, and it was clear to Foley that Moss was already making up his mind about Max. He found himself once again oppressed by the uncouth starkness of the judgement. Trying to discuss Max's delicate, hysterical equipoise in terms of happiness was like training a blunderbuss on a butterfly.

'I shouldn't think it's as simple as all that,' he said. 'Things never are, really.' He might have gone on, but he saw that Moss's face had already assumed a heavy, ironic patience.

'You'd better meet him,' he said shortly, and turned to start on the rather complicated journey to the bar.

'Just a minute,' Moss said urgently, and at the same moment Max turned his head and caught sight of them. Immediately he broke into that smile of terrific social delight which was all his own and flung an arm into the air. He held this pose for an appreciable moment, then began to make his way towards them with an undulating, slightly pin-toed walk.

'Dear boy!' he called from several yards away. His high, fluting voice caused a slight stir among the plus-fours group, who were still apparently immersed in criminology. They all looked round at Max and a certain stillness settled on their features. Max seemed to have some difficulty in extricating himself from this group. He began to make courteous, side-stepping motions, without getting any nearer to Foley and Moss. He nodded and maintained his smile, to show them he was still on his way. Some of his gin slopped out on to the carpet and Max said 'Oops a daisy' brightly to the averted face of plus-fours. In his yellow pullover, with that vivid smile and the agitated grace of his movements, he looked exotic, and frail, like an oriole among pigeons.

'Such a lot of people,' he said breathlessly, reaching them at last. 'And the men all look at me so *sternly*, it's divine. They're not *really* tough, though. What this pub needs more than anything, I always think, is a few *stokers*, scattered here and there, in their vests.' He grinned from one to the other of them, with cultivated impudence. 'So nice to see you. How are all the pixies? This must be the person you keep hidden away.'

Foley said: 'This is Michael Moss, my partner. Michael, this is Max Nugent.'

'How do you do,' Moss said ponderously.

'But you remembered my name, my second name,' said Max. He abandoned his smile and looked at Foley with ironical surprise. All his reactions had this quality of over-elaboration, and this made him at first appear artificial to the point of silliness; but after a while artifice impressed one as necessary poise, as touching and in a way brave, seeming to reflect Max's awareness of being in a hostile world.

He began speaking to Moss in a gossipy, mock-confidential manner: 'So few people do, you know. I am one of those whose surnames are seldom remembered, we are a race apart. I don't know why, I'm sure. It's awful, really, to be always Max or Maxie to absolutely everyone, as though one were a dachshund or one of those political cartoonists. It gives you no place in the world. I feel sometimes like the regimental mascot, if you'll believe me. Not that I'd *mind*, when you think of all those busbies.' All this time he had been keeping his deep-set, rather simian eyes fixed on Moss and now quite unexpectedly he marred the apparent seriousness of his manner by a sustained wink. Moss too had been regarding him with an unwavering intensity.

'I've heard a lot about you,' Moss said at last, in measured tones, and Foley, even while he winced, knew that this was just another example of Moss's tenacious sense of fitness. His sense of timing suffered like everything else, from his inability to judge the effect he was having on others. For Max, however, the remark at this juncture had a strong accusatory force and even his practised imperviousness was not quite proof against it. His face slackened with annoyance or surprise, it was impossible to say which, but a second later he was smiling again, his slightly wizened, durable smile, in which there was no mirth, and no real mockery, but a watchful, combative gleam – a duellist's smile.

'But he's priceless,' Max said, peering up at Foley. 'What *can* you have heard, my life is blameless. You must tell me sometime what it is, in private of course. Hearing discreditable things about oneself is one of life's greatest pleasures I always think, don't you?

It revives the illusions of youth. One felt capable of such wickedness then.'

There were no signs of drunkenness about Max now. The unsteadiness he had displayed at the bar had quite disappeared. All the same, there was a recklessness about his speech this evening that made Foley suspect he might be primed with something more than gin. He was usually quite free in his allusions, of course, especially when he felt sure of his company. And he displayed the usual air of keyed-up frivolity, as though he were convinced that all interlocutors were basically inimical and the main thing was not to be trapped into earnestness or anything approaching self-revelation. But tonight there seemed to be some extra quality of excitement in his speech.

'Don't you think, honestly?' he repeated, smiling up at them.

'You sound like your incomparable namesake when you say things like that, or perhaps Oscar Wilde,' Foley said, wishing suddenly to please Max. Max in fact was delighted. He raised his head and uttered his manic laugh on three ascending notes, the third one audible throughout the lounge.

'That was my period,' he said, reaching for their glasses. 'Dear boys, let me get you another.'

'Well,' said Moss, 'you might take that view, of course, or you might think that the good opinion of the community is well worth having and gives you something to live up to.'

If Max was like an overwrought Oscar considerably dwindled, reflected Foley, Moss sounded like Ralph Waldo Emerson at his least inspired. He was a little apprehensive of the effect of all this on Max whose poise was in some ways very precarious, but the latter had adjusted himself by now to the double tempo of the conversation.

'Get *you*!' he simply said. He took the empty tankards, holding them both in one hand. All his movements had a nervous, slightly unco-ordinated grace, a quality of struggle, as though he were, in some imponderable way, hampered. 'There's something I'm dying to tell you,' he said over his shoulder as, clutching the tankards and his own glass, he began to make his way back to the bar. As before, he side-stepped frequently with elaborate and unnecessary deference, as though to avoid collisons.

'Quite a case, isn't he?' said Foley, while they waited. 'All this archness, you know, you needn't take it seriously. It's Max's *persona*, that's all. I suppose it is necessary for him, but it's all talk really, just a habit. As a matter of fact after such a long course of gin I should think the poor fellow would be impotent, if it came to it.'

'I don't think we should talk like that about him,' Moss said. His gravity had deepened to the point of exultation. 'You're not going to tell me,' he said, 'that this is a happy man?'

Foley was rather puzzled for a moment, then he realised that Moss had reverted to that point in their conversation immediately prior to Max's joining them. Probably he had been put out by Foley's contradiction. He seemed in any case to feel that the interval had somehow proved him right.

'Oh, I don't know,' Foley said. He looked across at Max who, having reached the bar by now was talking with vivacity to the blazered manager and eliciting from him a series of reluctant smiles. 'He's happy tonight, I think. Don't you?'

Moss assumed his patient expression. 'I didn't mean on the surface, of course,' he said. 'A person surely is either happy or unhappy. Basically, that is. No one could keep his self-respect living on money sent by another man.'

There was such a depth of conviction in this last remark that Foley experienced a sudden weariness at the need to reply at all. Why had Moss taken up this issue with such firmness?

'I don't know why it is,' he said, 'but you always seem to choose the wrong sort of words to apply to people. Max is just constantly in a state, that's all. You seem to be taking it for granted that there's a sort of definite territory of happiness that Max has somehow wandered out of, that he could get back to again if he could find the way or someone would show him. I don't think that's true, not for anybody. I don't believe Max was ever in such a place, even in the early days with Simon.'

As usual Moss seemed somewhat staggered by the figurative turn the conversation had taken, but he was on the point of replying when Max rejoined them, holding the three glasses, two large and one small, between his palms with exaggerated care.

'I was just saying that you seem on top of the world this evening,' said Foley.

Max drew back his head and smiled from one to the other. His eyes were very bright. 'Well,' he said after a moment, 'what it is, my dears, you see, Simon's coming.' He said this with simplicity and a sort of finality as though this topic at least required no embroidering.

'But that's marvellous news,' Foley said.

'Yes,' said Max, with the same delighted explicitness. 'Yes. I had a telegram yesterday. He's coming on Saturday. He's going to stay for the week-end.'

'He doesn't come very often, does he?' Moss said, seeming to surface abruptly from some rumination of his own.

'He comes when he can,' Foley said, trying by his tone to convey a warning to Moss. 'Doesn't he, Max?'

'Yes, that's right,' Max said. 'He comes whenever he can. He likes to come down here, but of course he's a very busy person. He is in demand all the time. He's been in Africa for the last three months, filming. You can't expect him to get down here very often.'

'Of course not,' said Foley.

'Yes,' said Moss, 'I realise that, but how long actually is it since he was last here?'

'Well, it's a few months, but you can't expect a famous actor, an *internationally* famous actor, to be free to please himself, when he has all these commitments, literally all over the world . . .' Max was still smiling but his air of invulnerability had gone, and something anxious had crept into his tone, as though he were defending not Simon but himself, from some accusation inherent in Moss's words.

Foley noticed with horror that Moss's expression of patience had returned. 'Yes,' he put in quickly, 'we know how it is, Max. These celebrated people, they can't call their lives their own. It's like royalty, really; don't you think so, Michael?' He tried to catch Moss's eye, but Moss was looking steadily at Max.

'Is it more than a year since he was here?' Moss said. 'Or less?'

'He likes to get it right, doesn't he?' Max said.

'He could always fly,' said Moss. 'He's got the money. If he really wanted to come he could always fly.'

For a moment Foley regarded Moss helplessly, wondering how

such obtuseness could be possible. Then suddenly the conviction came to him that Moss was not being obtuse at all: Moss, amazingly, was speaking with deliberate intention. What made him so sure of this he could not have said exactly. Perhaps it was something to do with the fixed and intent way in which Moss regarded Max; or perhaps it was one of those moments in which coincidence has to be abandoned in favour of design, when blundering becomes too accurate to be any longer believed in. For whatever reason, he knew that behind that calm and still slightly surprised face some process of calculation was going on.

'It's really great news, Max,' he said, determined if possible to keep up Max's euphoria, collapses from which, as he knew, were apt to be sudden and complete.

'Yes, isn't it marvellous,' Max said. 'He comes here to rest, you know. The *strain* of an actor's life is terrible, absolutely terrible. He can forget all about the theatre here, for a while. Simon is at the top of the tree, of course.' Max said this with great pride, but glanced at the same time in a curiously supplicatory way at Moss, as though to see how he was taking this praise of Simon.

Foley, who had known Max to scream like a jay in fury at some slight to Simon and seen him keep off rudeness to himself with a close and quite deadly play of mockery, was astonished at this deference to Moss's opinion, this ascendancy established so quickly. He had never seen anyone else do it. He could only suppose that Max's usual imperviousness, his rapier arm as it were, had been dislocated at the outset when in his happiness at Simon's coming and his assumption of the pleasure others must take in it, he had been at his most vulnerable. Moss, at least, showed no signs of letting his present advantage be lost.

'Aren't you an actor, too?' he asked.

'I once did some acting,' Max said, raising his head and meeting Moss's gaze at last. 'A long time ago now. But I wasn't any good, really.'

'You stopped acting,' said Moss, 'and your friend, what's his name, Mr Lang, went on.'

'But I wasn't any good, duckie, I didn't have Simon's talent. I was just a camp-follower. Very camp.' Here, with an effort at jauntiness, he winked at Foley, who smiled back as encouragingly as possible.

'But you'll never know that, will you?' Moss said. 'You'll never know how much talent you had because you stopped trying.'

Max was now definitely becoming distressed by Moss's persistence. He had given up all attempts to smile and his low-browed, rather monkeyish face had a chided look. Suddenly Foley noticed with absolute dismay that there were tears in his eyes. He remembered someone telling him of an occasion in the Tolreath pub when one of the drinkers had quite inadvertently said something sympathetic to Max and brought out in him a mood of tearful self-abasement which, coinciding with an excess of drunkenness, had taken all power of movement from him, so that he had clung to people, weeping, confessing old sins. If that happened here among all these people it would be terrible: they would all be regarded as birds somehow of a feather, they would never be able to live it down. Foley felt convinced that Moss was working towards this, with a horrifying adroitness. What his motives were could only be guessed at. Perhaps he was simply trying in a drastic fashion to prove his point, to demonstrate Max's unhappiness. Or, as seemed more likely, something in Max's initial manner, that defensive insolence, had aroused a levelling instinct, brutality masked as plain speech, as it so often is. At all events he, Foley, was resolved at all costs to avoid being classed with persons who broke into hysterical weeping in public places.

'Well,' he said, intent on saving the situation. 'What *fibs* you tell, Max. You've never stopped acting, you know you haven't. You are not content with life as it is, that's the thing about you. You are always trying to make life finer, aren't you? You improve the quality of life, Max, that's what you do. Acting is a kind of courage.' He had spoken only half seriously. Now he waited briefly until he saw some slight stiffening of Max's demeanour, then added swiftly, 'But how can anyone say what you are like Max, you are so *peculiar*.' Fear of a scene had given skill to his speech. The affectionate deflation of this last remark, coming so soon after the praise, and in such contrast to Moss's bleak insistence, delighted Max and steered him back to exuberance. He burst out again into his loud, three-noted laugh.

'Peculiar, odd, *queer!*' he said. He handed his glass, empty now, to Moss and raised both arms, holding them out with a sort of dainty rigidity and snapping the fingers of both hands. Then he executed a lunging tango step, graceful and rather old-fashioned. Foley saw the figure of the manager hovering at the bar, no doubt wondering whether public feeling against Max was strong enough to warrant a rebuke. Foley had no doubt it soon would be. Moss for his part showed no awareness of being thwarted: he continued to regard Max with solemn interest and concern, rather like a naturalist who has just netted a new species, slightly wounding it in the process.

'It's fun to have fun,' sang Max in a clear tenor, throwing back his head and snapping his fingers.

At this moment he saw Gwendoline sitting with a young man whom he did not know at the far end of one of the alcoves. She had been concealed from view until then by the persons between them, but these had cleared a space around Max as soon as he had started his singing and dancing.

Max repeated the tango step, backwards this time and with a tricky little half-turn at the end. Moss put out an arm as though to prevent him from falling. The manager uttered preliminary coughing sounds. It seemed to Foley a good time to withdraw.

'Excuse me a minute,' he said. 'There's someone over there I know.' He made his way towards the alcove. Gwendoline saw him when he was still some yards away and smiled, but not in a very welcoming way. 'Hullo,' he said, 'I didn't know you came here.' He regretted this opening immediately: it sounded too injured.

'I don't often,' Gwendoline said, 'but we have a car tonight, you see.' She indicated the young man at her side, who was beginning, somewhat reluctantly it seemed, to get up. 'Ronald Foley,' she said. 'He lives here. Ronald, this is Bernard Scott, a friend from London who is spending a few days down here.'

Foley acknowledged the introduction without a great deal of warmth. He had a rather confused impression of a tall, heavily built man of about his own age, with a fleshy, big-nosed face and plentiful fair hair arranged in exact waves all the way up like benches in an antique theatre.

'Where are you staying?' he asked.

'Oh, I'm putting up at the village where Gwendoline is living. Landooly or whatever its name is. All these names sound the same to me.' He had a rich voice and the sort of assurance which would always make his difficulties discredit their causes rather than himself. He had now effectively designated the whole region as one not to be taken seriously, cancelling out whatever advantage Foley might have felt at being in familiar territory.

'Lanruan,' Foley said.

'What's that you say?'

'The village where Gwendoline is living is called Lanruan.' He had spoken with intentional flatness, but he could see that Bernard was far too complacent to be effectively derided in this way.

'You live here all the time, I believe,' Bernard said, smiling broadly. 'What a lucky fellow you are.'

'Come now,' said Gwendoline in an intimate, teasing voice. 'You know you adore London. You wouldn't live anywhere else.'

Bernard said, 'Oh well,' and smiled even more broadly at Foley. Now he had London too, supreme in both the Metropolitan and Regional divisions.

With a rush of aversion Foley saw that Bernard's eyelashes were very long and almost white and that he had combed his hair with a wet comb; the corrugations rose one above the other at exact intervals. He could picture Bernard carefully blocking them in with a sort of light rabbit-punch action. He knew that at this point he should have contested London, dropped a few names of smart bars or head waiters, but none came to mind. Moreover he was possessed by an irrational fear of giving Bernard any clue as to his way of life in London. He decided, as always, to play safe by confirming the assumptions about himself that the other appeared to be making.

'Of course,' he said, 'for we provincials London always seems the centre of the world.' I should have said 'us', he thought immediately, with a pang disproportionately large.

'Bernard is a solicitor,' said Gwendoline, 'in a well-known City firm.'

Bernard looked with mock resignation at Foley, but said

nothing. There was a short silence, then Gwendoline spoke again in quite a different tone. 'Won't you join us,' she said, and 'Yes, do,' urged Bernard.

'No thank you. I'm with friends,' Foley said, salvaging what dignity he could.

'Do you mean that funny little man who was dancing?' said Bernard, whose tone seemed to be getting more insulting. 'He looks as if he's had a few. Seems to have quietened down a bit now, though. Probably been chucked out.'

Foley said to Gwendoline, 'I'll look in and see you one of these days.' He wished Bernard a good stay and watched him beginning to slide down gratefully beside Gwendoline. Turning away he felt like one who has been given alms and dismissed.

When he got back to that part of the lounge where he had left Max and Moss he found they were no longer there. Not believing at first that they could have left the pub, he spent some time looking round the room and even thought of having another beer while he waited. But he did not want any more beer and as the minutes passed it became obvious they were not going to return, that they had left without him. This realisation so astonished him that for the moment even the disquiet engendered by the meeting with Gwendoline and Bernard was overlaid. One expected this sort of behaviour from Max, who was widely known as an erratic character – a habit of acting on the flawed impulse, a sort of impure spontaneity, had probably always characterised him. But for Moss this was a departure from all precedent: it seemed to presage the abandonment of all forms and ceremonies whatever. Standing alone in the crowded, noisy bar Foley felt the spectral presence of Anarchy.

10

He waited for a few more minutes to make quite sure, then went out into the car park. Their car was still there, so Moss must have gone in Max's. If he had, he would without doubt be regretting it by now: Max was an extremely dangerous driver with a colourful history of endorsements, not reckless but seeming unaware of elementary rules, as though he had learned to drive and always driven in remote places, accessible only to his own car. The thought of Moss in this predicament — having to keep up an appearance of composure for the sake of his moral ascendancy, yet filled with apprehension at every wavering bend — made a strong appeal to Foley.

He drove back slowly, stopping on the way to smoke a cigarette. When he had put the car away he wandered about the house aimlessly for a while, oppressed somewhat by the silence, which was emphasised rather than relieved by the very faint chime of the bell-buoy and thuds of a dazzled moth. He made coffee with a solitary, hypochondriacal sense of ministering to himself. His mind reverted continually to the latest lapse of Moss's. What chiefly intrigued him was the concerted action of two such dissimilar people. On what basis could this sympathy have been established — so rapidly and after such an unpromising start? And what in the world could they be talking about? He recalled Moss's attack on Simon, his deliberate attempt to undermine Max's happiness at the impending visit. Perhaps he had wanted to strip away Max's illusions and bring him to a rock-bottom view of his situation. If so, who but Moss would be so presumptuous? It was as though he were trying to get Max born again. And indeed there was something crudely evangelical about Moss, something of the spiritual bully, coercing people to admit their imperfections.

His thoughts turned unhappily to the meeting with Gwendoline. It was only now that the wounds inflicted during that conversation actually began to give pain. The tone of pride in which she had declared Bernard's profession, as though it were an Order of Knighthood; her acquaintance with his tastes and opinions, and the fluency with which she spoke of them: all this argued a good deal of intimacy. But most hateful of all to remember now was Bernard's insolence and the way in which he had swallowed it, almost with deference.

It had been, on the whole, a wretched evening. Still, as he sat on, the silence gradually supplied a balm, as though his present purely accidental loneliness were willed, a retreat from the stresses of the world and therefore healing. His temper indeed was almost restored and he was beginning to think of bed when he heard voices in the yard, the sound of car doors, and a few seconds later Moss himself appeared, blinking and smiling in the light.

'Well,' said Foley, 'what have *you* been up to?' He spoke lightly, almost playfully, having decided that it would be both more polite and more dignified not to seem to mind too much.

'I went off with Max,' Moss said. Something almost abashed about his stillness, and his thickened voice, told Foley he was drunk.

'I gathered that much.' Despite himself, his tone took on a certain tartness. He was irritated to see Moss's drunkenness, irritated too by the other's failure to explain immediately. 'You might at least have told me you were going,' he said. 'Not that it matters, of course, really.'

'Yes, I know.' Moss replaced the smile with a look of wooden contrition, an expression difficult for him to maintain, because of the confused delight he was experiencing at seeing Ronald at last as the injured party. 'We acted on the spur of the moment,' he said. 'It was wrong of us, really.'

'Yes,' Foley said, 'you couldn't have discussed it very long. I was only gone five minutes.'

'That was Gwendoline you went over to speak to, wasn't it?'

'Yes, that's right.'

'Who was that she was with?'

'Just a friend.'

'I should think it *was* a friend,' Moss said rather boisterously.
'What on earth do you mean by that?'

'That word covers a multitude, I always think, don't you? And then, when you got back, you found we'd gone. You must have felt a bit . . .'

Moss paused, as though inviting Foley to supply the word, admit his misery, and Foley perceived at last that the other was actually enjoying the conversation, a fact which if he had not been so taken up with the modified expression of his grievance he might have noticed sooner. Moss was definitely elated, there was no other word for it. The drink, probably. Still, Foley resolved to utter no more complaints. 'Well, anyway,' he said. 'Here you are.'

'Yes,' said Moss. 'Yes, definitely.' He knew he ought to explain, knew Ronald was expecting him to, but he himself had not yet understood the impulse that had driven him to suggest that abrupt departure. Or rather he had not yet put into communicable form his strong sense of the momentousness of those few minutes in the pub after Ronald had left them. He had known only, obscurely and with a sort of dark excitement, that this was an important, a crucial juncture of his life. In the silence which had fallen between Max and himself after Ronald had gone, this sense had brimmed in his consciousness, impelled him to action. It had been his idea, not Max's, to leave without waiting for Ronald. He had known that Max would agree – his certainty of Max's acquiescence was another element he would have found difficult to explain in any form of words; it had seemed anterior to calculation, like an instinct. So he had acted quickly, mindlessly almost, aware only of the urgent need to dissociate Ronald from anything further that might pass between Max and himself. This in fact at the time had seemed his only motive – to plant Max and Ronald as far apart as possible. He had seen how opposed to his own Ronald's attitude to Max had been, how Ronald was really concerned only to avoid anything unseemly. He had known that he would never get anywhere with Max while Ronald was about, because what Max needed was someone to be frank with him, not to confirm his weaknesses with tact. During the first few minutes after they had left the 'Jubilee', Moss had thought it was simply this, that the urgency came from his impulse to subjugate Max's self-damaging illusions. He had not realised for some time that now his own needs, not Max's, had driven him; not until they were in Max's car and on the road and he was talking Max out of stopping at the next pub. Not until Max had said, 'Let's go home then, duckie, plenty of gin at home,' had it really come to Moss, with a mixture of fear and exhilaration, that this very glibness was what he aspired to; that Max's style, his whole public identity, signified above all a high degree of initiation. Sitting beside a prattling Max, Moss had felt, as an increasing difficulty to breathe freely, the acknowledgement he now made less equivocally than ever before that he wanted, needed, an introduction into that world, a means of entry. This helpless recognition of his destiny had only failed, as he afterwards felt, to suffocate him completely, through his noticing that Max was driving on the wrong side of the road, a fact which changed the nature of his perturbation very considerably. Later, at Max's house, his excitement had returned, this breathless sense of irrevocability — not caused by anything personal or particular that Max might say, but by his increasing sense of the other's total commitment to that other camp. Max, who had suddenly become drunker, less taut, when they reached the house, seemed nevertheless to put on authority, being the first fully fledged homosexual that Moss had ever knowingly conversed with, the embodiment then of innumerable broken speculations and desires. Over the gin Max had become archetypal; for Moss too the bitter drink which he had always disliked seemed to signalise a change of heart, sufficiently unpalatable to be regarded as sacramental. He had a stealthy, metamorphosed feeling as he stood there, looking down at Foley.

'No,' he said softly. 'It wasn't very nice of us.' The gin, and the agitation of his feelings, had unsettled perspectives; things tended to slip sideways if he looked at them too long. 'Not nice at all,' he repeated.

'Well, it's not as bad as all that,' Foley said. 'It's just not like you, that's all.'

Moss took a slow step forward and stood still again, still wearing his smile. 'No, quite unforgivable,' he said.

'Did you have a nice drive with Max?' Foley asked, with a sudden gleam of vindictiveness.

'*I* drove,' said Moss. 'Max wasn't in a fit state. We started off with Max driving but he was going all over the road. I made him stop and change over.'

'My, my,' murmured Foley, quite foiled.

'Yes, we changed over. Max doesn't take proper care of himself. That's what I was telling him. "You don't take proper care of yourself," I said. "Do you want to kill yourself?" I said. "You'll kill yourself one of these days, driving like that." Do you know what he did when I said that? He just made these mooing noises like a cow. What it was, you see, he'd had too much to drink.'

'Yes, I rather suspected that was the case,' Foley said.

Moss took another step forward. He was quite close to Foley's chair. The tall standard lamp which Foley had been reading by was beyond the chair and a little to the rear of it, and Foley's shoulders and head were full in the rather harsh white light. With a drunken intensity and brilliance of focus – a kind of visual rage – Moss looked down at Foley's face in profile, the pale, immaculate parting in the hair, the long scornful lash of his left eye, the ear set gracefully close to the head and whorled more delicately than is common in a man. Moss was never afterwards to recall the events of the evening except in conjunction with this beauty of Foley's, this almost hallucinatory radiance under the lamp. 'Max has asked us to a party on Saturday, to meet Simon,' he said.

'That'll be nice,' Foley said.

Moss rested his hand on the back of the chair. 'Did I ever tell you,' he said slowly, 'that I am subject to these hot flushes?'

Foley glanced up quickly and then away again. 'No you didn't,' he said, 'as a matter of fact. Why don't you sit down?'

'I feel better like this. Didn't I ever tell you about them?'

'How do you mean, hot flushes?'

'It's difficult to describe. I've had quite a few of them lately. I sometimes get them in the day but more often at night when I'm in bed. There's a feeling of warmth in the chest, round my heart, and it spreads all over my body. It's not so bad at first, actually, because it's mixed up with feelings, usually like a sort of happiness, but after a bit it affects my breathing. Like drowning or something of that sort. And just before it starts to go away, there's

134

always a point when I feel that I'm going to die.' Moss paused for a moment, then added, 'I've never told this to anyone but you.'

'You ought to see a doctor about that,' said Foley. He was impressed. Perhaps because of the drink Moss was speaking more vividly than usual. 'I should see a doctor if I were you,' he repeated.

'I don't think a doctor can help me much,' Moss said, with a rather peculiar emphasis.

'They can do a lot these days,' he replied vaguely, bothered by Moss's nearness and immobility and by the possible gravity of these hot flushes.

There now followed a rather long silence between them, during which Foley could distinctly hear Moss breathing. The chief characteristic of Moss's breathing was the heavy downstroke through the nostrils. The sound of it tonight, together with Moss's proximity, Foley found unnerving enough to attempt eliciting more speech from Moss as an alternative.

'What did you talk to Max about?' he asked, directing the question at the ceiling.

Moss spoke immediately and smoothly as if responding to a cue: 'People don't understand Max, he doesn't take the trouble to explain himself of course, he lets people think what they like. Max has a lot of courage.'

'I don't doubt it,' Foley said mildly.

Moss looked straight before him and said, 'He's got no time for women, of course.'

'Well, you don't say,' said Foley. 'You must be joking.'

'He admits it,' proceeded Moss steadily, 'freely. He told me so himself, just tonight. He said to me, "I am as queer as a coot." Those were the very words he used.'

'But surely,' Foley said, 'surely you didn't need to be told.'

Moss could find nothing to say to this. The telling was precisely what had been needed, and for a long, long time. He might have gone on as always before, possessed by a guilt that came wretchedly prior to any action. In any case he had no skill at inferences. He could not see any way of conveying to Ronald the great difference between supposing something and hearing it admitted. No one in all Moss's life had said it to him, until tonight. He had heard it, of course, reported of others, and the more direct forms of that reporting had run in his mind from schooldays, a soft and contemptuous jingle, nancy-fairy-pansy-pooff: affecting his own modes of judging. Even the obliquer references had been slighting, or dismissive at least, pushing their objects away, beyond the rim of acquaintance, a disgracefully aberrant minority whose deviation was so great as to swamp all other human attributes they might have laid claim to – simplified to the point of monstrosity by this long course of innuendo. This then had been Max's gift, that he had told it, that he had embodied the quality of being queer – and with this all Moss's sordid or melodramatic associations – in himself; in his frail, consistently human and consistently present self. And, because he was so much more than this, particularly in his needs, Moss had been enabled to see that one may be this and yet go on being the self one was before. An inestimable gift. Max could not have known or even suspected the effect of his words on Moss; they had cost him nothing to say; and he had proceeded to talk of other things in a tone not much different. But a couple of gins later, as though he had indeed calculated his effects, he replied to a random question in a way which finally melted the pathetically thin membrane of reluctance and protest in which Moss had been sealed. 'Of course,' he had said, 'you can't go by me. I never got over Simon.' 'But it was twenty years ago,' Moss had said, expostulating. 'You can't go on feeling like that for twenty years.' And Max had smiled, shaping his mouth and widening his eyes with conscious charm, yet at the same time meaning it when he said, 'Well, I do, you know.'

You had to call this feeling love: it endured and remained generous through the stress of years, jealousies, separation; and though guilt and self-contempt could not be effaced at a blow from Moss's mind – the stain of the furtive could probably never be effaced – he was brought at the least to see clearly what had before only been part of his defiance: the folly of any attempt to grade such feeling by distinguishing among its human objects.

'He makes no secret of it,' Foley said. 'Personally I think he's asking for trouble going about so blatantly.' He paused, then added darkly, 'Max is going to come a cropper one of these days, you mark my words.'

'How do you mean?' enquired Moss. He had resolved on subtlety, thinking this to be at anyone's disposal, there for the putting on, like frankness. He felt secretiveness now to be a condition of survival, since he was encamped, so to speak, right under the enemy's cannon. There was nothing sensuous in his feeling, despite Ronald's luminous nearness. So far, it was his mind, not his blood, that was stirred. He felt simply as though he were a secret agent conducting a delicate and possibly dangerous negotiation.

'Well, it's against the law, you know,' Foley said. 'People are tolerant enough on the whole, of course. But there are those who are very much down on that sort of thing. Anyone who wanted to could get Max into real trouble.'

'But why should anyone want that? In any case, if he doesn't *do* anything, he's all right, isn't he? I mean, it's not what he says that matters. Besides, that sort of person, the sort who would go out of his way to get someone like Max in trouble, would be a latent himself.'

'Would be a *what*?' asked Foley, startled. He did not now for some reason find it very easy to support Moss's regard. The former constraint of drunkenness seemed to have quite gone and Moss looked ecstatic; there was no other word for it: his eyes were wide and shining moistly and his lips were pressed tightly together as though he were repressing sounds of joy. Foley had never seen him like this before.

'A latent,' said Moss. 'Max was saying that a lot of people who are very much against it are latent queers themselves.'

'Oh yes,' Foley said, with sudden angry sarcasm, brought out by his growing uneasiness at Moss's manner, 'Oh yes, we've all heard that before. Anyone who says it's disgusting must be grappling with his own guilt, anyone who actually likes women must at least be both ways. You can include anybody if you go about it like that. It's like the argument about great men, you can make quite an impressive list, with Shakespeare and Socrates and Leonardo at the top. But in fact the great majority of people who have achieved anything in art or politics or science have been ordinary heterosexual people.'

'But they are the great majority anyway,' Moss said. 'So what

137

you have just said doesn't really mean anything, does it? Besides, I should think that Max knows more about these things than you do.'

It was the first time in their association that Moss had made a deliberately derogatory remark like this, and Foley was strangely shocked by it. It was while he was still casting about for a dignified rejoinder that Moss, who also felt he had gone too far, said slowly: 'Max says he has loved Simon Lang all this time. He used that word. Do you think, yourself, that it is possible for a man to love another man like that?'

But this was too naive, even for Moss. Even while Foley was replying, was saying rather huskily, 'We're hearing rather a lot about Max tonight,' aiming thus at a dignified rebuke, he was realising with a sort of expanding suspicion what was wrong about Moss tonight: it was not only the suppressed exhilaration, disturbing as this was, but Moss was being too humble. Always, always before, in discussing such matters, Moss had put on his man of the world manner, prudish, essentially dogmatic, which he used as a substitute for argument. This present tentativeness had been assumed deliberately, and could only mean that Moss's conception of himself was changing, had changed. It came to Foley that Moss was not the person he had always thought him, that this creature standing so close, breathing heavily, waiting with a rather appalling docility, presumably for some sort of answer, was virtually a stranger. Even his face seemed different. There was something muffled, almost creepy, about this change. Suddenly he felt that it would be a bad mistake to prolong the conversation. He got up from his chair with a rather remarkable sideways rolling motion, ending up on the side furthest from Moss, with the chair between them.

'I don't know,' he said. 'Yes, I suppose so. There are cases of it, aren't there? One hears about it.'

'In what way?' asked Moss, who had not moved.

'Well, I mean ... Take David and Jonathan.' Foley was beginning to feel distraught. He held the Cellini book in one hand; with the other he smoothed down his hair.

'The trouble is,' he said, 'the word is made to do far too much – if you see what I mean – it's always the same word, isn't it? We should invent some more nouns ...'

Moss nodded his head sagely, as though he too had given the linguistic aspect some thought. He had noted Foley's rather extraordinary way of extricating himself from the chair, but had not associated this with any possible mental disturbance. He was too interested in his own feelings to be for the moment accessible to such an idea. He had fallen in fact into the trap of self-absorption that awaits all green conspirators, and could not regard Foley as anything but an element of his own sense of the marvellous potential of the situation. It was with a feeling, therefore, almost of outrage that he saw Foley adopting a particular kind of smile and heard him say: 'It's time for bed. I think I'll say good night.' But before he could find any way of stopping or delaying this exit Foley, moving quickly but smoothly, was out of the room.

On reaching his bedroom Foley uttered a great sigh. He felt completely exhausted. He had no wish to think things out, to analyse further either Moss's behaviour or his own. What he had, irreducibly, was the conviction of Moss's duplicity. He felt a reluctance to go beyond this, into any investigation of motives. Tomorrow, he thought, or at some suitable subsequent date, I will have a proper look at all this.

It was less than ten minutes later, before Foley had got into bed, while he was still examining his features in the looking-glass above the dressing-table, that he heard Moss's footsteps along the passage. They stopped outside his door. Through the glass Foley watched the door-knob with fearful intensity, but it did not move. He could hear nothing from beyond the door. After a few more moments of suspense, reassurance came suddenly to Foley, bred of the conviction that Moss would never enter his bedroom while the light was on. So strongly was he persuaded of this that he felt able to start a conversation.

'Is that you, Michael?' he called.

There was a brief pause, then Moss said, 'Yes it is,' in a rather grudging voice.

'Just going to bed?' Foley enquired, but Moss made no reply to this at all and under the stress of the ensuing silence Foley was driven to make polite mouths at his reflection, declining his head and nodding and simpering slightly. After a minute or two of this

139

he composed his face into a noble seriousness and looked at that for a bit.

Suddenly Moss, from beyond the door, broke into speech. 'It's funny though,' he said. 'I mean, of course you come across it. Take this time I was in London, I was about twenty I suppose, no, wait a minute . . . it was in April 1953, and my birthday isn't until August, so I must have been nineteen. Nineteen and a half I would have been. I was staying with my aunt in Cricklewood, she's dead now of course. I'm going back nearly ten years now.'

Foley watched himself listening politely, head a little on one side, eyebrows raised suavely. He narrowed his eyes just enough to denote alertness, not enough to seem suspicious.

'I was at the Regent's Park Zoo,' continued Moss, dates and ages now satisfactorily fixed. 'I was watching those little deer, what do you call them, gazelles. They were all in a big enclosure. It was very hot, for April. I remember seeing in the paper that it was a record for fifty years. I wasn't wearing a jacket. I was carrying my jacket. I was wearing one of those sports shirts with short sleeves. After a bit a man came and stood beside me. He was looking at the animals too. Suddenly this man put his hand on my elbow, partly on the elbow and partly on the upper part of my arm. He began speaking to me as well, no wait a minute, he didn't start speaking all at once, he just kept his hand on my arm. Then he said how beautiful the gazelles were, graceful and that. He said what beautiful eyes those animals have. They *have* beautiful eyes, of course. He said they were his favourite type of animals. All this time he was moving his hand up and down my arm. I didn't know what to say. He was very dark and he had curly hair. He had a foreign accent too. He was smiling and looking through the wire, not looking at me. He didn't look at me at all. I shook his hand off and moved away a bit, but he still went on talking to me. I left him there. I walked away from him. The funny thing was, I started shaking after that. I couldn't stop myself. I remember how strange it seemed, shaking like that on such a hot day.'

Foley sat motionless at the table. He had not been able to sustain his own regard during Moss's story and his eyes had dropped from the glass to gaze in a distracted fashion at the toilet articles laid out on the table. After-shave lotion, symbol of conquest; the stoppered bottle of Cologne water.

Moss leant forward until his hot forehead was resting against the outside of the door. He said: 'For some reason or other I always thought he was a Syrian. I didn't have any reason for this – it just happened that the idea came into my mind that he was a Syrian.' He could remember as if there had been no interval of time the details of the Syrian's face he had taken in during that quick look, the thickish, constantly smiling lips, the dark drowsy eyes, the way his hair, though not seeming oiled or wet at all, gleamed in the sunshine. He remembered too the daunting grace of the gazelles. He knew now also what he must always have known without acknowledgement, that it had not been anger or outrage that had set him trembling, but the awful consonance of his own desire with that gesture, that caress. The hand which had moved, so strangely without importunity, along his bare arm had distressed and frightened him only by its confidence, its assumption of his complicity. But his assent had been forged when he was helpless, before his life became sequential to him – it was antecedent to choice. Nevertheless, on that sunny April day it had seemed that life could be wrenched into other courses; and he had walked away from the Syrian, and trembled afterwards.

Now as he stood in silence with his brow still resting on the panel of Foley's door, some of that distress returned to him and it seemed almost that the vibrations of such a feeling must penetrate the room and reach Ronald's mind and cause him to understand without need for more words. Not only to understand, but to put things right. Ronald could fuse the fragments of his life, burning out the waste. Lumley and the smell of sin, Frank's purified regard from the shelf above the fire, the hand with the warm gold ring sliding up his nerveless arm; that announcer on the wireless whose voice he would have known among thousands; the terrible pauses before nude Apollos in museums. Ronald could make all this whole, if only it somehow could be brought before him. Moss did not feel he was being unreasonable, but what he was expecting from Foley was a miracle.

11

Moss said no more that night. After a short silence Foley heard his footsteps receding down the passage. He was too far gone to feel any relief at this now the damage was done, his obdurate understanding violated at last. The story of this drooling Syrian had finally, in spite of all his efforts, cleared things up. At about the time he had lowered his eyes from his reflection it had come to Foley with irresistible force that Moss was kinky, was in fact, not to put too fine a point on it, a pervert. But how could a person who wore a beret without even pulling one side down, and thick ginger socks in all weathers, how could such a person be a *pervert*? It was not conceivable. And where had he got that word from, anyway? He would never have applied it to someone like Max, who was quite open about the thing. It was a term of abuse. He had thought of it, he realised, because it resembled *perfidious*. Moss, the perfidious pervert.

He undressed as quickly as possible and got into bed. His eyes wide open in the dark, he tried to cope with the problem of what to do with Moss. It was impossible that he should actually *encourage* him, even to keep the business together. But could he, on the other hand, at this late stage, try to divert desire from himself by such feeble palliatives as introducing Moss around? He already *was* introduced if it came to that.

He cleared his throat, with a sound that was cautious and rather prim, after the pain and intensity there had been in Moss's voice. He was lying on his back with his knees drawn up sharply. For an appalled moment or two he tried to think what it might be like actually to be Moss, and have such a sting and not know whether acid or alkali was needed and no one to tell you, but almost immediately he became confused between two images of

Moss as yet quite unreconciled: the Moss of tradition, reliable, exploitable; and the Moss revealed latterly, a tortuous queer. He had known other homosexuals, that is he had detected this tendency in men from time to time, in the streets, in pubs. During his modelling days he had actually worked with them; but it had always been with the sort of indulgence that seems to absolve one from any need for deeper understanding. He had never considered more than their external vagaries. Usually these young men had been marked from the first by a sort of preening, excessive even in that *milieu*, and by a waspish and jeering camaraderie. They had been blatant, people you could spot a mile off. He had not liked working with them, because they were not respectable, they lowered the tone. But he had never at any time thought of their condition as involving complexities of emotion, practices that bodies and minds were deeply engaged in. And now here was Moss positively clamouring, albeit deviously, to be associated with these others, the Moss of monumental decencies and Harris tweed, whom he had thought he knew, whom he had seen almost daily for three years. In the abstract he felt no particular hostility – he lacked the quality, perhaps it was simply imaginative energy, which could have made such considerations very real to him. But when he thought of Moss actually taking part, adjusting his heaviness and solemnity to whatever postures such loves might demand, the whole idea became repugnant and comical too.

Sleep came to him finally and he slept deeply and dreamlessly and woke unusually late the next morning. Moss was not to be seen or heard in the vicinity of the kitchen. This in itself was not unusual since they always made their own tea and toast separately, taking it together of course if they happened to coincide, but more often bearing it off to their respective working quarters. Moss always made tea for the mid-morning break and they were accustomed to take this together, usually talking over matters related to the business.

So Foley merely assumed that Moss had taken his tea along to the casting-room and started work. He was relieved at this since he had an extreme reluctance to set eyes on Moss just then, and for some time to come. He was himself disinclined to begin work this morning, although there was much to be done. They were behind with the orders, and at a time when the peak period was beginning. They should both have been working full out. Even if they worked steadily through July and August they would probably still lose money now.

This morning, however, the very urgency of the work seemed to intensify Foley's reluctance to engage in it, and after a very short struggle he decided to take the morning off and walk down to the village by the cliff path. The decision which, once made, he did not think of changing, nevertheless filled him with gloom. Such irresponsibility on his part, such a neglect of duty, of self-interest, seemed like a further element in the disintegration which threatened from all sides.

He walked slowly, in dejection at first, but brightening gradually as the cottage and with it all disagreeable calls to action receded behind him. It was a fine morning. The sky was a tender blue with a high tremulous haze of cloud, the kind of sky that in Cornwall promises hot, still weather. The sea was pale hyacinth and calm to the horizon, greening in the shallows. On the landward side the sloping fields were stiff with wheat or ploughed black. Foley's passage along the cliffs was marked by puffs of gulls that he scared off the ledges; they did a couple of screaming turns before settling down again behind him. The turf under his feet was dense and springy, sown with the dark blue vetches that endure all summer. As Foley walked on an optimism that was entirely of the body grew in him, characteristically deep-centred in himself, in the mechanisms which propelled him along so smoothly, the steady carriage of his trunk, his marvellous, swivelling head. His delight in himself served as a substitute for purpose and destination.

As he drew nearer to the village the path became easier. A sharp turn brought him within sight of the pronged headland, its cleft containing the harbour like a puddle in a furrow. He had decided to miss out the harbour area and particularly The Smugglers' Den. This he managed by taking a circuitous route through the narrow cobbled streets above the harbour. He emerged on the far side, quite close to Barbara Gould's house. It was earlier in the day than he had ever visited her and as he stood on the doorstep he was assailed by the dismaying thought that she might still be in bed. But she called out to him immediately in her clear, harsh voice.

She was sitting at the table with writing-paper before her. Foley noticed at once that she looked different, less elaborate in appearance. That would be because of the time of day. Her hair was parted in the middle and came low over the temples at each side, softening the cheekbones and making her whole face look gentler. She did not seem to be wearing very much make-up; there were faint lavender-coloured shadows beneath her eyes. The eyes themselves were as brilliant and reptilian as ever as she looked up smiling.

'How nice of you to come just now,' she said. 'You have saved me from having to write letters.'

For some reason Foley felt disconcerted by this remark and he remained silent for a moment or two. Barbara regarded him, still smiling.

'I believe you are blushing, dear boy,' she said at last, in exactly the same tone as before. This tone of hers, completely without warmth or sympathy, too dispassionate even for mockery, frightened Foley and helped him to recover. He smiled and wrinkled his nose slightly, one of his favourite charm expressions.

'It's supposed to be a sign of grace, isn't it?' he said, holding the expression for a moment before dissolving it in a broader, heartier smile.

Barbara replied, 'Yes, so they say,' and got up from the table. 'Come and sit down,' she said. 'No, not there, this is more comfortable.' She pointed to the black divan against the wall.

It was the first time he had sat on the divan, as far as he could remember. On previous occasions he had used a straight-backed chair and the slight discomfort of this had marked the formal expository character of his visits. He could not help wondering whether his present posture, which he tried hard to make unsprawling, signified the beginning of a new phase.

'I'll go and make some coffee,' Barbara said. 'I expect you'd like some.'

'Heavenly,' Foley said, nervously, but with a definite sense of keeping his end up. He observed that Barbara had well-defined muscles in her calves. He was again visited, while she was in the kitchen, by a gloomy sense of impermanence. Everything seemed to be slipping out of his grasp. Suddenly it came to him that the rot had started with Bailey and the skulls. Since that irregular request there had been nothing but trouble for him. He experienced an upsurge of malice towards Bailey, recalling that moon face, that neurotically billowing, too Protean personality. However he was soothed by the recognition, which instantly followed, that Bailey would come to grief before long.

'Well, what's happening down on the farm,' asked Barbara, returning with the coffee.

'Well, Moss rather let himself go last night.'

'Do you mean he made a pass at you?' Barbara asked, and took a sip of her coffee. 'I can't say I blame him,' she added.

Foley looked at her in amazement. 'Do you mean to say that you suspected something?' he said.

'Do you mean to say that you didn't?'

'Of course he didn't make a pass at me; the idea!' Foley said carefully. 'But he did admit, or rather he talked himself into the position of not needing to admit in so many words, that is he told me things about himself which amount to an admission – although I don't know if he knows it himself yet, knows that I know, I mean – '

'That he's a raving queer,' she interrupted, on a rising note of triumph. 'Anyone would have known that.'

'Indeed, would they?' Foley said, with extreme coldness. 'At any rate he is certainly not raving, you are being melodramatic. Moss is quite calm about the whole thing.'

'Well of course,' she said, with a sort of overbearing gaiety, 'but he must be quite batty with it underneath, so repressed and that. I wonder what he's been *doing* all these years. My dear boy, you are a simpleton for all your airs. Did you think they all lisped and minced? I should have thought anyone would suspect Moss. Never any girl friends or anything. And have you never really noticed, there's a sort of *muffled* quality about him. About men like that. Surely you must have noticed?'

Barbara looked sideways at Foley, smiling. Her head was inclined a little and the dark hair had swung forward, partially concealing her face.

'As a matter of fact – ' Foley began.

'They seem muffled up, they don't move freely. Moss is a big strong chap, isn't he, but have you ever seen him do anything . . .

sweeping? Have you ever seen him make a single expansive gesture? When he points at something does he stretch his arm right out or does he bend it at the elbow?'

'I've really no idea,' Foley said. He was disturbed by the quality of Barbara's excitement, in which there was neither scorn nor pity for Moss but only a sort of relish at the accuracy of her judgement. Above all he was appalled by her perspicuity. She had detached Moss from his protective background, like taking a crustacean off a rock, with one twist. She had winkled him out and now here she was holding up to the light the poor little gobbet of transparent jelly. It was inhuman.

'You saw it all right, my dear,' went on Barbara, with a return to a sharper tone. 'You see things as quickly as anyone. But you're capable of suspending conclusions indefinitely if they're not convenient, aren't you? People are only real for you at the points where they impinge on your little life, otherwise they might as well be *plankton* for all you care. You simply ignored about four-fifths of Moss. Exploiting people doesn't matter, but you didn't care enough to try to understand the nature of the instrument. It comes from trying to form alliances with people all the time, instead of friendships. You have permitted yourself to become an object of admiration to Moss, basked in it, acted up to it. Now you are probably going to suffer for it, which you richly deserve. Lads like Moss have their sprouting time sooner or later and he has had the good sense to break out of the role you had cast him for.'

'I hadn't cast him for any role,' Foley protested. 'He just seemed to be *like* that. I took him as I found him.'

Barbara made no reply to this. Her face slowly lost the expression of delighted percipience with which she had been speaking. She looked at Foley in silence for some moments. He himself was filled with a sort of furtive resentment against her. So great was her authority now that this could only have been expressed in some very primitive defiance, such as nose-thumbing. So he swallowed rather noisily and said nothing more. All the same, it irked him terribly to sit chidden on the black sofa. It was the grossness of perception imputed to him which hurt him most, much more than selfishness or any unkindness. He felt instinctively it was this quality that Barbara herself most despised.

147

'Never mind, Ronald,' she said at last in her customary, somewhat jeering tone. 'You are a very decorative fellow.' She was smiling again. The pale mouth curved upward, slightly tremulous at the corners; the steady black eyes regarded him unblinkingly, without tenderness or any detectable expression save zest. She would not have regarded much differently, he felt sure, a forkful of pâté. She obviously thought of him as neither ally or friend, simply appendage. Yes, Barbara was detestable . . .

Her skin, he noticed, allowing his eyes to dwell on her face in an effort to escape the marked down feeling her eyes gave him, was faintly moist-looking. It was very pale and delicately pored and there were no spots or blemishes anywhere. It was a face inured to expensive preservatives. He could picture her applying, each night before she went to bed, a paste of cold cream, until her face was a stiff white mask and only the derisive eyes lived in it. How old was she? Forty? Forty-five? What was her life in London like? He had no means of knowing. He felt sure she had always taken the proper exercise, used the best type of corsetry. Unwanted hair had been razed tenderly from her body. He was beginning to feel excited by all these private things she did, and repelled too. He took refuge in a deliberately renewed rage against Moss.

'It's the deceit I can't stand,' he said. 'His keeping quiet all this time about it. He should never have agreed to come in with me, not without telling me first. I suppose he was hoping I'd come round in the end.'

'Yes, but don't you see, my pet,' Barbara said, 'what a dim and pathetic hope that was, not even consciously a hope at all probably, but worth it for him, worth giving up years for? He might have gone on all his life like that. You don't call it deceit unless there is some process of calculation. He liked being associated with you, that's all. Only this year it became clearer to him, who can say why? Perhaps he felt his security threatened. Moss might have gone quietly dotty over the years if something hadn't stuck in his throat. Much better for him that it did, whatever you may think. Much better than going on making pixies all his days and thinking all he wanted was companionship. I expect he knows what he wants now, doesn't he?'

Finding no adequate reply to this, Foley stood up and said he thought he'd better be getting along. The visit had not gone at all according to plan. Again she accompanied him to the door. It seemed to have become settled practice. It was at once more formal and more intimate and Foley found it vaguely intimidating, as though Barbara had reassessed him, revised his status in some way. At the moment of parting he experienced a strong desire to prolong his visit by some means, but he could think of no plausible pretext.

'Whatever,' he said, 'shall I do with him now?'

'Do with him? There is nothing much for you to do, is there? You must put up with the way he will look at you, that's all.'

Foley pondered this remark as he proceeded through the village. He had decided to return by the road. How would Moss look now, sheepish, reproachful? He had a disagreeable conviction that fresh shocks were in store. Absorbed in these thoughts he took the shortest way back and this led him past Gwendoline's cottage. He was walking very fast when she tapped on the window to attract his attention and a moment later she opened it and called softly across to him. He stopped, and after hesitating a moment crossed the street towards her, assuming as he did so a certain nonchalance.

'I've been hoping to see you,' she began, speaking it seemed to him rather hurriedly. 'I feel that I owe you an explanation. You must think me very rude.'

'Oh no,' said Foley. Gwendoline obviously had not been long out of bed. She was wearing a dressing-gown of dark blue towelling and her hair, pinned up hastily, had strayed loose here and there around her face, which still carried the pallor of sleep. Foley sensed rather vividly, as she leaned towards him out of the window, the languidness, the compliant heaviness of her body, before the brisker juices of day had began circulating properly.

'I just happened to see you passing and I thought . . .' she said, trying vaguely to secure her hair.

'My!' said Foley lightly, 'you get up late, don't you? Are these your London hours?' He was pleased with himself for having found this vein of careless ease right at the outset, so much so that he could not resist giving Gwendoline his sexy, down-from-under look. Unfortunately, she wasn't looking at him, but gazing rather worriedly down the street.

'I don't usually,' she said. 'I just saw you passing and I felt that I owed you an explanation. No, I don't usually get up so – ' She stopped abruptly and stared down at him, widening her eyes slightly. 'Oh dear,' she said.

'Only when you have visitors?' supplied Foley, with bitter alacrity, for he too had heard the sounds which had caused her to break off, a wanton joyous splashing from within, mingled with throttled bursts of a baritone voice. Beyond any doubt it was Bernard, having a bath. Foley looked grimly up into her eyes. She must have thought the coast was clear while he was in there, forgetting Bernard was the sort who would splash about and sing, even in other people's baths.

'He must be having a lovely game with the loofah,' Foley said. The sounds were those of a man in full possession. The image of Bernard wallowing there, the warm water stirring his pampered genitals, was suddenly too much for Foley. 'I'll be getting along then,' he said.

'Oh dear,' Gwendoline said. 'No, wait a minute, don't go yet.' She regarded him helplessly for a moment. 'I *am* sorry, really I am,' she said.

'Never mind, never mind,' Foley said. All he wanted was to get away.

'But I felt that I owe you an explanation.'

'I think I understand already.'

'No, you don't. Listen, Bernard goes back to London the day after tomorrow, that's Friday. I could see you in the afternoon if you liked. We could go for a walk.'

For the sake of dignity Foley appeared to consider for a few moments. 'All right,' he said at last. 'Friday then. I'll call for you.' He had already begun to move away, and Gwendoline closed the window quietly, shaping some final words, which he did not understand, through the glass.

The walk back was a gloomy one. He was tempted, on his arrival, to go straight upstairs, but Moss had to be faced sooner or later and so after a minute's struggle he proceeded directly to the casting-room expecting to find him at work there.

Moss however was nowhere to be seen. Nor was there any sign of work in progress. On one of the benches there was scattered

150

debris of plaster chips. Foley took these at first for scrapings off the mould, but looking more closely he found them to be the fragments of pixies. He stood beside the bench for some time fingering the minute pieces, wondering what accident could have befallen them. They could not simply have fallen and been swept up or the pieces would have been much larger. They could not be diverse sweepings from the floor; they had an unmistakable appearance of belonging together; and besides, it was new, fresh plaster. Rather it seemed as if something heavy had fallen squarely on to them as they stood in a row on the bench. But what object so heavy was there in the room? And where, in any case, could such an object have fallen *from*?

Foley abandoned the problem abruptly and stood for some time looking around the room, rather at a loss. The ovens were quite cold. It was apparent that Moss had not spent much time here this morning. He crossed to the window, which was so dusty that it was quite impossible to see out, and rubbed with his fingers a clear oval in the middle. His action startled a huge, fawn-coloured spider that had been lurking in the crack between the pane and the sill. It shot diagonally across the window and up the wall towards the ceiling, making in its haste a disagreeable, dry, whirring sound.

He stooped a little and looked through the oval at Moss's view. The farmyard was quite deserted. One of the farm dogs, a thin, black, shivery bitch with mangled ears, came trotting up the defile of the farmyard holding something in its mouth. It held its head up high and rigid, and trotted on stiff legs, looking neither to left nor right, but seeming apprehensive of both quarters at once. The unusual nobility of its demeanour – quite different from the slightly hysterical ingratiation it showed at all other times – was due, Foley realised, solely to greed and the fear that the thing in its mouth might be detected and disputed by one of the other farm dogs before it could be taken somewhere private and bolted. The thing itself was difficult to identify. It was black and wet-looking; shreds of it hung down and dripped on either side of the dog's jaws, though perhaps the drips were merely saliva. Still moving at the same stately pace the dog, whose name he thought was Betty or Maria, disappeared through an opening in the fence at the top end of the farmyard.

He was just about to turn away from the window when he caught sight of Moss, some way off, making diagonally across one of the high fields that bordered the lane. He was clearly heading for the house. While still several hundred yards away he stopped dead, as though struck by a sudden thought and remained motionless thus for several moments while Foley peered at him through the oval. Then the distant figure crouched slightly and the next moment broke into a series of fierce and inexplicable motions, bounding from side to side and flailing the air. Foley was inexpressibly startled by this. For a moment he thought that Moss had gone mad out there in the middle of the field. But as Moss drew nearer it became apparent that he was slashing about him with a stick, knocking off thistle tops. He was striking out with all his strength and the seed-cases of the thistles were bursting and glinting like sparks all around him. There was a savage energy in this display, and a quality of adroitness too, which Foley found disturbing. He recalled the broken thread on that bolt, the way Moss could heave sacks of plaster.

He was through the gate now. In a matter of a minute or two he would be in the house. Foley was in doubt as to the best course to follow. He did not really want Moss to find him mooning about in this room; it might seem like snooping or, worse still, give Moss the feeling of having been missed. On the other hand Moss had to be met and spoken to, a semblance of normality to be maintained. He decided to stay where he was.

Moss came straight into the casting-room, still holding the stick, the whole lower half of which was wet with sap. When he saw Foley he smiled, but at the same time seemed to stiffen and become more deliberate in his movements. He held the stick now with diffidence as though he had only just picked it up and didn't know quite what to do with it. After a moment he rested it carefully against the wall.

'I've just been out for a walk,' he said.

'Jolly good idea!' Foley exclaimed immediately, putting on to his face an expression of delight.

A silence followed. Foley felt his nerve slipping. 'Tell me,' he said, 'whatever happened to those – ' He stopped abruptly. He had been meaning to ask about the crushed pixies, but some

152

intimation made him wary. He glanced at Moss's large hands. 'I've just seen one of the farm dogs,' he said, 'with a bloody great black thing in its mouth. It looked pretty foul, but it might have been meat. Can Royle have taken to feeding his dogs at last?'

'No,' Moss said. 'No, it's not that.' Solemnity had descended on him with this question and Foley recognised with relief a familiar expression – Moss the imparter, the doler out of facts.

'I know where that came from,' Moss said. 'Do you remember that ram I told you about? I found it stuck in the bog down below the farm.'

'It was dead, wasn't it?'

'Yes, that's right, it was. It didn't look dead at first, mind you. It was upright in the mud, the mud was holding it up.'

'I remember your telling me,' Foley said.

'Yes, well. The dogs must have found it about the same time that I did. They've been eating it piecemeal ever since. They bolt down there when they feel like a snack, and pull a bit off. They have to scramble about a bit in the mud to get at it – that's why the stuff looks so black. It's rotten too by this time, of course. And the ram was probably diseased to begin with.' Moss paused, then added: 'It's filthy, really, isn't it? Royle should feed them properly.'

'Yes, he should,' Foley said quickly. They stood silent for a few moments, united in disapproval of Royle. Then Foley said casually, 'I suppose we ought to be thinking about lunch.'

It was the right remark, at this juncture, restoring their respective roles almost unimpaired. Moss assumed a placid, inward look. 'We've got those sausages left,' he said. 'I was thinking we might have toad-in-the-hole.'

'Splendid,' Foley said, stretching his lips laterally without actually opening them, to show a kind of beaming appetite. They were back, he reflected as he went upstairs to put on a bit of work on the pixies, they were back, for the moment anyway, in the pre-Max era. He thought of this period as a sort of Golden Age when he and Moss had lived in the undifferentiated garden. He felt sure Moss had been meeting Max – probably that was why he had gone out this morning. His new knowledge of Moss, at least, could never be eradicated, he was certain of that. But the knowledge, paradoxically, had rendered Moss unpredictable. As he took up his little spray and took aim at the nearest pixie, Foley wondered with some dismay what thought could be churning in Moss down there in the kitchen, busy with his toad-in-the-hole.

12

His forebodings were soon realised, during that very afternoon and evening in fact, and all the next day. If he had not at the time understood Barbara Gould's remark, he came to understand it very quickly. What he had not seen and what she presumably had was that he was now, in Moss's eyes, a deliverer from travail, a means to freedom.

The plain fact was that Moss had begun to look at him with open desire. He found a hundred pretexts in the course of the next couple of days for visiting the floor above, and he would remain a long time, looking on, trying to engage Foley's attention with sudden questions, such as what he would like for supper or whether he wanted his trousers ironed. Foley grew nervous, listening for footsteps on the stair, even fancying once or twice that Moss had slipped unnoticed into the room and was watching him from some hidden point of vantage. It became increasingly difficult for him to avoid the suspicion that he was being stalked by Moss about the house. All urge to expostulate vanished immediately in the burning intensity of Moss's regard. The fear of precipitating a crisis was always with him, though what he really was afraid of was not clear. He dreaded any explicit recognition that things had changed.

It was in the evenings above all, when he could not feign absorption in work, that the strain became greatest. He was aware of Moss's gaze the whole time, wherever in the room he happened to be. The light of desire seemed to have expanded the pupils, given them a blazing quality, which Foley found impossible to confront. He had never been the object of such desire before and did not know how long he could stand it. It affected his sense of identity, so that his simply continuing to inhabit the room began to seem like acquiescence. Yet he could not summon the resolution to go out.

To make things worse Moss had returned, except for these brief, dreadfully solicitous questions, to his habitual taciturnity. That former spate of words had been like a phase in a malady, the ramblings of fever. His eyes now contained all that delirium. The result was that conversation between them was halting and marked by long pauses, made urgent by Moss's loud breathing. All this oppressed Foley terribly. Yet in ostensible ways Moss was the same as he had always been; he wore the same clothes, had the same attitudes to the business, the same practical, pedestrian way of life. And this too struck Foley as treacherous: he could not help expecting Moss to break with the past in some obvious way, however slight.

Moss did nothing of the sort. He merely continued to keep Foley in unwavering focus. Such an intense regard was in-distinguishable from hatred: there was no placating it without self-damaging consequences. Foley felt persecuted; but he was nevertheless constrained to act in a consciously elegant way. He took more care over his appearance. When he stood anywhere within Moss's range of vision he could not help wondering whether he composed well.

All things considered, it was a positive relief for Foley to get away on the Friday afternoon. He slipped out of the house immediately after lunch without saying anything to Moss, though there was not much hope of concealing his absence now that Moss was continually popping up to see him.

Gwendoline was quite ready when he arrived and they left immediately without his being asked to wait. He felt sure that this was part of a deliberate policy. She was afraid that his grievance would grow too large and insistent within four walls. No doubt she reckoned that outside in the open, whatever reproaches detonated between them would be more easily dispersed.

It was rather a windy day. Gwendoline was wearing a tweed skirt and a woollen cardigan over her blouse. Her hair, which was of that fine variety easily blown about, was confined in a silk scarf tied below the chin and this gave a naked, patient look to her face, a look of endurance. Foley noticed too with a peculiar bitterness that she had taken great pains with make-up this afternoon, even to the extent of applying mascara, which she did not normally use; her mouth, which was set and serious, glistened slightly with lipstick.

They skirted the harbour and took a path which would lead them up out of the village, across open fields, and eventually to the cliffs again at the next bay down the coast, Ralland Bay. For the first few minutes neither of them said anything. Several times Foley was about to speak but a sort of obstinacy, an unwillingness to sue, prevented him. As the silence continued he began to have a doomed feeling. Glancing surreptitiously at her face he noted how grave it was, almost exultantly so. His bitterness increased. How she must be enjoying this. She was rounding the thing off, gracefully. For this she had made up her face and was observing now a ritual period of silence and solemnity. It was she who had wanted the explanation – she had been determined not to be cheated of it. Where did they learn this trick of prolonging, this mistimed, infuriating honesty? Better to have let him slink away out of her life to the sound of Bernard's sated gurglings in the bath. Then at least he would have had her treachery to assuage him. But no, she had to seem blameless.

'Bernard will be back in London by now, I expect,' Foley said. 'Will he be starting work again straight away? The senior partners must be waiting with agonised impatience for Bernard to take over the helm again.' This sneer had been irresistible, but as soon as he uttered the words Foley regretted them, since they exposed him to Gwendoline's kindness.

'Yes,' Gwendoline said with predictable forbearance, 'I suppose he'll start more or less straight away. Look, let's not talk about Bernard just yet, shall we? It's such a beautiful afternoon.'

They were approaching the sea again now. They heard the harsh clamour of the gulls and then saw them, as it were, flung and littered against the sky, motionless on spread wings as though skewered on the wind. The path narrowed and sloped more steeply as they followed the descent towards the sheltered bay. They were obliged to walk one behind the other. For most of the time Foley led the way but during the last few minutes, when the path got easier, Gwendoline was in front. Then he was able to observe the steady carriage of her shoulders and head, the grace and certainty of her steps on the rough path, the movement of her thighs in alternate definition against the thick skirt, the brief flexing of her calves. She was big-boned without being angular, and the evident strength of her body was not of the athletic type, which he detested, but seemed a strength that sought only to be expressed in traditional ways, in docility. For these few minutes, while he was able to look steadily at her undetected, he felt an emotion akin to grief for what he had lost. He would never sleep with her now – and here his mind flickered a curse towards whistling Moss – nor had he even the power to harm her. She was out of range. His regret had nothing to do with her character; he had never sought to understand this; and for what seemed to him the systematic and self-regarding way she was conducting this final walk he had nothing but contempt. But she represented now an impoverishment of his life – he had the illusion that she could have aggrandised him.

The path ran level for a few yards through patches of brambles already weighted with green fruit, and then turned sharply, bringing them within sight of the little bay spread just below them. They came to the foot of the cliffs and walked across the shingle to the far side of the bay, through the bleached refuse of the spring tides, corks, floats, sticks and bits of fishing tackle, tangled in the tough, thick-bladed grass.

'Some of these cork floats are very decorative, really,' Gwendoline said. 'Something could be done with them.'

'The shapes are interesting,' said Foley. 'They might do for bookends or bases for lamps, something of that sort. They'd have to be weighted, of course.'

'Painted in contrasting colours,' Gwendoline said.

They became interested in the possibilities of rope-mesh and bits of net and lobster pots, as though planning to set up house together. Talking in this way they reached a grassy level area on a knoll above the shingle, overlooking the sea and sheltered by the overhanging cliffs. Here, by common consent, they sat down together.

Immediately their bodies were at rest the former constraint returned, and the topic of marine décor withered rapidly. Clearly, the moment for Gwendoline's explanation had arrived. For some time, however, she said nothing, merely stared out to sea, while Foley studied her profile covertly.

'It's lovely here,' she said at last. She sighed and took off her scarf, shaking her head sharply so that her hair settled straight behind and did not get caught in her collar. At the same time she compressed her lips with what might have seemed determination; but Foley felt sure she was merely checking on the distribution of her lipstick. He had not thought it possible that he could ever again regard her as anybody's victim, but something dutiful and childish about these preliminaries touched him strangely. They were impersonal, as though she were taking part in a ceremony almost, in which her own judgement counted for nothing. She was Bernard's victim, now; still practised upon, if not innocent.

'We could come again tomorrow if you liked,' he said.

Gwendoline smiled gently. 'I shall have too much to do, I'm afraid,' she said. 'I'm leaving at the beginning of next week.'

In order not to seem too affected by this, Foley seized on a minor aspect of the situation. 'Do you mean to say you're giving up the cottage?' he said. 'Now, in the middle of the season? That's hardly fair, you know, the landlord will find it difficult to let now. People have all made their arrangements by this time.'

Gwendoline maintained the gentle smile without apparent strain. She said: 'It can't be helped, I'm afraid. I can't be thinking of his pocket when it's a matter of my whole life. He overcharged me anyway.'

'That's not the point,' Foley said.

'Bernard has asked me to marry him,' said Gwendoline. 'That's the point as far as I'm concerned.'

'I see. He came and asked you, just like that.'

'No, I'm afraid you don't understand. We've known each other quite a long time, getting on for four years now.' Gwendoline paused, and her tone when she went on had become perceptibly more stately. 'We were together, as a matter of fact, in London, all this last year. You see, I'm telling you all this so that – '

'Together?' interposed Foley, but he knew from her dignified manner what she must mean.

'But he began to take me for granted,' Gwendoline said. 'That was the trouble. I told him I wouldn't stand it. He kept me out of his life, out of his real life. He was used to having me around. Then in the end I found out he was seeing another girl. Taking another girl out and then coming back to me! I could smell her on him.' She was speaking rapidly now, wholly possessed by her narrative. 'So I told him I'd had enough. Quite calmly, you know — we didn't have a row or anything like that! I don't believe in quarrelling, do you? I simply told him I was clearing out. That's why I came down here for the summer. I had a bit of money put by. I don't believe in being too dependent, do you? So I came down here. I felt I owed it to myself, if you see what I mean.'

Foley saw that she was trying to enlist his support, to make him feel for her. But the immediate effect of her words was to antagonise him further. He felt that such frankness belittled him, neutered him almost, as though he was being regarded as some sort of eunuch retainer, his capacity for all but sympathy denied. Moreover, what she said induced a reluctant admiration for Bernard's prowess and insolence: it was something, after all, to leap into bed with a girl like Gwendoline without so much as a pause to wash off the amorous residue of the girl before.

'You took care to leave your address behind,' he said.

'I didn't want to lose touch altogether. I meant it as a sort of test for him, you see. To find out whether he really cared.'

'Well it did the trick,' Foley said. 'It came off.'

'I want you to understand,' she said. 'I always loved Bernard, but I couldn't go on making myself cheap.'

He wondered for a moment at her facility with these terms of love. It was strange, also, that in speaking of this, no doubt one of the crucial events in her life, her vocabulary seemed to drop several notches of sophistication, as though the material itself were too dramatic to require more than the immemorial clichés.

He looked away from her in silence at the famous Ralland rocks below them which, though always called red by the local people, were in fact a dark lilac above the water and zoned in colour below, as though the sea contained acids of varying strengths: rose pink in the upper band, shading to cinnamon, then mauve, and black finally in the crabby depths round the base. Foley was struck by the flexing, spiralling light on the rocks. He saw after a moment that this was being caused by reflections from the crests of very small waves ridged up as the bay narrowed. He watched one, trying to calculate the extent of its life. Nine seconds, perhaps, from start to finish. Long enough, however, he thought, for almost anything: long enough to realise your death, for example, or for an orgasm, or the apprehension of beauty, or for any of the degrees of pain.

He no longer had any deep sense of loss. What rankled now was a feeling similar to that which he had experienced after Moss's revelations, a sense of having been duped. It was as though Gwendoline had advertised misleadingly, putting out fictitious details of her availability and her innocence. But why had he persisted so long in this belief? Looking at Gwendoline now he found it inexplicable. Her confession had debauched her before his eyes. Her very skin under the identical clothes would seem muskier now. The haplessness which had attracted him and roused his ferocity was clearly inalienable, however many times she was brought to bed.

'Where do I come in, in all this?' he asked finally. 'I suppose I was just a way of passing the time.'

'No,' Gwendoline said. She put a hand lightly on his arm. 'You mustn't think that. You did me a lot of good, you know. You gave me back my self-respect. I was missing Bernard terribly, but I had to go through with it. I wanted to see just how strong this thing with Bernard was, and, of course, you are so good-looking, you *are* you know, I thought, well if someone as attractive as this can't take my mind off Bernard, nobody can.'

'But that afternoon,' Foley said, 'at my place, you remember.'

'I didn't mean anything like that to happen, honestly. I mean, I don't think you should, unless you love somebody, do you? It was the sight of that poor old man upset me somehow, made me feel, you know, why *not*? And then, you seemed to want it so much. But I was glad afterwards that nothing happened.'

'Were you?' Foley said.

'I want to thank you for everything. And don't think too harshly of me, will you?'

'No,' Foley said. 'There must have been something, though, that caused you to dislike me. I never asked you what happened that afternoon, did I?'

'I never disliked you. I don't dislike you now. It's difficult to explain, really. A girl likes to feel that there's a place for her, I didn't get that feeling with you, at all. And there was a sort of *cosiness* about things at your place that I didn't like, it didn't seem . . . manly, somehow, and when your partner was praising you up, I could tell you liked it, and something seemed wrong somehow, I can't quite explain. He didn't like me either, your partner, what's-his-name, Moss.'

'Moss, yes. Why?' said Foley quickly. 'What did Moss say to you? Was it because of Moss that you left so quickly that afternoon?'

'It was, yes, as a matter of fact. I know it was rude of me to leave like that. He was just being loyal to you, really. He's absolutely devoted to you, of course.'

'It was while I was out of the room, wasn't it?' Foley said urgently. He remembered Moss's placid face, and the demoralised bullocks. 'What did he say to annoy you?' he asked.

'Oh, I wasn't annoyed. He rather frightened me, you see, at the time. It was the way he looked at me, rather than anything he said, as though he would have liked to hurt me. Quite frightening. Of course he was just being – '

'Loyal to me, yes I know.' Foley began to feel rage. 'He had no right,' he said loudly.

'It didn't make any difference, really. I mean, I was upset at the time, I don't mind telling you, that's why I rushed off like that, but I was still intending to see you again if you had wanted. Then Bernard came and asked me to marry him. The very next day. He said he'd come to realise since I went away how much he needed me.' She smiled at Foley with a sort of wary happiness, wanting him to see the marvellous element in this declaration, but Foley could find no response to Bernard's whirlwind proposal and general princeliness, because of his mounting fury with Moss.

'We'd better be getting back,' he said. All the way back to the village and right up to the time of bidding Gwendoline goodbye, almost certainly for ever, he was quite unable to find appropriate replies to her gentle and elegiac conversation. This culminating treachery provided a reason more acceptable than any deficiency of his own for his failure with her. Perhaps because of this he nursed his rage.

'I wish you all the luck in the world,' he said, when they reached the door.

'You can kiss me if you want to,' Gwendoline said, and he was surprised at the warmth of her lips. None the less, before he had gone two steps towards home he was thinking only of Moss.

13

Foley nevertheless withheld all expression of his resentment until late that evening. He did not want his denunciation to be spoilt by an intervening, practical issue of work. Moss was not going to wriggle out of this. So convinced was he of the rightness of his quarrel, that he forgot both his fear of Moss's violence and the conciliatory feeling lately bred in him by being so unequivocally the object of Moss's love.

His opportunity came soon after his bath. Dressed in pyjamas and a dressing-gown of imitation Japanese silk with red, whiskery dragons embroidered on it – dressing-gowns were a weakness of Foley's; he had five altogether – he was sitting turning over the pages of the *Listener*. This was normally a sealed-off, unimpassioned time. Pores unclogged and limbs still dazed from the mild scalding, he felt all gross secretions had been for some little while suspended, and this trance of the hormones seemed to him supremely civilised. Leafing through the *Listener* he felt languid, a connoisseur. Whiffs of the lavender bath salts he used liberally rose now to his nostrils from the depths of him as though distilled from his own essence. Under these circumstances the wrath he had been nursing against Moss was too liable to go drowsy. He resolved to speak at once.

He looked up from his *Listener* when he was sure that Moss was not for the moment regarding him. Moss in fact was busy repairing the radio. His head was lowered, presenting Foley with a rather endearing view of the round, cropped crown. His large, blunt fingers moved gently, without haste, amongst the intricacies of valves and transformers.

'I spent the afternoon,' Foley said in a meaningful voice, 'with Gwendoline.'

Moss looked up immediately. 'I wondered where you'd been,' he said. There did not appear to be anything guilty in his expression. He returned Foley's gaze with the intensity characteristic of him these days. 'I took you up a cup of tea at about three,' he said. 'But you weren't there. I thought you must have gone out.'

'Yes,' Foley said. 'I was out with Gwendoline.'

'So that's where you were. Is she still around then?'

It was perhaps the slight shade of surprise in Moss's tone which – presenting itself as unrepentant insolence – revived Foley's rage. 'You thought you'd got rid of her, didn't you?' he said loudly. His own words angered him further. He flushed and tears pricked his eyes. 'You thought that was the end of it, didn't you? That's what you thought. How dared you try to bully that girl?' Moss's face seemed to be slowly drawing itself into an expression of astonishment.

'I hope you are pleased with yourself, anyway,' Foley went on. 'You succeeded in frightening her away on that occasion. You must be crazy, that's all, you must be crazy, even to imagine for a moment that you could have had any lasting effect on her. She is far above you.'

He was distinctly conscious of over-praising Gwendoline now, especially after her performance that afternoon; but the desire to wound Moss was so urgent that he could not care about this. He recalled with a fresh access of fury how he had tried to cover his own discomfiture by inventing the story of the phone call and how Moss had listened impassively, known the real reason all the time.

'You are poles apart, don't you know that, poles apart,' he said, staring wildly at Moss.

'I have nothing against the girl,' Moss said.

'Nothing against her? That's very tolerant of you, I must say. She's done you some injury, I suppose, that you are generously overlooking.'

Moss still seemed bewildered. 'No,' he said. 'She's done nothing to me. Nothing at all.' He began to glance round the room as though noting the objects in it. 'What's she been saying, then?'

'She has not been saying anything,' said Foley, more collectedly, 'if you mean by that spreading stories. She has simply told me what happened on that afternoon when she came here for tea.'

His first rage had passed, leaving him somewhat depressed. He watched Moss's slowly travelling gaze, still lighting on object after object.

'You threatened her,' Foley said quietly. 'You made her frightened to stay in the room with you. Why did you do that?'

Moss rubbed his hands on the insides of his knees. 'I quite liked that girl,' he said. 'I didn't like her name, though.'

Foley stared at him, amazed. The enormity of this lie made his voice gentle when he replied, as though he were talking to an afflicted person. 'But you know you never liked her, Michael,' he said. 'Right from the start.'

'I did,' persisted Moss. 'I did like her. I thought she was a nice girl.' He looked at Foley with a sort of solemn obstinacy. 'She was a bit flighty, of course,' he added. His face slackened, attempting to convey indulgence for girlish follies. 'A bit immature, you might say.'

'But good heavens – ' Foley began, then checked himself, feeling suddenly sure that Moss meant what he was saying; meant it for the moment, anyway. Moss took one in by his extraordinary, almost infantile simplicity. He had divined that the affair with Gwendoline was finished and had chosen the attitude he thought would be most acceptable. It did not seem to occur to Moss that the past could in any way invalidate his claims: he expected others to effect the same severance of past and present as he himself did. Whatever beastly things he had said to Gwendoline belonged to another plane of existence altogether. They had no reality now. He was not accountable, any more than a child who waves a broken toy in proof that a new one is needed. He even praised Gwendoline in the past tense, as though she were dead. It was a little sinister, but neither cunning nor hypocritical, this freedom from the past. It had given him the advantage over Max, that evening in the 'Jubilee'. It was threatening to give him the advantage now.

Foley took a deep breath. There was no sense, he perceived, in arguing. It seemed that he had Moss completely in focus at last.

'She might have misunderstood something I said,' Moss ventured after a lengthy pause.

166

'You told her to keep away from me,' Foley replied. 'There was only one way for her to understand that, surely?'

'I was thinking of your interests. Anything I might have said was in your interests.'

'So you admit it, that's something,' Foley said. He was tired of the whole conversation and pursued it only from a sense of justice. 'What do you know about my interests?' he enquired, reaching again for his *Listener*. 'Anyway, things can't go on like this much longer.'

'Not know your interests,' Moss said, warmly. 'I know that better than you do yourself. Supposing I did say something to her. Supposing I did. Do you think I was going to stand aside and see you throw yourself away on a girl like that? She would never have settled down, here, burying herself in the country. She was a town girl. She'd have had you back to London.'

'You've got no right to interfere in my life,' Foley said. 'No right at all.'

'You may be feeling upset now,' said Moss. 'But in a little while, when you can see more clearly, I know you will thank me for what I did.'

'God, you *are* talking rubbish,' Foley said. 'It's my resentment at your interference I'm trying to express to you, not my sorrow at losing Gwendoline. And anyway, it wasn't anything to do with what you said that broke us up. She's getting married to someone else, someone she knew before she came here.'

'A friend,' said Moss in vibrant tones, 'sometimes has to do . . . distasteful things, for the sake of his friend. Things that go against the grain.'

'I don't think it was for my sake at all,' said Foley sharply. He laid his hands on the arms of his chair, and leaned forward, preparatory to rising. 'It's no good,' he added, 'we're not on the same wavelength.'

Moss stood up suddenly, anticipating him. Odd pieces from the interior of the wireless fell from his lap to the floor and were disregarded.

'Careful,' said Foley, alarmed. 'You're dropping things.'

'You won't understand, will you?' said Moss loudly. His face had suddenly become flushed and patchy, strange looking. 'You only think of yourself,' he said. He took a step forward so that he now stood directly in Foley's only possible line of retreat from the armchair.

'We used to be happy, didn't we?' he said. 'Why can't we be like that again? Everything that was unpleasant for you, I did it. I always tried to make things easy for you. I did the cooking, kept the place clean, made out the shopping lists. I always looked after the money. Who would have done it if I hadn't? You? You never had to worry about anything, only getting on with the business. And we've done well, haven't we? We've built up a good business here.'

Trapped in his armchair, Foley looked up warily. 'I don't deny it, Michael,' he said soothingly. 'I owe a lot to you. You were marvellous,' he added, faithful to the traditional phrases of acknowledgement. 'The way you managed! Absolutely marvellous. But you must see for yourself that things – '

'Don't give it all up now, Ronald,' said Moss. 'We can go back to what we were before.' His emotion seemed to express itself mainly in an increased stiffness, even woodenness, of feature; but Foley, looking upwards, saw that his mouth hung open a little and the lower lip was minutely quivering. 'We used to get on so well,' he continued. 'We had our own ways of doing things. You can't just wipe out three years. Maybe I was wrong, speaking like that to the girl . . .'

'But it isn't only the girl, or even mainly,' said Foley. 'Don't you see? The whole situation is changed now. We can't go on . . . How can I go on living with you like this, knowing that I can never reciprocate this special feeling you have for me? I should always be feeling as though I were exploiting you.'

'Of course,' Moss said, 'I shouldn't dream of . . . I wouldn't do anything to offend you.' But there was no conviction in his voice.

Foley again prepared to escape, now that Moss seemed milder, more amenable. Privately, he was still amazed at the other's disingenuity. Thinking in terms of heterosexual relations he knew that if he were in the same position he would constantly be trying to change the girl's mind; all his actions would have a quality of ingratiation. It was not conceivable that just being with a loved person could suffice the need for involvement – if Moss thought so, he was deceiving himself.

With the situation thus under control, and Moss seemingly tamed, Foley rose from his armchair, saying at the same time in a casual tone: 'Well, I can't at the moment, I'm afraid, see any solution to all this, except, of course, for us to live separately. Extra rent, but it can't be helped.' He was attempting, on the tide of these remarks as it were, to flow past Moss in the direction of the door, when he heard a harsh intake of breath like a sob. The next moment he felt himself seized with painful firmness by the upper arms and he was looking down at one side of Moss's face — the other being pressed with considerable force against his dressing-gown. The side he could see was very pale and had its eye closed and was contorted about the mouth. In order to get his face low enough to press against Foley's chest, Moss had had to adopt an ungainly, crouching position and for the first second or two Foley's feeling was one of startled solicitude: he thought that Moss had been attacked by some sort of cramp. But he realised almost immediately, from the wordless tenacity of the grip and some abasement in the posture, that Moss was in fact embracing him. Immediately upon realisation of this he began struggling, gently at first, then more firmly, to extricate himself; but Moss, breathing now in great noisy gulps partially stifled in the folds of the dressing-gown, continued to hold him in a clutch that demonstrated clearly — if any demonstration had been needed — the relative quality of their muscles.

'Let me go, Michael,' he said, but Moss for only answer turned his head so that it was hidden completely, and held on. For a space of time they were locked together, Foley pushing away with all his strength and Moss clinging. Foley began to pant from his exertions. He felt the lacerating absurdity of his situation but lacked the physical strength necessary to disembarrass himself of Moss. 'Let me go, I tell you!' he cried again, breathlessly. The terrible, unbudging deference of Moss's stance horrified him further and added to his sense of nightmare. 'You're hurting my arms,' he said. He was desperately considering a kick in the region of Moss's shin when, with a sound between gasp and moan, the other released him, so suddenly that he staggered back. Moss straightened up and put both hands over his face, standing there for a full minute, while Foley confusedly adjusted his dressing-gown.

'I'm sorry,' Moss said, through his hands. Foley felt unable for the moment to utter any words at all. The crudely practical nature of Moss's next remark shocked him into composure. 'What would you have done,' Moss enquired slowly, uncovering his face, which was completely drained of colour, and looking steadfastly at Foley, 'if I hadn't let go?'

'I think I should probably have kicked you,' Foley said as coldly and promptly as possible. He felt upset but determined to make no concessions. Above all he must not allow Moss to think there had been any prospect of his resistance collapsing. The very fact that he could frame such a question at so delicate a juncture brought home to Foley, as perhaps nothing had before, Moss's essential unscrupulousness, the urgency of his need. 'I should *certainly* have kicked you,' he said. 'On the shin. I don't know whether I've ever told you this, but I know a bit of judo. Anyway, I hope this has finally convinced you that things can't go on like this. It's not fair to either of us.'

'Not fair? How do you mean, not fair?' Moss said quickly. 'Why is it not fair? I can stand it if you can.'

'I don't mean it's unfair to me because of the temptation,' Foley explained patiently. 'It doesn't present itself to me as a temptation at all. It's just a bloody unpleasant and embarrassing position for me to be in.' I suppose, he thought, Moss can't quite believe in anybody not having a dash of it, since it bulks so large in him. He decided to end the conversation on a man of the world note.

'I sympathise, don't think I don't sympathise,' he said. 'I'm all for revising the laws. Consenting adults in private is fine with me. I mean, don't think I'm *prejudiced*. But I don't want to join in these revels. They are not for me. And I'm hardly likely to change now. After all, let's face it, the majority are with me.'

'Don't be too sure,' Moss said. He spoke in a gruff and argumentative tone, wanting to hide the extent to which Foley's jaunty and unfeeling remarks had wounded him, setting him without distinction among the merely tolerated. Ronald spoke as though it were simply an activity, like a game of cards; more strenuous than this perhaps, but similar, requiring only a shared inclination, a knowledge of how to play. Did he think of girls in this way? Surely love should permeate all other relations. It should commit, even the hypothesis of love that is, all the person to it. What consenting adults did in private: Ronald knew more about this than he did. But love did not stop when you put your clothes on. It occurred to Moss suddenly and without irony that Ronald's attitude to sex was unhealthy.

'Don't be too sure,' he said again.

'Oh well, yes,' Foley said. 'I know you enlist them in their thousands. But we can't really argue about what is latent. The point is that the majority act as though they agree with me. And it's acts that count, surely.'

'I should have thought it was feelings,' Moss said.

There was silence between them for a short time, then Foley began to move towards the door. 'Be that as it may,' he said, with deliberate unconcern.

'Wait,' said Moss. 'Don't go yet. Don't go like this. If I promised it wouldn't happen again . . .'

'What would be the use of that?' Foley said. He turned at the door, looked back at Moss. They stood regarding each other for a long moment in silence. Suddenly a kind of ripple passed over Moss's features. He opened his mouth as if to speak, making at the same time a shrugging movement. Then Foley saw that his eyes had filled with tears. While he watched a tear spilled over and went coursing down Moss's left cheek until it was arrested at the corner of his mouth. He made no attempt to brush the tears away or to turn aside, but went on looking at Foley steadily, even raising his face a little, as though wishing to exhibit his tears as proof of the gravity of the matter.

The sight of this naked weeping in one normally so stolid was horrifying, and Foley did not know what to do. He felt a desire to comfort Moss, and even experienced a sympathetic moistening in his own eyes which for a moment hindered his vision. But at the thought of actually approaching Moss his nerve failed him. After a further moment of helpless gazing, he turned and with a muttered 'Good night, Michael,' made his escape. He had at least, he told himself, spared Moss further humiliation. But almost immediately, as he was mounting the stairs, he was assailed by an extremely disagreeable sense of his own inadequacy. He should have found a way of smoothing things over, instead of scuttling away like that. He paused halfway up the stairs and stood wondering whether to go back. But presently the sheer relief at having escaped swept over him again and he proceeded up the stairs more quickly.

Moss noted the pause and the acceleration. He had not moved since Foley left. He could hardly see for the hot tears, but he made no attempt yet to brush them away. He had not really believed that Foley would come back but his breath caught when the other stopped and he released it only when he heard the bedroom door closing. His throat was wrenched and painful with the effort of quelling sobs that kept rising. He felt some wonder at this fit of crying which had come upon him so suddenly. It was many years since he had cried. He did not feel pity for himself and the tears had nothing in common with his most constant memory of crying, the harsh, angry crying of boyhood fist-fights when victory had not been signal enough. They were tears of sorrow. It was Ronald's tragic obtuseness that he mourned for now. So intimately had Ronald been held in his thoughts that he could not believe the pain of this division was confined to himself. The intricate, daily spun and ramified coil of their association was ruined, and this was because Ronald had refused to accept his place in it, and his place, his topmost place, in the hierarchy of Moss's affections. He had not seen how he fitted in there, how he was the heir to all the moments of pain Moss had endured and the treasures of devotion he could now dispose of. Ronald had simply turned his back on all this. He had fought to keep Ronald fixed in his habitual assessment, which had seemed to him, and still did seem, the same as fighting to keep Ronald a perfect human being. And it was from this height that Ronald had coldly and without compunction descended. Ronald had abdicated from his own perfection and torn out of Moss in the process some capacity for belief in such perfection. It was a violation quite unforgivable. Moss knew he would never forgive it.

He returned to his chair and settled himself down deliberately to think of Ronald as unfavourably as possible. His was a nature incapable of compromise and now it was necessary for Ronald to be reduced to the ranks as soon as possible. He had always known that Ronald was weak and vain. These qualities had formerly seemed endearing. But Ronald had forfeited indulgence now, and it could readily be seen that he was a very bad character indeed. Moss reviewed in his mind the three years of his life with Ronald. The business meant nothing to him as such. It had been for him simply the symbol of their covenent. It had made Ronald happy to see it expanding and Ronald's happiness had been his happiness. Three years of his life he had given, and for what? So that Ronald could make a little money, persuade himself he was an artist, put on airs, make those cherubs dangling upstairs? Those cherubs . . . Ronald had always been discouraged immediately at the smallest setback. Ten times over the business would have crashed. What had he, Moss, got out of it all? Ronald's gratitude had gone into those bloody angels and cherubs dangling about upstairs . . .

Patiently he cultivated animosity towards Foley, but reminiscence was not good for this, cluttering his mind with remembered images, each peculiarly characteristic, each with its colour deepened by the pain of his present rejection: Ronald standing, walking, sitting, grave, smiling. On the little beach below the cottage Ronald in brief black trunks that did not reach to his navel, his hair sleek from the sea, shook himself like a puppy scattering drops around him on the sand. Ronald came in with a bunch of daffodils and could not untie the string that held the stalks, the sap wet his fingers and he pretended to be disgusted by thinning his lips. In the attic among the cherub lamps Ronald was holding up his feather brush and rays of sunshine from the high windows fell on him. His arms glowed through the thin white shirt.

Moss thought again of that miraculous conversation in The Fisherman's Arms down by the quay in Lanruan, where it had all begun. He remembered the details of this as though they too were elements in his deception. Water on the flat cobbles along the quay, the sky reflected in it. The swoosh of someone's swill going stealthily into the harbour. The bright fishing-nets on their tarred poles. Himself shy with the accomplished stranger who began so casually to speak to him. He had had too much sun in the afternoon and his shoulders were sore under the rub of his shirt. Ronald had seemed from the start so much the sort of person to whom this never happened, who never peeled, but was always smooth-skinned, even and urbane. That talk of theirs! Begun so carelessly by Ronald, pursued with such diffident persistence by himself, while the light waned outside and the harbour water glassed over with evening. And that thunderous proposition which seemed to grow out of it almost by accident. He remembered his excitement as he walked back to his boarding house, the promise of the summer night and the stars. He had not known then, but he knew now – and he faced it squarely – that it was the prospect of associating with Ronald that had caused that excitement, not any hope of commercial success, not the thought of a change of job. Then and always it had been Ronald.

And how did Ronald himself regard that first meeting? For the first time, and with considerable effort, Moss asked himself what Ronald must have felt, seeing in the bar this raw-looking, lobster-faced person in a hairy jacket, clutching a glass of Guinness. It must have been clear to Ronald after a short while that he lived alone, was unmarried, did not much care for his work, and possessed – though this transpired somewhat later – two hundred and fifty pounds, the savings of four years. Why then had he always insisted on believing these overtures, this proposition of Ronald's to be generous? He had needed from the beginning to feel grateful to Ronald and protective also. He had needed to refashion Ronald into an object worthy of devotion. Ronald had been luckier than he could have dreamed possible, finding a person not merely credulous but desperate to be exploited.

No simple withdrawal of love could disengage him now. The experiment having failed, the equipment too must be broken. Only an act of vandalism could effect this severance. Moss's face settled into a vindictive expression which was not now merely an exercise.

14

Next day they spoke little to each other, barely saw each other in fact, since each kept strictly to his own working quarters.

Even getting ready for Max's party in the evening they did not exchange many words; and the ten-mile drive to Max's house passed in complete silence. Moss drove, with the blank and rather sad expression he always had when concentrating. Foley wondered idly, as the car snouted through these devious lanes, further and further from the coast into the rural hinterland, why Simon Lang had installed Max in a remote hamlet like Treleath, not even near the sea. Perhaps he had wanted to keep the association as quiet as possible. But in that case he had certainly miscalculated. Max's constant drinking and his chichi manners would have attracted attention anywhere; in this retreat he must be almost grotesquely conspicuous, chattering and flaunting among the softly scandalised village people. Perhaps Simon had simply wanted to keep Max as far as possible from London, to avoid the embarrassment of drunken, recriminatory visits.

They were rather early – it was only about eight o'clock, so it was not surprising to find no other cars outside the house. Max himself let them in, but a changed and indeed almost unrecognisable Max, so collected and responsible his whole manner. He shook hands with them both, looked straight into their faces and said, 'So glad you could come,' with an exactly similar intonation to each of them separately. His appearance, too, had changed. Gone was the Monte Carlo insouciance of his normal drinking kit, the gay scarfs and coloured pullovers. He was dressed in a charcoal-grey suit and maroon woollen tie and these clothes made him look frailer than ever and somehow seedy.

When they went into the large and comfortably appointed

living-room they saw a young man, willowy and beautiful, in a dark serge suit of sober elegance. Max introduced him in the same careful manner as Eric.

'He has come down from London a little ahead of Simon,' he explained, flicking his cuffs and smiling. He was quite sober and did not seem to be drinking anything. Eric had a gin. 'To prepare the way,' Max added, after a pause of considerable length. It was difficult to judge whether this last remark had been intended humorously, because although Max grimaced as he said it, Eric did not seem to find it funny.

'Oh yes,' Foley said, smiling at everyone in a non-committal way. Moss said nothing at all. Eric, who had beautiful slanting eyes and a charming manner, smiled and said, 'Oh not really, Max, just the trains were more convenient this way.' His voice had a kind of RADA resonance and would obviously carry well. This was obviously the talker, the fixer, the advance guard.

'What will you have?' said Max and his mouth twitched twice. 'We have gin, and gin, and whisky, and gin . . .'

Foley asked for whisky and Moss did too. 'Did you have a good journey down?' Foley asked Eric.

'Not very,' Eric said. 'The train was crowded.' His smile diminished somewhat. 'We didn't know we'd be coming to a party,' he said.

Foley's imagination was stirred by the proof of Simon's power that the presence of Eric afforded. He obviously used human beings like counters, sending them here and there to construct a required atmosphere, a desired set of relations. Foley had never met anyone with minions before, and he looked forward more than ever to Simon's arrival. He wondered suddenly what Moss was making of all this. Moss was sitting on his own in a corner, holding a large whisky and staring austerely straight before him. Eric went over to speak to Max who was standing against the far wall of the room. The doorbell rang and Max disappeared, coming back a minute or two later leading a baldish, youngish man with irritably mobile eyebrows, and a blonde, rather expensive-looking woman.

Max and Eric were standing close together, talking. 'But who else is coming, Max?' Foley heard Eric say. 'Surely you remember how many, at least?'

'Just a few friends,' Max said, flicking his cuffs again, and tugging slightly at his left lapel. 'Friends of Simon, mutual friends.'

'But Simon has no friends here in this part,' Eric said.

The doorbell rang. 'Excuse me,' Max said.

Several more people now arrived together and among them Graham, in a dark blue fisherman's sweater, looking surprisingly amenable without his cap. Suddenly the room seemed crowded. Except for Graham, Foley found that he knew none of the guests. They did not seem to be local people. And in these first few minutes, while Max and Eric were getting drinks for everyone, it became apparent that they were all complete strangers to one another. Everybody seemed surprised and politely resentful at finding so many other people present. On what basis had Max selected these people to meet Simon? Max had no fixed body of acquaintance from whom to select. He had no friends, no permanent attachments except Simon himself. His contacts with people were intense, drunken, dissolved at closing time, forgotten the next morning. These invitations must have been issued during the past week or so in all the bars where Max happened to find himself, to all the people who appeared to recognise Simon's name.

The doorbell rang again and this time Eric went to answer it. He looked, not flustered exactly – he would rarely look that – but certainly put out. It must have been a distinctly unpleasant experience for him, seeing wave after wave of people entering, not knowing anything about them. And Simon expected any minute . . .

The new batch of arrivals seemed livelier. Foley thought it probable they had been drinking somewhere on the way. Now he heard Simon's name mentioned for the first time by a middle-aged man of dishevelled appearance with glasses and a fair, forked beard. 'As Simon said to me himself,' he heard the man say. He was the centre of a small group in the middle of the floor. 'This boy, there was this boy wearing earrings and a Salvation Army bonnet, and he said to me, Simon said to me – you know that sudden . . . whimsical way he has – "How camp can camp get?" he said, you know that sudden, whimsical way he has of saying things. I thought it was rather good. On the spur of the moment. "How camp can camp get?" ' The man laughed delightedly, levelling his pronged beard at people. Some of those listening smiled, but others seemed rather bewildered.

'But why was the boy wearing earrings and a Salvation Army bonnet?' he heard a plump girl say. 'And at a camp, of all places.'

'Of course, it's some years ago,' the bearded man said. 'I daresay he wouldn't remember me now.'

'What are you doing here?' Foley said, reaching Graham at last. He could not remember having spoken to a capless Graham before and found the difference striking. Graham drank some whisky, winking over the rim of his glass.

'I borrowed a bicycle from a bloke in the village,' he said. 'Well, the bicycle was lying around, so I took it. You never *ask* the Cornish for anything. They clam up on you. Bloody hard work, cycling. Worth it, though. Plenty to drink here, and some food later I expect.'

'I doubt it,' said Foley. 'I didn't know you knew Max.'

'He bought a water-colour from me once, years ago. He knows something about painting. And I used to see him sometimes in the pub at Lanreath, before I was barred for using improper language, and insulting the Cornish. I'm barred from every pub in the district now. I worked it out that I'd have to travel twenty-five miles altogether just to get to a pub I'm not barred from. And back again, of course. Twenty-five miles. He's not a bad bloke, Max isn't. Doesn't matter a monkey's to me what he gets up to, you know what I mean. A lot of these chapel-goers get up to a lot worse. He's asked me round here once or twice, but I never came before, it's too far. I thought I'd come tonight, though. It's by way of being a farewell party.'

'You don't mean you're leaving?' exclaimed Foley.

'Looks like it, boy. Life is getting too difficult here, with these bloody Cornish. And not being able to get to a pub, that doesn't help. Besides I've sold that painting.'

'Not the big one?'

'Yes.' Graham collected saliva in his mouth and swirled it around for some time. 'Sold,' he said without jubilation. 'Chap came last week, said he'd heard of me from a friend, asked to see the picture. Then he said he'd buy it, just like that. I don't know who the friend was, I thought it might be Max but he says not. He's not himself tonight, is he? Standing about fiddling and smiling, not saying anything. He isn't drinking either, is he? He must have turned over a new leaf.'

'He's being kept on his best behaviour ready for Simon Lang.'

'Who is Simon Lang? Oh, you mean this mate of his, this actor. I don't think much of actors. I got three hundred pounds for the picture.' He turned uneasy eyes on Foley. 'To tell you the truth,' he said, 'I don't know what I'm going to do without that painting.'

'There'll be others,' Foley said, as lightly as possible. He too felt appalled at the selling of the picture. He had never thought of it as a commodity at all, but as a sort of self-perpetuating activity. 'What will you do now?' he asked.

'I might go to Belgium,' he said, 'stay there for a bit. I've always wanted to go to Belgium and see the pictures there. I don't like the Belgians much.'

'What about that mural you were doing for Bailey? Did you finish it?'

Graham smiled. 'Oh yes,' he said. 'I finished it all right. I've had half the money as a sub. I'm not likely to get the rest.'

'Why not? He'll pay you sooner or later. He's probably a bit pushed just at present. He owes me money too.'

'You'll be lucky!' Graham said. 'Bailey is in trouble.' He drained the remainder of his whisky and took a step in the direction of the drinks. 'Bailey,' he said over his shoulder, 'is in the shit. Well and truly. I hear he's talking about doing me up, but he'll never get to me. I'm taking the plank up.'

'Why?' said Foley. 'What sort of trouble?' But Graham had stepped out of earshot.

Max still stood at the far side of the room, not far from the swishing of the drinks, the clink of ice and sussurations of soda, all of which must have been trying for him. However, thought Foley, he probably feels better there than if he were out of sight of the stuff altogether. Eric now, as Foley watched, moved over and stood beside Max, a head taller, incontestably in command of the situation. They spoke together for some time. Eric urbane, Max's face somewhat puckered, supplicatory. Foley felt sure that Max was pressing for a gin and Eric was stalling him. Eric must have had pretty strict instructions from Simon not to let Max have any, at least till Simon himself arrived; and this, in its inhuman way, was wise, because Max could never have stopped at one drink; once he started he went on and on; and on. By the time Simon came he might have been beyond everything. One could never tell with Max because it didn't always depend on the amount of alcohol he consumed but on some sort of interior equipoise. So they were right to be careful. It is undesirable, after nearly two years, to be unable to articulate a dozen words coherently to your eminent protector.

He was moving towards them with some idea of listening to what they were saying, when he found his way blocked by the man with the forked beard, who seemed to have already achieved a measure of intoxication. His glasses were quite thickly misted over as though someone had breathed very heavily on them. From behind these steamy lenses Foley felt himself observed and, returning the look, saw the man's eyes, dark and strangely inert, like prunes viewed through a plastic lid.

'Hey,' said this bearded person. 'Have you heard the latest about Simon?'

It was at this point that Foley, reviewing the matter afterwards, decided that the whole temper of the party changed. Over the bearded man's shoulder he saw Moss, bearing down with a certain deliberation on Max and Eric.

'Excuse me,' Foley said. He sidestepped the bearded man and was in time to see Moss hand Max a large, brimming, gin.

He saw the look of outrage on Eric's face, the gratitude on Max's, and he was near enough now to hear Eric say in well-modulated but pointed tones that Max was on the wagon, didn't he know? For answer Moss nodded and said cheerio to Max who it seemed had been waiting only for this magic word and now downed the drink in a gulp, without a further glance at Eric, and when this was done stared intently at the empty glass in his hand.

'Go and get yourself another one, Max,' Moss said, with a quite astounding air of authority. So far he had ignored Eric but he now turned to him, nodding his large head. 'Did you really think I was going to sit back and let you put Max at a disadvantage with every single person in this room?' he said.

It is surprising how quickly people scent discord. Although he had not been speaking particularly loudly, these words of Moss's fell on a certain hush. Even the bearded man, having now recovered from Simon's rich humour, seemed aware that something was wrong.

Under this blow to the authority he had been establishing throughout the afternoon, Eric's poise was visibly impaired. He said: 'It's better for Max not to drink. Surely you know that, whoever you are?'

'Better for Mr Lang, you mean,' Moss said, in the same ponderous way. 'I don't see why everything should be made easy for Mr Lang.' This use of the formal mister, implying a culpable lack of familiarity, clearly put Moss beyond the pale with the other people in the room. An indignant muttering was to be heard here and there. Eric tossed his head. Mortification had fixed a sort of Mephistopheles sneer on his face. 'You are quite obviously,' he said, 'incapable of understanding the situation.'

Moss regarded him with an increased intensity. 'If I were you,' he said, 'I'd push off back to Swan Lake or wherever you come from, pretty sharpish.' The physical menace in his voice was unmistakable and Eric did not mistake it. He put a hand on his hip and turned away, flinging the single word 'charming' over his shoulder. He retired in good order but Moss's dangerous stillness made it all look like a tantrum. And Moss was left in undisputed possession of the field.

Conversation gathered again but with a difference now. People seemed slightly distracted. Moss had driven a breach in the general tone of the evening; he had cut across the mood of adulation and insinuated a discord, the prospect of a scene. Now he remained beside Max, and Foley saw they were talking earnestly, or rather that Moss was talking and Max listening, and disposing of his third − or was it fourth? − gin.

He glanced at his watch. Ten past ten. Simon Lang was bound to be arriving soon. Foley was wondering where Max had got to when Max suddenly appeared at his side, a different, ginned-up Max, bright-eyed, chirpy, disposed to mockery. 'So there you are,' Max said.

'Nice party, Max,' he said.

'Fine body of people, all friends of friends of friends,' Max said, and passed a hand completely over his face as though he were wiping it clean of something. Obviously he had been making up for lost time, since Moss set him going. The delay in Simon's arrival was demoralising several of the guests. The fork-bearded man had sunk to the floor, with his back propped against the wall, and appeared to be asleep. Foley saw with some surprise that he had no socks on.

Max said: 'Did you see how Michael put down that Eric? Michael is a wonderful person. Eric is Simon's current number, you know. Did you know? He always gets his boy friends to run errands for him and do his mopping-up. It's a sort of training in deportment. Like royal pages. Eric has rather ballsed this one up though, hasn't he?' Max giggled. 'Her Majesty will not be pleased. It could make all the difference to Eric's career of course, that's why they all *mind* so much. They don't care who they sleep with so long as it gets them forward a bit, do they? I suppose Simon has promised him a part. Still it's a bit strong, isn't it? Michael says it's a bit strong, too.'

'What is?' Foley asked.

'Well, as Michael was just saying to me, I ought to mind Simon sending down his boy friends to make sure I'm fit for company. Michael says this is insulting to me.' Tears appeared quite suddenly in Max's eyes without effecting any visible tremor of his features. 'Don't you think, honestly?' he said.

'I'm sure he doesn't mean it like that,' Foley said, very carefully. 'He is trying to protect you. And after all, he is a very busy man, a famous man.' Saying this he felt a certain malicious pleasure in undermining Moss's influence. 'Don't forget, Max, that Simon is a very well-known person,' he added.

'Well, of course,' Max began eagerly, the tears quickly vanishing in the pleasure of discussing Simon's fame. 'Well of course, he *is* famous. In my opinion Simon is a great actor. I would go so far as to say — oh, excuse me, I must see what Michael wants.' Moss had in fact at that moment made a sort of slow beckoning gesture, like Hamlet's father's ghost. Max scuttled back to him at once, and at once Moss began talking to him earnestly. Max again listened, his face seeming to express a precarious composure. Eric hovered nearby, looking both anxious and disdainful. He did not, however, try again to intervene.

Foley helped himself to another drink. He was beginning to feel that expansiveness that marks the early stages of drunkenness. Also he found that he was enjoying the party very much.

Suddenly Eric appeared beside him and said, 'Excuse me, can I speak to you?' He drew Foley a little to one side, then went on: 'Look, can you do something with this friend of yours, this Moss person? You did come together, didn't you?'

'What do you mean?' asked Foley.

'Well, look at him,' Eric said in a controlled voice. His face was pale with vexation. 'He's simply pouring gin into Max and saying the most ghastly things to him the whole time. All the wrong things. And Simon is due at any moment. I've been working all day to keep Max on the rails. Max hasn't seen Simon for nearly two years and it's going to be a terrible failure if we can't get this person away from him. There'll be a ghastly row and Max will be bitterly sorry when it's too late. And it will all be your friend's fault. What is he trying to do, anyway? Is he queer or not?'

'I don't know what he's trying to do,' Foley said. 'Yes, he's queer, I suppose.'

'You don't seem very sure. What about you?'

'No, I'm not, not at all.'

'I see. That's why you don't seem to mind how he behaves. I thought, that since you came together . . . Anyway, I think you ought to go and try to reason with him. Surely he wants to do what's best for Max?'

Eric made a scornful gesture that embraced the whole room. 'Just look at the appalling collection of people he's got in here. Just whoever was in the tatty lounge bars he goes to. He doesn't know himself who they are. Simon will be utterly furious when he sees them here. Max knows he comes here to be secluded. Just look at them. There's a man there who isn't wearing any socks and a person in a navy-blue sweater has eaten all the cheese.'

'Graham, that would be,' Foley said.

Eric's harassed expression had given way to one of dismay.

'You don't know what Simon can be like when he's upset about something,' he said. 'Please see what you can do. *I* can't do anything, he snaps at me like a *mastiff*, my dear, whenever I go anywhere *near* him.'

'All right,' Foley said, 'I'll try, but I can't promise anything.' He moved towards where Max and Moss were sitting, stepping as he did so with some distaste over the extended legs of the bearded man. When he reached them he saw they were holding hands. Their two faces turned to him at the same time, Moss's expressionless, Max's showing wonder and something like apprehension, like that of a child who has been listening to a gripping fairy story with sinister elements.

Foley said, 'How goes it?' and worked his way round to the side furthest from Max. He began speaking to Moss in low tones. 'Do you really think, Michael,' he said, 'that Max should be encouraged to drink quite so much? You know what he's like. You don't want to cause a row with Simon, do you? Eric seems to think that you are upsetting – ' He broke off abruptly, checked by the sudden darkening of Moss's face.

'Go away,' said Moss.

'Well, really!' Foley exclaimed.

'I might have known you'd take their part.'

'I was only trying to help,' Foley said, wishing he did not sound so plaintive. 'I hope you know what you're doing, Michael, that's all. You're certainly not doing Max any good. Simon Lang is all he's got, you know.'

Moss glanced sideways at Max's face before speaking again. 'It's a good job for you Max didn't hear that,' he said, speaking with almost closed lips, so that the words came out slurred and fierce. 'Now, *go away*.'

For a long helpless moment Foley looked into the other's face, which so recently had pleaded with him, and wept. It was closed against him now, irrevocably. There was anger and obstinacy in it, and something else, something like exultation.

'Very well,' Foley said. 'No one can say I didn't try.'

Moss stopped looking at him the moment he began to withdraw. He reached over and with surprising gentleness and dexterity adjusted Max's tie. While he was doing this Max brought his glass up over Moss's arm and took a long drink. The moment, in this particular conjunction of activities, seemed symbolical to Foley. He was about to return to Eric and report his failure when the slam of car doors was heard outside. It was an expensive slam. Foley realised that Simon Lang had arrived at last.

Things happened quickly but at first smoothly. There was a reshuffling and repositioning among the people present. Eric moved towards the door, smoothing his hair. Moss spoke to Max who stood up and broke into a smile. Simon Lang appeared at the door followed at his heels by a barrel-bodied hound with huge jaws and little bloodshot eyes. He stood there for a moment frowning in what looked like surprise. Everybody stopped talking at once and the only sound for some moments was the slight wheezing of the dog. It was an effective entrance.

'Well, well, well,' Simon Lang said, smiling a little, raising his eyebrows, giving them all time to take him in.

Foley studied the famous features, making the same adjustment as everyone else there to the flesh and blood presence of the actor, after so long an acquaintance with the heroic image. He found it a difficult adjustment to make. Simon Lang had made his name in films, and in the sort of films that featured Simon Lang the concern was always with the character in action, athletic, law-enforcing-or-defying, amorous. Even his static moments were stressful, as when he faced unblindfolded a firing squad, or teetered, monosyllabic, on the brink of a proposal. One never got a glimpse of the banal interludes that take up so much of ordinary life. But here in this room Simon was to be taxed in a different way: he was standing on the same carpet as everybody else and they knew how far from heroic *they* were. A sudden drop was inevitable. What Foley chiefly felt, apart from this, was that Simon's features had, as it were, suffered in transition from the pure empyrean, a certain blurring, almost a melting. The famous aquilinity was there of course, the profile passionate and ascetic, that had wet the hankies of millions. But, full on, the face was heavier than might have been supposed. Almost it could be said to have jowls. There was a certain brutality of confidence in it, and the lips were considerably fuller, more everted, than the cosmeticians had ever permitted to appear publicly.

He stood for a few moments longer at the door, his eyes going over the group, which had pressed itself together as though to be introduced as a unit, as though feeling not sufficiently important singly to claim his attention. Max still had the welcoming smile on his face, but Simon had not once looked towards him. Fastening at last a deliberate eye on Eric, he said:

'Who are all these people *littering* up my house?' The gay, rather fluting emphasis went a little way towards mitigating the rudeness. Eric performed a rather elegant sequence of gestures with shoulders and hips, to indicate non-culpable helplessness. 'People Max invited,' he said.

Max now advanced somewhat unsteadily. He seemed to have become drunker since Simon's arrival. 'Friends and admirers of yours, my love,' he said. 'Gathered here.' He advanced on Simon, taking short steps, his arms raised slightly and fully extended, as though to embrace him.

Simon stepped past him into the middle of the room. His face looked angrier now. 'They may be *admirers*,' he said. 'There isn't a single person here whom I have ever set eyes on in my life before.'

So far none of the guests had said anything. On the faces of all, however, was registered the awareness, not yet veering to resentment, that their presence was failing to gratify Simon Lang. Being prepared to revere, they had not thought they could be unwelcome. Only the man with the forked beard, who had by this time got to his feet, ventured a remark. He took a step or two forward out of the ruck and said with extreme affability, 'Did you have a good journey down then, Simon?' Foley realised at this point that the man with the forked beard was not in his right mind.

Simon ignored him completely. 'My friends,' he said, making his cheekbones stand out, 'I am very grateful to you for coming along this evening, and I am sorry you have had such a long wait, though some of you seem to have borne with that tolerably well, tolerably well. The journey down from London was uneventful, the roads quiet, the weather fair. Just now I have a headache and I am feeling rather tired. I cannot entertain you now, but under other circumstances, of course . . . Thank you. I know you will

186

understand.' He ended these remarks with a practised, almost a benedictory, gesture.

'That's show-business,' said the man with the forked beard, nodding his head resignedly. None of the others said anything much at all. They trooped out meekly as though they had known all along that the party would be over when Simon actually arrived. Nobody made any claim to Simon's acquaintance.

Foley was making doorward shuffles with the others, when Eric signalled him to stay. So great had been Simon's impact that it was only now that Foley noticed Moss had made no movement to go, had not even risen to his feet when Simon came in. He had a premonition of more trouble to come.

'Well,' said Simon, when the last of them had gone. 'Let's have a drink, if there's any left.' Standing at the drink table, pouring himself out a gin, he contrived to look suddenly haggard as well as dashing. Handling the bottle and the glass he revealed broad, spatulate fingers and thick wrists. He plopped three little white onions one after the other into his gin and swirled them round.

'You've been a bit mean with the onions, haven't you?' he said to Eric. 'Is this all there are?'

'There *were* some,' Max said. 'I put them out.'

'I think that man with the divided beard ate them,' Foley said. 'At least, I saw him standing there at one point, eating.'

Simon looked at him without expression.

'Simon always has onions in his gin,' Max said, to everybody else.

'It's rather an unusual drink,' Eric said. 'Distinguished, I always think.'

'There are some more, Simon,' Max said. 'I always keep a stock in, just in case.'

'Just in case?' Simon said. 'Just in case of what? In case your ragged-arsed friends feel hungry?'

The dog was recumbent just behind him, belly flat to the floor, its heavy jaws resting on its forelegs. Every time Simon spoke its ears moved.

'I haven't had an explanation yet,' Simon said, into his glass. He sipped and then looked at Eric again. 'I'll deal with you later,' he said. Eric looked distressed. Max now emerged from the corner of the room to which he had retreated for another drink.

'I keep a stock of them in, bottles and bottles,' Max said, 'in case we get a visit from you, darling. In case Simon Lang honours us with a visit, drops in unexpectedly some decade or other, he's like that of course, not a bit conventional. You never know with Simon. They get frightfully *mushy*, of course, after a while, onions I mean, not actors, even though preserved in brine and kept in a cool place. They actually begin to ferment after a year or two. I could have onion wine if I wanted to, all the year round.'

'Try it, duckie,' Simon said, and no film-goer had ever heard this note of brutal contempt in his voice. 'Do try it. Pickle your little liver for you, less expensively than my gin. It's all mine, you know,' he said, turning his head and addressing the others. 'She'd be on the parish if it weren't for me, trying her luck along the Fulham Road. I don't know why I keep on with it. She stinks of gin and knickers and then she wonders why I prefer to drink with the boys.'

Max, weaving his head slightly from side to side, more than ever resembled a frail duellist on guard against rude cudgels. 'Yes,' he said, 'we met one of your boys tonight. Such camaraderie is touching, Simon, you sound so *butch* to anyone who doesn't know you. Such a bond as there obviously is. Clearly you have grappled them to you with hoops and hoops. You should be all wearing your sou'westers, darling, running before the gale and having cups of cocoa. It's all such a sham, Simon. What you would really like, of course, is to be in full drag and have a bloody great stoker after you.'

'By God,' Simon said thickly, 'I won't have this in my own house!' The dog behind him heard the anger in his voice and growled a little. 'Turning my house into a whorehouse,' Simon said. He had flushed darkly with rage, but for some moments said nothing more, seemed indeed somewhat at a loss. A certain unimaginativeness, a stupidity in fact, had been apparent in the crudely frontal attack on Max, in the immediate recourse to the obvious advantage Max's dependent position gave him. And this impression was strengthened now rather absurdly when after a longish pause Simon took a step or two forward and pretended to look closely at the front of Max's body. In a tone he struggled to make urbane and with a sort of baffled smile, he said, 'I believe you are growing breasts, Max.'

It was so venomously irrelevant that Max himself giggled a little and did not immediately reply. And it might have passed off thus if Moss had not chosen this moment to intervene. He seemed to take this remark of Simon's more seriously than any of the others, in spite of Max's giggle.

'No, he is not,' he said. The contradiction, delivered in Moss's flat tones, sounded absurdly positive for the point at issue, like the stubborn assertions of children when they dispute verifiable facts.

'Who the hell is this?' shouted Simon. 'You are turning my house into a whorehouse. What bloody tout is this?' His face glistened with the exertions of his rage and his voice was developing a tendency to shrillness. The dog behind him had raised its muzzle, and kept up a continuous, minatory growling.

'He's an impossible person. He's been causing trouble all the evening,' Eric said. 'When do you *moult?*' he added spitefully, looking at Moss's hairy jacket.

'Do you think you're doing Max a favour, keeping him here?' said Moss, who had not moved nor altered the tone of his voice. 'He'd be much better off without you. You only keep him here because you can't give up anything. Don't you know that you can't own other people? Max has more talent than you have, in my opinion. You are a marsh-mallow, in my opinion.'

There was no time to wonder what Moss intended by this extraordinary term which he must surely have dredged up from a controversial childhood, because Max began to speak again, advancing towards Simon with a sort of bravado. Moss's intervention had disturbed his puny, duellist's poise, and his face now was desperate and jeering.

'Yes, you see, Simon,' he said. 'Someone believes in me. You never thought anyone would take my part against you, did you, not against the great Simon Lang, the well-known procuress, the *doyenne –* '

Simon swung his arm suddenly. There was the sharp sound of a slap and Max stepped back a pace. The dog sprang up and seemed about to attack Max in its turn, but Simon spoke to it and it subsided slowly, its lips wrinkled back in a prolonged, soundless snarl. Max buried his face in his hands and a single sweet-toned sob broke from him. Then, while the others were staring aghast, while Simon was still half turned to admonish the dog, Moss acted. He rose from his seat with a ponderous springing action, covering the distance between Simon and himself in two long strides. Using the impetus of his body, as well as the full weight of his arm and shoulder, he struck Simon a swinging upward blow, high on the cheek, just as he was turning to face them. It was a formidable blow, rather sickeningly audible throughout the room. Simon was a heavy man but he was knocked back several feet and would perhaps have fallen, but for the wall. Without a pause Moss shifted the weight of his feet and caught the springing dog with a kick full on its muzzle, which deposited it near its master. Blood thinned by saliva ran from its jaws. Foley remembered suddenly the heavy metal toe-caps Moss always wore. The dog, however, with the indomitable nature of its breed, seemed to be gathering itself for a fresh attack.

'Get that brute under control,' said Moss, 'or I'll kill it.'

Simon stood still against the wall with his hand to the side of his face, which shock had emptied of all expression. 'Down, get down, Roland,' he said indistinctly through his hand.

Moss watched him carefully. The fist with which he had struck was still clenched. 'You won't be hitting Max again, ever,' he said quietly.

The final divergence now took place between Simon's public and private personas. He would never have taken a blow like this in one of his films. He had had some hard, brutal, slogging fights on the screen, sometimes against considerable odds, taking and dealing out twenty or thirty such knocks as this, but he had always fought on, even when victory seemed remote. And he had always, as far as Foley at any rate remembered, finally emerged victorious. A bit of blood, a displaced necktie, the congratulations of the township, the honourable embraces of the principal virgin. Now, however, he showed no signs of intending to retaliate. He removed the hand from his face after some time, and straightened himself.

'I didn't know you had hired a bully to protect you,' he said. His left cheek was mottled red. 'The police will deal with him,' he said. He looked at them for some moments with vague eyes and Foley realised that he was still partially stunned from the blow. 'Come, Eric,' he said finally. 'We will find an hotel for the night.' At the door he paused and turned. 'By this time on Monday,' he said, 'I shall expect this house to be vacant, unless I get a full apology and assurance you will never see this person again. You can clear out, Max, for good.'

Max, still silently weeping, made no answer. Simon turned again and was gone, Eric and the wounded dog following with a sort of appalled docility behind him. They heard the slam of the car doors outside, and the sound of the car being driven away.

Max raised his head. His face was blubbered with tears. 'It's not the first time he's hit me,' he said.

'It's the last time, though,' Moss said with solemn exaltation. 'This is the beginning of a new life for you, Max.'

'He's always been too free with his hands, always,' Max said. 'People don't know.'

'He's a bully,' Moss said. 'You are well rid of him.'

Max said with invincible pride, 'Do you know, he once pushed a whole table over with all the tea-things on it, and scalded my arm.'

'Don't think about him any more. This is the beginning of a—'

'He'll never get the lawyers, of course.' Max said. 'He wouldn't.'

'Never mind about what he will do. It's what you're going to do that matters.' Moss spoke urgently, perhaps perceiving now the precariousness of his own position. Simon would not be easily dislodged. 'You are not going to apologise, of course,' he said, looking hard at Max.

'Apologise to Simon?' Max smiled. 'Everyone apologises to Simon. Do you think it matters?' He reached for the gin bottle.

'I shouldn't drink any more now, Max,' Moss said firmly. 'We'd better have a talk, get a few things straight.'

Max, with his hand on the bottle, looked at him in dismay. Moss turned to Foley and said with distant politeness: 'Would you mind leaving now? I shall stay here tonight. I don't want to leave Max alone just now.'

Foley followed this suggestion with some relief. Certainly he had no desire to listen to Moss and Max getting things straight. What Moss obviously in any case meant was warping things his own way. He wondered if Moss really understood what a wrenching this would mean for Max. He wondered if Moss really understood anything. Still, it was not his business. He drove back slowly and thoughtfully. The evening had been full of incident but he could not quite believe any of it. It was vivid but lacked probability. Almost he felt he had been imposed upon. It was not until he was putting the car away that it occurred to him that he was going to be quite alone in the house.

15

Moss did not put in an appearance the following day. Nor the day after. Foley stayed at home possessed by a languid sense of crisis. He worked listlessly for a while on some pixies, but most of the time he spent reading the Cellini book or listening to the wireless, which seemed to be all palm court strings on the British stations and lewd French voices everywhere else, talking about de Gaulle. An unflagging wind blew from the sea and the powdered clay of the farmyard swirled everywhere, mixed with hens' feathers and the year's first crop of fallen leaves. Morning and evening a red-faced, cursing Royle herded his bullocks through.

Foley spent long periods in the attic with his cherub lamps. The sight of them clustering above reassured him, like a familiar constellation seen in the wastes of the sky. Standing among them he experienced a suspension, a stillness, the distancing of all need for decision. The slight discomfort of posture made necessary by the overhead positions of many of them promoted those feelings of reverence and loneliness associated with the interiors of cathedrals. The silence was skeined with minute crepitations, mice capering behind the walls, the sorties of spiders, the shifting of dust. Foley dusted the gilt limbs with his feather brush, setting up amongst them ecstatic vibrations, fugitive gleams of light. In the midst of this multiple shuddering and shining he was aware of the action of his own heart. The bland sightless faces seemed to express a wantonness, a dimpled lubricity. Foley felt the stirrings of idolatry in this room filled with the creations of his commercial enterprise.

Apart from this he did little but wait for a sign. He neglected to eat now that Moss was not there to cook for him. Old Walter turned up on the Sunday afternoon, wanting to know what there was to do. Foley had not the remotest idea – all that had been Moss's concern. Besides, the sight of Walter was painful to him, reminding him of that afternoon with Gwendoline. He gave the old man ten shillings and sent him away.

He wondered continually what Moss and Max could be talking of, how they could be passing the hours. Moss of course would be consolidating his position, bullying Max, preventing him from crawling back to Simon. It was the sort of admonitory role that he would relish, the self-appointed keeper. But what about Max? What was his role, now that Simon, stricken, had declined below the horizon?

By Monday afternoon he could bear his inactivity no longer. He took the car and went down to the village, having made the reservation that he would not visit Barbara Gould, would not go near her house at all. He still remembered with shame his slithering performance under that bright pleased stare of hers which, without being malicious exactly or ironical, was so belittling. When he tried to fix precisely the nature of this regard of Barbara's, the nearest he could get to it was *familiarity*. He felt that she was completely acquainted with the sort of person he was.

He left his car in the large municipal park above the village and walked the half-mile or so down to the harbour. It was most inadvisable to take a car further down at this time of year, especially such a large and cumbersome car. This was the peak of the season and the village was packed with visitors. He was surprised to find The Smugglers' Den locked up and apparently deserted. He tapped on the window and looked inside. The barrels and nets and lamps were all set out in their proper places and the skulls hung at spaced intervals, softly gleaming. The walls were newly whitewashed and there was no sign of a painting on them. There was no sign of Bailey. He tapped again and after a further pause heard noises from the interior. Bailey appeared from some inner recess and came shambling towards the door. He was in shirt-sleeves and was wearing candy-striped braces, pink and white, which hoisted his trousers well up towards his armpits. After some preliminary fumbling with what sounded to Foley like a chain, he opened the door. He regarded Foley flatly and without apparent recognition for some moments. His little eyes looked slightly glassy.

'Oh, it's you,' he said at last. 'You'd better come in.' A heavy breath of whisky enveloped Foley. He stepped inside the café and heard Bailey busy again with the chain behind him.

'Go through to the back,' Bailey said. 'We don't want anyone spying on us. There's some whisky in there.'

'But what's the matter?' asked Foley. 'I was expecting to find you on the crest of the wave.' Behind him Bailey uttered a single throaty laugh. They went behind the counter into the small kitchen. It was stuffy in there and spiritous fumes once again assailed Foley. A half-empty bottle of whisky stood on the little aluminium draining board.

'Would you like a drink?' Bailey enquired, in lifeless tones. There was a marked absence of bounce in his whole manner.

'Yes, I would rather,' Foley said. 'What's the matter, why aren't you open?'

'Do you mean you don't know? I thought the whole bloody village would know by this time.' The prospect of repeating the story seemed to enliven Bailey somewhat. He got a tumbler from the shelf above the draining board and poured out a liberal quantity of whisky. 'Water with it?' he said.

'Just as it is, please.'

'I never take anything with mine either.' Bailey settled himself down again on to a small kitchen chair over whose confines he spilled out in all directions. The seat of the chair ended just under the fleshy part of Bailey's thighs, squeezing them so that they swelled tightly inside his voluminous grey flannel trousers. The thighs thus expanded were each of them thicker than Foley's waist. 'Never spoil a good drink by mixing things with it,' he said. 'That's a maxim of mine.'

'Cheers!' Foley said, resolving to wait in patience on Bailey's sense of the dramatic.

'Cheers, cheers,' responded Bailey, with bitter alacrity. He downed half his tumbler, then opened his mouth in a sort of snarl to let the heat of the whisky out. 'Why don't I open?' he said, and repeated the throaty laugh. Still fixing Foley with his eye he attempted to lean forward in his chair, no doubt to lend intensity to the words he was about to utter, but he suffered a temporary loss of equilibrium which caused his head and trunk to go on slowly and helplessly declining until he was looking down directly at Foley's knees. This apparently was his point of balance, because from here he was able slowly to hoist himself backwards until Foley's face came once more into his line of vision. Arrested at this angle of inclination he stared at Foley speechlessly for several seconds.

'Yes, why?' said Foley, rather nervously. Deceived by Bailey's bulk and ponderousness of movement he had not realised how drunk the latter really was.

'Because I bloody well can't, for fear of proceedings,' Bailey said loudly, slapping one knee and only just hitting it. 'As soon as I open that door to the public there'll be a court order against me.'

'Good heavens!' exclaimed Foley.

'Have another drink,' Bailey said. '*I'm* having one. As a matter of fact I've been having the odd one all morning.'

'All right,' Foley said. 'But what on earth is all this about?'

'I'll tell you,' Bailey said, when their glasses were full again. 'That painter chap, you remember, the man I hired to paint smugglers on the walls, he lives in a shack up above the village with a bloody great *moat* all round him . . .'

'I know, yes I remember,' said Foley. 'You mean Graham.'

'Graham,' repeated Bailey, and his eyes almost disappeared into his head. 'Graham,' he said again in a voice charged with hatred. 'That's the one I mean. Him. He's done for me. He might as well have blown the place up. Those pictures he did . . . I should never have taken him on, something warned me against it. I had a feeling from the beginning he wasn't the right man. It was a hunch. That's what I did, I went against my hunch.' With this word his American accent had returned, its plangency subdued but still quite unmistakable.

Foley allowed his glass to be refilled. He was drinking to keep pace with Bailey, which was a mistake really, in view of the latter's evident capacity and the fact that he was already well lubricated and running smoothly.

'He let me down,' resumed Bailey. 'He didn't paint smugglers at all, he painted wreckers. You know what wreckers are?' Bailey's trunk began another slow and rather majestic roll forward. He got Foley in focus again with something of an effort. 'Those fellows who brought ships on to the rocks then pinched all the cargo. They did the crew in first, of course. Well, that wouldn't have mattered. I mean it was all the same to me whether they were smugglers or wreckers, only that bastard painted real people.'

He paused for so long at this point that Foley felt constrained to put in a remark. 'All artists use their personal experience,' he said, but he knew quite well what Bailey meant.

'Local people,' Bailey said. 'Important people, people of standing. They all had nasty expressions but you could recognise them. They *were* recognised. Not by me, of course, being a stranger here. The vicar and the curate were in it and the landlord of the pub and there were aldermen in it, sticking knives into injured sailors, drinking rum out of the bottles, and an old chap called Brigadier Martin, maybe you've heard of him, he's a Justice of the Peace, he was in it, receiving stolen goods, and his wife too, with her hair in bloody great rollers. He even brought the women into it, you see, nothing was sacred to him, nothing.'

Bailey brooded for some moments, nursing his glass. 'Well, I didn't *know*, you see,' he said. 'At the time.'

'It was naughty of Graham,' Foley said.

'Naughty?' repeated Bailey. '*Naughty?*' He looked at Foley unbelievingly. His head had now developed a tendency to wobble, very slightly. 'He might think he's got away with it,' he said. 'But I'm going up there later. Paid him his money, I did, on the dot.'

'In full?'

'I paid him *half*,' Bailey said, and nothing could have been more impressive than this truthfulness, nor shown more convincingly Bailey's state of shock. 'I thought he gave me a funny look from under that bloody cap of his,' he went on. 'He's keeping out of the way now, but I'll find him. I'll have the money back for a start. Then I'll do him up. I'll squash him.'

Taking in once again the dimensions of Bailey, Foley felt some complacency that he was not himself the object of this intention. Whatever the other's commercial buffooneries, his bulk compelled respect.

'I never did like these little runts,' Bailey said, and all his travails with his own bulk gave poignancy to this. 'I just thought I'd have a drink or two first,' he added.

'No more for me,' Foley said, but he was too late, or Bailey didn't hear him. He had protested over this drink because he felt it to be the one which would allow him no further illusions of sobriety, would in fact change the nature of his visit, turning what he had envisaged as a sociable couple of drinks into something like a session.

'Don't worry,' said Bailey, mistaking the nature of his reluctance. 'Got another bottle here.' He raised himself a little and reached behind him, bringing out from somewhere a sealed bottle of Vat '69.

Bailey took a large swallow from his glass. His capacity to absorb whisky seemed endless. 'I was taken in,' he said, with pathos. 'I didn't know, you see. Being a stranger here. I opened for business last Wednesday – a bit later than I expected. The place was packed within an hour I tell you, they were queueing outside, mostly visitors of course, they didn't know any different any more than I did. But there were a few people here and there taking quite a bit of interest in the paintings. I thought Graham had done a good job then. I even felt grateful to him.

'Then about midday a fellow came in and asked for a word in private. I brought him in here. He said he was on the Council and a captain in the Territorials. I found out afterwards that he was in the picture too, egging the others on he was, in a sneaking sort of way. He said he had spoken to his solicitors, who had told him it was actionable. I tried to tell him I didn't know any of these people he said were in the paintings, but all he would say was that they'd prosecute if I didn't close down at once. "You'll have to close down," he kept saying.'

Bailey changed his delivery from the bitter staccato of disastrous narrative to a tone ampler and more rhetorical. 'What could I do, I ask you, what could anyone have done? What would you have done in my place, a stranger here with nothing behind you? I have had to keep the place closed ever since, turning good money away.'

'You don't mean you believed him?' Foley said. 'Did you close

198

down only because of that? He was only trying to frighten you. I mean, what could they actually do?'

'They could prosecute,' said Bailey. 'I asked him, I saw the whole situation at once, I put it to him man to man – I've always believed in the man to man approach – I offered to paint over the pictures myself, on the spot. Nothing doing. I painted them over just the same.'

'Exactly,' Foley said. 'Those paintings don't exist any more, anywhere. They've got nothing on you now, have they? They're trying to put you out of business, that's what it is. Anyone who isn't a native, they're against him from the start. I should fight it, if I were you, call their bluff.'

Bailey emitted a snorting sound, jerking his head up to give it free passage. 'Call their bluff,' he said. 'What bloody well with? I keep telling you I've nothing behind me. Listen, supposing someone took photographs of those murals. I don't *know*, do I?' He raised his head and endeavoured to fix Foley with a keen gaze. The whisky seemed now to be taking delayed effect on him. It was like watching the slow, gentle death throes of a sick and elderly elephant. His great head that in the passion of explaining had wobbled incessantly was now motionless again, sunk on his breast. His chins multiplied indefinitely there, and all the reclinations of his body expressed torpor. From time to time a tremor ran through him, his limbs stirred as though in protest, and he raised his head seeking to fix Foley in a glassy and truculent regard. Suddenly he began speaking again.

'Bloody swine,' he said, referring to the Councillor or perhaps to Graham. 'I can't stand a court case; I've nothing behind me. Everything I had went into this place, the alterations, the improvements, the . . . décor. I'm in debt. I've been living on what the caterers sent ever since last Saturday. Meat pasties and potato crisps . . . Everything I had, all my savings. I had a good job, I was in the Co-op. I might have been manager, but I wanted to have my own business. I *studied* it, gave up my evenings, took correspondence courses. Ask me any question, function of the wholesaler, different types of retail organisation. I am well up in the subject. My sister, I lived with my sister, she was against it from the start. Nothing venture, nothing win, I told her.'

Bailey somehow got the last of the whisky into his glass. 'It ought to have been a certainty,' he said. 'Catering business, expanding resort. This has just come at the worst time, before I could get going properly. If I could only have had a couple of months to pay back, I'd have been all right. Just a season, that's all I needed.'

The pathos of Bailey's being denied what every butterfly and bug can confidently expect, a summer season, moved Foley. Was his own season not blighted in mid-career by Moss's vagaries? Bailey, he now saw, was no mere money grabber, but an idealist, like himself. The impulse that had taken him, in spite of a sister's protests, from the safety of the grocer's counter and the prospect of managerial rank to this debauch in a cramped kitchen was akin to that which causes other, wieldier men to engage in remote explorations or sail single-handed across great oceans. And although he lacked the grit to defy the councillors, who could blame him for that? Through correspondence course and visions he might have prepared himself for almost anything but Graham. Graham belonged to the class of calamities which men cannot guard against.

Leaning forward, Foley put a hand on one of Bailey's spongy knees. 'Why,' he asked earnestly and almost tenderly, 'do you sometimes speak with an American accent?'

Bailey reared up again, breathing stertorously. 'American accent?' he said in an indignant voice. 'What do you mean, American accent? Wass the *marrer* with you?'

'Never mind,' Foley said.

'Who are you saying got an American acshent?'

'It's all right,' Foley said.

'I come from *Middlesboro*,' said Bailey. 'I shall have to sell up and get out. I had everything ready, the barrelsh, the netsh, the lampsh, everything. The skullsh.'

'Ah yes,' Foley said.

'I know what you're going to say.'

'What?'

'You're going to say you want your money for them skullsh. And I don't blame you. No shentiment in business, keep shentiment out of business. That's a macshim of mine . . . But will

200

you wait a bit, that's what I want to know, till things are shettled up?'

'Yes, I don't mind waiting,' Foley said, perceiving there was no choice.

'You're a white man,' said Bailey. 'You're a good guy. True blue.' His head had begun to sag again, declining on to his chest. His eyes slipped quickly over Foley's face and came to rest in a fixed stare at the floor between them. His remaining words came out slurred and indistinct. 'I can always tell a good man, pick him out of a hundred, what am I shaying, a thousand. Never wrong. I – am – never wrong. Knowledge of human nature,' said Bailey. 'You'll never get far in business without it, never.'

'But how can you know?' asked Foley. He felt suddenly eloquent and responsible. A spokesman. 'How can you ever know human nature? All the knowledge you are talking about is retrospective and it doesn't help much in the present because nothing is ever the same twice in your life, no situation is exactly repeated. Where do you get your criteria?

'I think experience is overrated, actually. You still have to start all over again every time with every new person. So it seems to me that what you need is energy, not experience. These good judges of human nature that people talk about are usually just old men and women who have lost their energy and try to apply some sort of preconceived standard to people.

'Take my case. My partner, Michael Moss. Three years we've been in business. You can't help making assumptions about a person in three years. People have got to be supposed to be calculable to a large extent, whatever their ultimate mystery and all that.

'I was wrong about Moss. Moss is a homosexual. Keep it to yourself, of course. How could I be expected to know that? He doesn't show any of the obvious signs of it. At least I didn't notice anything odd about him. He didn't tell me. He should have told me when we formed the partnership. Then I should have known what I was getting into. He deceived me, wouldn't you say he deceived me?' Foley paused, challengingly, but Bailey made no answer.

'He *did* deceive me. He might say he didn't know at the time.

But he must have known in some way. He must have *suspected* something. He's not such a fool. You know why he said nothing about it? He was hoping I'd turn out that way inclined as well. That's what I find so difficult to forgive. And do you know that Moss *blames* me now for not having seen through him? He actually holds it against me. If you asked him at this very moment he'd almost certainly say that I'd injured him. What it comes down to is that my assumptions about Moss were mistaken but his about me were dishonest. No two ways about it.'

Foley fell silent for some moments, possessed by a sense of injustice. Bailey breathed regularly, showed no disposition to intervene.

'Now you're going to find this difficult to believe,' Foley continued, 'but I can't help feeling that Moss is in the right somehow. You know what I mean? I feel that he's in the right and I'm in the wrong. In spite of everything. He's on my conscience, I can't quite explain it . . .'

Thus for a moment Foley came near to apprehending the reality and tyranny of Moss's love. But the effort was too difficult to be sustained for long, and when he spoke again he had returned to that level on which Moss could be wholly blamed. 'He has deserted me,' he said. 'In the middle of the season, just when our commitments are heaviest.' He leaned forward and prodded one of Bailey's knees. 'What do you think of that?' he demanded in impassioned tones.

Bailey made no reply, but a long and trailing sigh escaped him. His head, supported by a neat scaffolding of chins, still rested on his breast.

'Without a word of explanation,' Foley said. He lowered himself in his chair and leaned back, tilting his head in order to look into the other's face. Bailey's eyes were closed and his moist, childish mouth a little open. In sleep he looked quite guileless and curiously pagan.

Foley sat forward on the edge of his chair, advancing his face as close as possible to Bailey's without actually rising. 'You *have* got an American accent,' he said softly, straight into Bailey's still face. 'And it's no good pretending otherwise. I think you started using it because you thought it sounded high-powered. Well, I should drop it if I were you, it makes you sound untrustworthy. And another thing, Bailey, let me give you a bit of advice, don't you go in for maxims and sayings so much. Try to use your loaf a bit more.'

He smiled for some moments into Bailey's unconscious face, feeling pleased and powerful. Then, rather dizzily, he stood up. He was beginning to go from the room when a charitable impulse visited him. Turning back he looked round the room for several moments without seeing what he wanted. In the café itself, however, he found, rather pathetically, a little pad for making bills out, in a leather case, with a pencil attached to it by a string. Bailey had clearly neglected none of the appurtenances. Tearing out one of the bills, Foley wrote on the back of it in block capitals: 'It's no use going to Graham's place, you will only fall into the stream because he has taken the bridge up and besides he has probably left for good by this time.' He went back into the kitchen and laid the paper on Bailey's lap, hoping no sudden motion of an unquiet dream would dislodge it. Then, feeling virtuous and somewhat lightheaded, he made his way through the café, braving the fixed disdain of the skulls. In spite of his fumblings with the chain, Bailey had not succeeded in locking the door, having forgotten to close the padlock, and Foley let himself out without difficulty.

It was quite late in the afternoon. The sky, which had been a clear blue when he entered Bailey's, was curdled now with cloud, but still luminous. The sea was calm beyond the harbour wall, glazed-looking, as though it had a skin on it. Water was flowing back into the harbour, raising the little boats from the silt. A steamer crawled across the horizon, but the effort of following it hurt Foley's eyes. His head ached a little, otherwise he felt no ill effects from the whisky. He went along the harbour, past The Fisherman's Arms to a very small snack bar called simply 'Snax', whose owner had a side-line selling souvenirs and bought a few pixies from time to time. Here Foley had a rather scrappy meal of beans on toast and exchanged with some spirit remarks on business and the weather with the proprietor, who took a uniformly pessimistic view of both. Afterwards, however, he could remember nothing of this conversation, only the tendency of the proprietor's right eye to water.

16

He drove home with conscious dexterity and found Moss waiting for him in the living-room; a Moss no longer attired in the homely habiliments of the casting-room, nor even in the hairy sports jacket of former outings, but in a square-cut, grey, double-breasted suit of old-fashioned appearance, which Foley could not remember seeing him wearing before. Nothing could have more firmly marked his break with the business. Sitting there, not quite at his ease, in the armchair, he looked like some sort of unfriendly official. He had darkened his hair with oil and swept it straight back from the forehead, emphasising the almost complete roundness of his head.

'You ought to lock the door when you go out,' Moss said. 'Anyone could get in here.'

'Someone did, it seems,' said Foley, trying not to sound defiant. 'You ought to be glad,' he added. 'Since it gave you somewhere comfortable to wait.'

'I didn't come just to wait for you. I came to pack my things.' He indicated two large and battered suitcases standing against the wall. Foley looked at them steadily for some time, trying to find a way of gaining the initiative.

'So you're moving out,' was all he could find to say.

'I'm going away altogether,' Moss said. He chewed briefly at something, then stopped and looked watchfully at Foley.

'Do you mean to say,' Foley said, 'that you are clearing out now, without a second's notice, in the middle of the season? How am I going to cope with all the work on my own?'

'You didn't think, did you,' Moss said, 'that I was going to stay on here after what happened?'

'You speak as though I have done you an injury of some sort,' said Foley coldly. 'Do you consider that I have done you an injury?'

As soon as he had said this he realised that Moss was not going to answer him. It was quite clearly useless to expect Moss to embark on any analysis of the situation at this point, when he had decided to leave. Foley understood that his own rejection was implicit in this decision and that whatever anguish it had caused Moss at the time to make, nothing now could alter it, nothing could render it even discussable. The sense of his being disapproved of by Moss was what emerged most strongly – so strongly that Foley felt his comportment deteriorating rapidly, like a stage hypocrite's when his plots have been at last detected.

'Don't think I'm going to plead with you to stay,' he said as nastily as possible.

'Nothing you could say would make any difference, I'm afraid,' Moss said.

'I'm not asking you to stay,' snapped Foley. 'You seem to imagine – '

'I'm sorry,' Moss said, 'but my mind is made up.'

Clearly, he had come determined to be pleaded with. Foley perceived that the subject needed changing. 'Where are you going, then?' he asked, with deliberate carelessness.

'You don't care where I'm going,' Moss burst out suddenly, losing his composure and flushing slightly.

'Of course I do,' Foley said. Moss's sign of distress had given him some hope of an advantage, but even while he cast about for a telling phrase the other's expression returned to its former lowering calm, and the moment had passed.

'We are going, if you really want to know, to Siam,' Moss said.

' "We," meaning you and Max?'

'Yes. Max tells me he has business contacts there, and it is far enough away from all his old associations.'

'Far enough away, certainly,' Foley said. He had not really intended to infuse this remark with any derisive quality, but Moss stiffened and said angrily, 'I suppose you think it's all very funny.'

'I don't think it's funny at all, God knows,' Foley said. He looked at Moss for some time in silence, at the square unlovely forehead and chin, the perpetual slight surprise of the eyebrows, the vulnerable, anticipatory mouth. The plastered hair, swept back over his almost perfectly spherical cranium, exposed his features in all their bluntness. It was not a face to stay the eyes in a crowd. It was the sort of face in fact that would never get the indulgence accorded to the more obviously and trivially eccentric, when the obsessions working behind it resulted in some sort of action. The owner of this face would always be subject to the shocked surprise of other people, because his deviations would always seem like a betrayal of conventions he so patently embodied and guaranteed. Moss might look at you over a garden gate with the same expression, and say good evening in the same way for twenty years, then after one such good evening no different from the others, go off and cut his throat or indecently assault a minor. Here he was in his clumsy suit talking about Siam.

'I didn't mean anything against Max,' Foley said at last, conscious suddenly of his cold, rather hateful wonder.

'Max is a wonderful person,' Moss said immediately, with his trick of ignoring or not perceiving the intentions behind words addressed to him. Having established Max as a person to be defended he would go on detecting criticism where only appeasement had been meant. 'He needs someone to look after him,' he said. 'Someone who understands him, who will give him the stability he needs in order to create.'

Suddenly at these words Foley knew what Moss had reminded him of earlier, what this new appearance signified. The lounge suit, antique enough, with its vast lapels and wide trousers, to be regarded as donned in the course of duty. The rather ghastly spruceness of the hair. Not an official, a nurse: a male nurse. He had all the qualities; he had acquainted himself with Max's infirmities; he was padding already round Max in his mind as though Max were in a hospital bed. Foley could see him, in plimsolls, patting the pillows softly, bearing oranges and grapes and magazines. He would want Max to ail for ever, the two of them involved in an endless convalescent dream in which full health was at all costs to be avoided. Gentle hands, all germs slaughtered, aseptic as the body under the orderly's suit. Hands that knew also strangleholds, if the patient grew obstreperous . . .

'People like you,' Moss said sharply, 'wouldn't understand.'

'I told you I was not speaking against Max,' Foley said, feeling suddenly tired of the conversation, and strangely discouraged too. Moss had simplified the relationship with Max to one of gifted invalid and devoted nurse. There was nothing now to be gained by hinting at complexities beyond this. A person like Simon Lang could not be rooted out cleanly, he was an integral part of the whole meaning of Max's past. And yet it was unlikely that Moss would try to deaden the roots by making concessions to Simon and the past. His scheme of therapy for Max would tolerate no rivals, even retrospective ones. Foley felt sure he would be unremitting in his hostility to everything that Simon had ever been in Max's life; and the roots, thus cut, would fester. He recalled Barbara's saying that Max was beyond help. She had meant that he was untranslatable from his present context. Simon, after all, had sustained Max, more than materially. Those flying visits and long absences had given him resentments and jealousies to brood over, as well as the memories of love; and Simon's fame had been a career for him too. What had Moss to put in place of all this? A time would surely come, in Siam or elsewhere, wherever an erratic prospecting led the pair, when all this would blow up in their faces. Foley wondered which of them would be the greater victim.

'How will you manage for money?' Foley asked.

'I have saved a little in these three years. You didn't know I had a separate account, did you? I was keeping it in case the business went through a bad spell. Max has a little of his own too. Simon didn't support him altogether.'

'No, I should think not,' Foley said, waspishness once more getting the better of him. 'Simon would hardly have given him so much drink allowance.'

An expression of vindictive pleasure came over Moss's face, a startling and unpleasing lightening of the features. 'Have your little joke while you can,' he said. 'You needn't offer to buy me out, if that is what you are going to do. I've taken my payment already.'

'Well, I must say that is magnanimous of you,' Foley said, disturbed by the other's expression but relieved at his words.

'Goodbye, then,' Moss said heavily, moving towards the suitcases.

'Take the car if you like,' said Foley, 'and leave it with Reg at the garage.'

'No thank you,' Moss said. He had lifted the cases now.

'At least let me wish you good luck.'

'We don't need your good wishes,' replied Moss. 'And you won't feel like that for long anyway.' Nevertheless, he turned to face Foley, still holding the cases. Their weight effectively prevented any gesture he might have liked to make. For a moment his face had the open, stricken look which with him indicated emotion.

'What do you mean?' Foley asked, but Moss turned abruptly and went out, carrying the cases. Foley watched him go down the path towards the gate. He did not look behind him. The cases, which must have been quite heavy, did not appear to incommode him. For a few seconds, watching that stalwart back in the ill-fitting suit, Foley was swept quite unexpectedly by feelings of envy. Moss was brave and strong and loving and had, or thought he had, a destiny which he was striding off with his horrible suitcases to meet. Moss boldly accepted the necessities of his life, while he – what did he do? Cowered here, spiritless, without substance, afraid of the abyss.

Moss had barely passed through the gate and disappeared behind the hedge before Foley's mood had passed to one of cautious rejoicing at the thought of not having to pay him any money. Moss had been most generous. He had asked for nothing when he might have demanded much. He might at least have asked for his capital back. Plus interest. It would have been awkward, finding a sum like that at present. He needed the money behind him, now above all, when he was about to branch out a bit, get out of the pixie business. Moss had not even asked for the fare to Siam. He had in fact behaved like a gentleman. Foley felt an appreciative warmth. Good old Moss.

He became aware of hunger. The beans on toast had not been very sustaining. He went into the kitchen but had no idea what to cook. Moss had always done that. After rather aimless explorations he found some eggs. He would have boiled eggs. He put three eggs in a pan of water and lit the gas under them. Later, perhaps, he would engage a cook. Cook and housekeeper, female of course. He would advertise. Please send a recent photograph with your application. He went back into the living-room and sat down to wait for the eggs. The silence of the house settled round him. Dusk was gathering outside and after a moment or two he got up again to light the lamps. Almost immediately several moths began fluttering and thudding round the milky globes.

Pixie production, of course, was more or less at an end. For this season, anyway. He couldn't do the work of both of them. Besides, he didn't really understand the preparation of the plaster, nor the process of casting. Too late in the season now to engage anyone, even if a reliable person could be found. Perhaps a female assistant. Please send a recent photograph. No, this season would have to be written off. Some money perhaps would have to be returned. He would have to live on capital for a bit. In the autumn, when he could get around with the cherub lamps, none of this would matter anyway. No one with half an eye could fail to recognise the excellence of the cherub lamps. Moss had prevented him from getting ahead, had been too cautious. He had meant well but he had no vision, that was his trouble, you had to have enterprise, you had to be capable of the large gesture. That's a maxim of mine. Something continued to trouble Foley without his being able for the moment to fix it precisely. Something about Moss? 'I've taken my payment already.'

It was quite dark outside now. Foley got up to draw the curtains and sat down again in a different chair, one of the two hide-covered club armchairs they had got from a local sale for three pounds each. A bargain. He lit a cigarette, remembering how Moss had carried the chairs in himself one after the other on his back into the house. He had obediently put them where he, Foley, had thought they looked best. He had always deferred, in matters of taste, to Foley, the arbiter of elegance.

Through his mind as he sat smoking there passed a succession of images of Moss, each one sharply distinct: Moss as it were frozen in characteristic attitudes, swinging an axe to chop wood, lifting a bucket of water, prising out the pixies from their rubber pods. And despite the diversity of the actions, Moss's expression remained almost constant: always credulous, possessing only the narrowest range. For nearly the whole period of their association, Moss's face had scarcely changed at all.

Then, abruptly, as he reviewed the last few weeks, that calm surface was damaged, cracked across. Moss's hurt and confiding voice in the dark, his eyes brilliant with desire, then full of tears, his face mysteriously contorted in that embrace, then closed and sullen with hostility. Moss had cracked up in the stress of this particular spring. It was the fire of spring that had buckled him. With gathering speed the images flashed through Foley's memory, dangerous now and violent, always violent: the bolt stripped of its thread, Moss's numbing grip on his arms, the slashed thistles, Simon staggering back with his hands to his face, the blood on the dog's muzzle. He knew now what had happened to those crushed pixies on Moss's work-bench. And he remembered suddenly the last expression of all, that curious and uncharacteristic expression of malice or vindictiveness that had lighted Moss's face with a sort of happiness in the moment before he had turned to go. *I've taken my payment already*.

A dreadful suspicion chilled him, for a moment, with a goose-flesh awe, then with sweating apprehension. He got up and made his way out to the passage. There he was arrested by a strong smell of burning coming from the kitchen. Rushing in he found that all the water had boiled away. Charred remnants of eggs adhered to the blackened bottom of the pan. Pausing only to turn off the eggs, he went back along the passage to the rear part of the house and began to mount the stairs towards the attic. He ascended mindlessly, not comparing his sensations to anything, not fully admitting his fear, rather as though he might just conceivably have lost something of great value or unique beauty and was, without conceding the possibility of loss, checking up stealthily.

Looking into the room he knew with anguish, even in the darkness, that all was not well here. Instead of sweet dust and cobwebs there was a sharp smell of slaughter and from all sides intimations of violation and disarray. For some moments he stood there in the dark, mustering what fortitude he could. When he moved to the switch of the overhead light, he trod underfoot something substantial yet yielding, that resisted briefly before subsiding with a dry grinding noise.

The light revealed a scene of carnage worse than he could have imagined possible. His seraphs and cherubs, defenceless on their stands or brackets or suspended from their beams, had been battered to pieces. Systematically. By what seemed blows of some heavy but wieldy instrument, blows of extreme violence which had sent mangled limbs flying to all corners of the room. The floor was littered with golden fragments bleeding white. In the clarity of the first shock Foley saw that pieces still hung from their wires or adhered to brackets that resembled model gibbets now, draped with dismembered felons. Here a body had been struck off at the neck and sent flying to shatter into fragments against wall or floor, leaving a trunkless golden head, its curls intact, its blind ecstatic gaze unwavering. Here nether limbs still writhed beneath a bent lamp shade, the torso gone, stark white dust spilling out like powdered intestines.

Foley stared about him, aghast at the thoroughness of the execution. This had been no random, petulant gesture. Nothing had been spared. His pride, the large angels planing on out-stretched wings high up in the ceiling, had all three of them been dashed to the ground. Even the lamp shades and the stands had been twisted and rent and glass from the shattered bulbs littered the floor and made it treacherous. His feather brush lay amidst the debris. Moss's onslaught – it could not be anyone but Moss – had exposed without pity the unenduring, tawdry nature of these creatures. The suavely rippling limbs, clad in gilt, would never without this wreckage have given the beholder cause to suspect that they were stuffed with dust only, lacking fibre and grain. It was this that rendered their remains so disgusting, denying them the dignity that would have been retained by fragments of metal or wood or stone. There they lay, leaking their vile dust, not even remains, simply rubbish now, a litter to be swept up quickly.

Now he understood the contempt there had been in Moss's voice when he had referred to the unlocked doors. With the strange and probably slightly mad discontinuity of his nature, Moss had been able to regard with scorn that carelessness, which had been through his agency – impersonal now, all passion spent

— the cause of Foley's loss. In the last moments, before the extent of that loss overwhelmed him, while he was still able to consider the havoc as a sort of universal disaster, not to be supported by him alone, Foley considered the pitiful shreds of angels that still hung from the ceiling and thought that they bore a strong resemblance to the revolving clay figures that he remembered seeing at fairground rifle ranges, hanging splintered and formless after the shattering pellet.

He switched off the light and turned his back on the scene with a sense of discretion, descending the stairs with a certain composure, as though he had terrible news to break to someone waiting below and must in duty restrain his own natural grief. Back once more, however, in the well-lit, familiar but curiously changed living-room, the magnitude of the blow came home to him fully. He was alone here, abandoned even by his assailant, with nowhere to turn. Three years' patient work gone into those lamps and not a trace left, not a single survivor. Worst of all was the brutal severing of the line by which he had clung to his craftsman's pride, his sense of his own distinction. He was as other men now, no samples, no showroom. It was the cruelty done to him that hurt him most, since it seemed so gratuitous. It was the first time in his life he had been dealt with so. The wrongs that are done with an object to be gained, however slight that object might be, he understood. He had suffered them, dealt them out, the petty forms of commercial deceit, the treacheries of sex, partial damage, incidental cruelties: all the attacks from which there is a refuge in custom. But before this blow he felt without resilience. There was not, however desperately he sought for it, any precedent for that shambles upstairs. He was exposed, raw. Gazing blankly from object to object in the room, Foley felt acute pain.

To escape from it he tried thinking of Moss again. Moss must have suffered a spasm of rage while waiting for him, or while packing in silence the sheer familiarity of things must have envenomed him, so that he could not bear to leave without effecting some radical change, something to record that he had lived and suffered in the house. The thoroughness of the destruction, of course, was typical. Moss was mad. One or two, in

213

a temper, you could be sane and break. But to break them all, systematically. That was mad. How had he got at the high ones? Thrown things up at them, probably, an aerial cherub-shy. Like knocking fruit off a tree. No, not that way. The feather brush, that was it. Moss was tall. He would get a chair and stand on it and hold the brush by the feather-end and stretch as high he could and lash out. He had actually used that feather brush, and then thrown it down among the wreckage . . .

Moss's using the feather brush, instrument of cherishing and symbol of loving care, for his brutal purposes, was the last straw of outrage and Foley's fortitude broke under it. He felt his face crack into a grin of grief and thick tears welled into his eyes. He wept for several minutes, gulping and sniffing. As his weeping became less abandoned, it occurred to him that he was standing in exactly the same place as Moss had stood, when *he* had wept. It struck him as a remarkable coincidence and went some way towards restoring his composure. How long ago had that been? A week? All that was undifferentiated now, non-sequential, belonging simply to the time when he had possessed his cherubs.

After a while he found the familiarity of the room unendurable. He wandered for some time around the house, his face still wet with tears, pursued by pungent smells of burning from the kitchen. Finally he went to the door and stood looking out into the darkness. Nothing here could be perceived except in the sky to the seaward side a faint glow from Royle's upper storey lights. They were in bed then. The night was dense, moonless. No sound came from the sleeping sea. But while he stood there an owl hooted once sharply and in a few moments repeated the call and after this, as though his senses had been refined by it, he became aware of a stirring around him which was not so much a sound as a sort of texture or graining of the night: moths' and bats' wings, trembling of grasses and leaves, the wrinkling skins of rats in the barns. He made out the vague bulk of the car where he had left it near the gate and with the sight, as though the decision had already been made and needed only that reassurance, he knew what he was going to do. He stopped only to make sure he had the car keys in his pocket. His intention grew urgent so that he dreaded finding some mechanical fault which would prevent or delay him. But for once the car started at the first attempt. The lights lit up suddenly an expanse of field and the laneside hedges, a whole new dimension culled from the darkness.

He drove quite mechanically, squashing what might have been a hedgehog at the end of the lane, as he came out on to the road. The headlights, swinging from side to side as the car nosed round the bends, lit up tangles of vegetation in the high banks, held them transfixed and frozen-looking in the white beam, like weeds trapped in ice, then slid past, releasing them. Occasionally brilliant moths or gauzy flying creatures swirled in the beam as in a vortex, sucked down against the glass of the lamps.

He came to the first houses. The village was quite deserted, the houses closed and containing their kindness. Foley felt a stab of desolation at the thought of all those people warm and safe in rooms, their ambitions intact. The Fisherman's Arms was long since closed. The harbour water lapped softly against the walls, as Foley walked the last few yards or so to Barbara's cottage. As he reached her gate someone on the hillside above whistled a few bars of a song and a second later there was the sound of laughter. Courting couples. He knocked softly and almost immediately heard her coming. She opened the door wide and peered out with her head thrust forward. 'Who is it?' she said. 'Oh it's *you*. But how sweet of you to come in the dark. I was beginning to associate you only with pure morning. Come in.'

Foley stumbled blinking into the blinding white room. He had a confused impression of the black divan, Barbara in some sort of cyclamen-coloured garment: a kimono? The glossy skull grinned at him from a bare white wall. Foley stood still in the middle of the room, bewildered by his emotion and the brilliant light. He closed his eyes for a moment.

'Is the light hurting your eyes?' he heard her say in an entirely conversational voice. 'I like a strong light, personally.'

He opened his eyes again and saw her face quite close, raised towards him. Sloe eyes, unblinking; the opulent, Semitic nose.

'Moss has cleared out,' he blurted. 'He's broken all my lamps.' The enormity of it, experienced again with this utterance, caused his voice to break. The knowledge that his distress was public, now that Barbara knew it, upset him even more. Only the sense that Barbara despised him kept his features stiff, braced against that former cracking.

'That was naughty of him,' Barbara said.

'Naughty?' The understatement increased Foley's sense of helpless humiliation. 'He has broken all my lamps. Every single one. Deliberately.'

'He could hardly have broken *all* of them accidentally, darling,' Barbara said, 'Now could he?' She had moved again and was now standing very close to him, so close that her thighs touched his legs. She did not seem to be wearing much under her robe.

'You don't understand,' he said. 'I didn't keep the moulds. Moss has ruined me.'

One of her windows must have been open because now in the silence he heard distinctly a double note from the sea-bell. It had the effect of a warning or a reminder. He wondered whether any woman could be unkinder than Barbara. 'You don't understand what it means to me,' he said. 'Can't we have this light off?'

'It's the only light there is,' Barbara said. 'I like to see what I'm doing.'

'I burned the eggs, too,' he said, gulping a little.

'Never mind,' Barbara said. 'You'll get over it.'

She raised her hands without haste to his breast and as he closed his eyes once more, against the harsh light, he felt her thin, hard fingers undoing the buttons of his shirt.